The Virgin of the Discos

The Virgin of the Discos

A BOOK OF TALES

Mike Harding

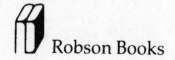 Robson Books

Tell me a story, tell me a story,
Tell me a story before I go to bed.
Tell me about the flowers and trees,
Tell me about the birds and bees.
Tell me a story before I go to bed.
Hank the Cowboy Puppet

Now this didn't happpen in my time, or in your time, but
it must have happened in somebody's time, or how could I
be telling you about it?
How a Seanchaí traditionally begins his tale

First published in Great Britain in 1993 by
Robson Books Limited Bolsover House
5-6 Clipstone Street London W1P7EB

Copyright © 1993 Mike Harding
The author has asserted his moral rights
British Library Cataloguing in Publication Data
A record for this title is available from the British Library

ISBN 0 86051 895 7

Typography and design by Mike Harding
Set in New Baskerville 10/13 and Windsor 24
by Thomas Meyer using an Apple Mac and Pagemaker 4.2
and printed in Great Britain by
St Edmunds Bury Press
Bury St Edmunds
Suffolk

Contents

Hopalong Cassidy and the Pigeons on the Roof

James Michael Patrick Cassidy was his real name, but the boys he played with all called him Hopalong. And that was dead funny, really, because Hopalong Cassidy was his hero and he used to see him at the pictures nearly every Saturday morning, when he went with all his mates to the matinee that everybody called the 'Sixpenny Rush' – because it was only sixpence to get in and the kids used to queue all round the block and when the doors were opened they used to rush like mad to get a ticket so they could get in first and sit near the front, only not on the front row because you got cricket in your neck. About three or four rows back was best.

There were two picture houses you could go to. The ABC had an ABC Minors Club, but that was ninepence and it was full of posh kids. He and his mates liked the Bijou better. It was only a tanner, and sometimes there were special days when you got in for thrupence and they gave all the kids an orange and a penny chew for nothing.

The Bijou looked like a palace out of the Arabian Nights book that his Aunty Kitty had given him for Christmas. because it had towers and minarets and was all gold and red inside. It looked like the palace in the story about the Flying Horse, where the horse flies right over the minarets to get the princess, only the one in the book didn't have a big gasometer behind it.

The Bijou was on the main road near the swimming baths and the café called The Witches' Brew, where you could get hot Oxo with a slice of bread for thrupence after the swimming baths when it was very cold in winter, and the steam ran down the café windows when you were inside, and your hair was all cold on your head because you hadn't dried it properly and you'd get *noomonyar* and die, his nanna said.

At the Bijou there was a man in a uniform that all the kids called Sparky. He had a big torch, and he ripped up your tickets, and chucked noisy boys out, and went mad if you called him Sparky – or if you tossed orange peel up into the beam from the projector so that you got shadows on the screen. Sometimes, when the film was boring, the kids would start whispering, 'Sparky… Sparky… Sparky…' and they would get louder and louder, and he would get really mad and shine his torch all over the place trying to catch whoever was doing it. Once he switched all the lights on, and stopped the film, and told them that he was going to throw them all out. They'd put another film on of the Three Stooges and they were everybody's favourites so it was all right after that.

His favourite funny films were the Three Stooges, the Bowery Boys and Our Gang; and he liked all the cartoons, especially Heckle and Jeckle and Bugs Bunny. But, when it came to cowboys, Hopalong Cassidy was the best of them all. He thought Roy Rogers was soppy, and he hated it when he took out his guitar and sang. Hopalong could punch a man and knock him right through the saloon doors, *Whaaap!,* just like that. He liked Gabby Hayes, too, because he was funny and had no teeth. He did the cooking for the cowboys and always gave them beans, and they didn't like beans and they pulled faces, and if there was a fight Gabby used to hit people on the head with his frying pan, *Doynnnng!,* like that, and they used to slide down the side of the chuck wagon into the dust with their eyes crossed and tweety birds going round in their heads. All the kids used to laugh and jump up and down in their seats when that happened. He didn't like it when the cowboys sang songs or when a lady tried to kiss Hopalong. Nobody did. When that happened all the kids booed and whistled and shouted. He liked it best when they chased the baddies through the deep canyons and across the desert, and the wheels of the wagons went backwards even though you knew they were really going forwards, and the cowboys all fired their guns dead loud, and all the kids cheered and jumped up and down, and it was dead dead good! That was the best.

When they were coming home from the pictures they used to chase each other down the streets, pretending they were Hopalong Cassidy and his men. They used to hide in the back-yard gateways and jump out and ambush each other, and they used to tie their raincoats round their necks so they flapped out behind like cloaks, and then they would pretend they were the Three Musketeers and fence each other, and Barry used to stand on the dustbin like Douglas Fairbanks and once he pretended to be stabbed and fell right off the dustbin on to the floor like they did in the films, *Bash!*, dead hard. He said it didn't hurt him – but it probably did a bit, because he was quiet the rest of the way home.

Anyway, the film had been brilliant this morning, and the sun was shining when they came out of the Bijou, and it was dead dead hot, and they'd played a really good game of chasing and tiggy-off-the-ground. Now he was in their street, and they were all going in for their dinners, but he'd see them all after and they would play some dead good games like Batman and Robin, or hide and seek, or they might even go on the croft and make a den! That would be best of all.

He could hear the noise as he turned the corner. It was his mother and father, and they were shouting and the baby was crying. They were shouting really loud, and he felt his stomach go hard and he wanted to wee-wee and cry at the same time. He opened the door and everything went quiet. His father looked at him from where he stood on the other side of the room, holding on to the mantelpiece, and his mother sat in a chair by the fire with her pinny to her face.

He walked over to the baby's cot. She was looking at the ceiling and crying really loud, so loud she was sucking air in between each cry – like he sometimes did at the baths when he'd swum dead fast and was out of puff. He put his hand in the cot and found the baby's dummy, and held it to her fat lips. She sucked it in hungrily. But she kept sobbing and whimpering while she was sucking, and then she shook all over just once and went quiet, sucking on her dummy and looking up at him with eyes that were all full of tears. He took a corner of the sheet she had kicked off and dried her eyes.

'I think she's hungry,' he said, without looking at either of them.

They didn't say anything and he could hear the clock ticking dead dead loud and the fire was lit and he could hear that, too because gas was hissing from one big lump of coal like a volcano and it was catching fire now and then in a long thin flame, like on that planet when Flash Gordon was trapped and nearly burnt to death. He'd liked that film.

'What's the fire doing lit?' he asked. 'It's dead dead hot outside.'

'We needed some hot water,' his mother said. 'I was going to have a bath before you all came in.'

'A bath! At this time in the day? It's not bedtime, and anyway it's not Friday night!' He stood on his tiptoes and looked through the window at the tin bath hanging from its nail on the yard wall.

'Your mother's going to have another baby, James,' his father said in a strange voice, like the one he used when he was really angry but didn't want anybody to know. His teeth would be all close together, and his mouth would hardly move at all, and he used to say things like 'I've told you for the last time,' or 'This is your last warning, me boyo.'

He looked from the baby's cot over to his mother.

'Yes, won't that be nice now, James?' she said. 'You'll have another little baby brother or sister to play with, and there'll be somebody for little Helen to play with, too.'

She smiled at him, but her eyes were red, and her voice was funny as though she was dead tired but didn't want to show it, like sometimes when he brought friends home from school without telling her. She'd make them something to eat even though there wasn't enough in the house; and she'd smile at them and be nice to them, but he'd know she was worried about there not being enough, though she wouldn't say anything, or she'd say one thing but she'd mean another. That was what it was like now, only there was something else.

It was like when his grandad had died and they hadn't wanted to tell him in case he got too upset but when they did tell him he was upset anyway, so they should have told him in the first place. It was just like that now.

'What would you like?' she asked in that strange voice. 'A boy or a girl?'

'I want a brother this time. We don't want any more girls. Anyway, where's our Helen gone?'

'She's gone to the market with your nanna, they'll be back at teatime.'

'Why aren't you at work, Dad?'; his dad normally worked on overtime on Saturdays.

'There was no more work for us today, so they sent us home early.'

He didn't say any more, he just stood looking into the fire. Then he lifted his head up and stared at a clear glass bottle on the table with some stuff like water in it. He looked at it for a long time, as though he was trying to sort something out in his head, and his lips started moving as though he was talking to himself. There was a packet of Epsom Salts there, too. James could read that and he could read the label on the bottle dead easy. It said Cork Dry Gin. James knew gin was a drink, his nanna called it 'mother's ruin'.

'That's stupid,' he said, pointing at the bottle. 'How can it be dry? It's a drink, it's as wet as anything. Anybody can see that.'

His father nodded towards the table. 'You'd better put that away, Frances,' and his mother stood up and opened the cupboard doors and put the bottle on the top shelf where all the rent-book stuff and other things were kept that had to be hidden and were 'for grown-ups'. He'd climbed up once and had a look when they were all out, but there wasn't much there – just some insurance books and a rubber bulb thing with a long tube in a tin box and some cotton things with loops on the end in a brown paper bag.

'Anyway,' she said when she sat down again, 'I'm not having a bath now, not with you two in the house. James, you can go out and play for a bit longer. I'll shout you when your dinner's ready.'

But he didn't want to go. Something was wrong, and he didn't want to go in case it was something he should know about, like grandad dying.

'But I want to play with the baby!'

'You heard what your mother said!' his father was almost screaming at him now. 'Would you ever get out of the house and play! God knows you're hard enough work to find when we want you in of a night-time!'

James could tell he was really angry, because he hardly ever shouted at him that loud. 'But I want to stay in!' He was almost crying now, he could feel everything inside him, all hot and mixed up, coming up as if he was going to be sick.

'Want! Want! That's all I ever hear from all of you in this house – want, want, want! You'll drive me into my grave, the lot of you!' His mother shouted, she was crying again now. 'For the love of God, James, do as your father says and go on out and play, and try and be good for a change!' The baby started crying again, too.

He went out and down the steps into the back yard and into the coal shed where, in its deep, cool, spidery dark, among the smell of firelighters and damp wood, his secrets box was hidden, wrapped in a bit of tarpaulin on a high shelf where his dad kept a jam jar full of rusting nails and a hammer with a broken handle. It was hidden behind some tins of paint that had gone hard and hadn't been moved for years.

It was in his secrets box that he kept his most precious things. There was a tiger's tooth that a boy at school had swapped him for a brilliant catapult his dad had made him; there was a glass ball with a village inside it and when you shook it snow fell, covering the houses, and then you turned it upside down and back again and it all fell again over and over; there was a medal with the king's head on it. He was dead now, and they'd had prayers for him at school. There was a queen now. He'd been given a coronation cup and saucer with her head on and a pencil with her head on, only his dad had kept the cup and saucer and put them somewhere safe saying they would be valuable some day, even though he didn't believe in the queen because he was Irish. There were four cats' eyes that had come out of the road and they shone in the dark; there was a badge with a German swastika on it that had come off a dead German's uniform; there was a really old brass whistle that had come off the railways – he'd swopped a broken roller-skate for it. And there was the gun.

He took down his little biscuit-tin safe and levered the lid off. Nobody knew about the gun. It could fire pellets if he put a new leather washer in it; he was trying to find out where to get one from. Someone said the sports shop on the main road that sold balsa wood aeroplane kits had them and he was going to go one day and ask. He knew his mother would take it off him if she found it because he might put somebody's eye out. Lots of things could put your eye out, like spears and whips off 'whip and top', and there was a boy in the next street called Jeffrey Clark who somebody had fired a bow and arrow at by mistake. His eye had been put out, and now he had a glass one and some of the other boys said he could take it out and suck it like a gobstopper and put it back.

He knew lots of people who had had accidents. There was another boy who had an accident when some big boys pushed him on to a bonfire and the skin on his back got burnt so that now it was all white and rippled like tripe and you could see kids looking at him in the swimming baths.

He'd swapped a mountain of comics and a broken camera for
the gun, with a kid called Bruce who had just moved into the street
and lived near the chip shop. He'd swapped nearly a hundred
Beanos and *Dandys* and *Hotspurs* and *Wizards*, all mixed. The
camera was too broken to work properly again since his dad had
dropped it in the sea at Llandudno and it got all full of salt and the
metal had gone green and crusty but you could still look through
it and pretend. But the gun was brilliant, it was his bestest secret,
and though he had no slugs for it and the leather washer had dried
and split, it still made a dead loud bang when you fired it.

The voices in the house grew louder and louder and the baby
was crying nearly as loud as they were shouting. It was dead dead
hot and the heat was coming up from the stone flags and the
cobbles. He walked through the gate and down the deserted back
alley. The smell of dinners came from the open windows with the
voices of people talking and knives and forks clattering on plates.
He could still hear the sad shouting voices from his house, too,
even when he was half-way down the back alley.

The gun was hard and cool inside his jumper and when he was
sure no one could see him he took it out and squinted along its
shining blue barrel at the pigeons on the roofs of the terrace, only
the pigeons were Apaches now, and they were on the canyon's rim,
and he stalked them along the palings, holding his breath.

'Bang!' he shouted. 'Bang! Bang!' as the tormented voices
followed him down the alleyway and the savage redskins flew up
into the Saturday air in a flurry of wings and purple breasts to circle
over the burning slate roofs of Dead Man's Gulch.

Some People Don't Even Know There's a Town Round Here

There is a salmon river, a castle on the hill, a road in and a road out, and roads that filter away up the glens to become shooters' tracks and forestry roads. There is a small town square with a branch of the Bank of Scotland; there is a lawyer's office where Campbell and Imlach preserve the titles, deeds and misdeeds of the populace; there is the office of the Laird's factor, Hector Imlach, brother of the lawyer, and there is the Tartan Bar that carries in its window a sign, hand-lettered in black poster paint on a bright green day-glo background, advertising *Dougie McCalman and the High Chaparral – Country and Western – Every Friday Night – Bar Meals and Raffle*. There is a hardware shop that sells everything from cattle drench, rabbit snares and plastic sweet pea netting to twelve-bore shotguns, firelighters and fly rods; there is a small police station with two beef-fed policemen and a thick-ankled policewoman with a boyfriend in Glasgow she sees once a fortnight, and there is a barber's where the red-faced farmers come to have their heads cropped and talk about bovine mastitis and lamb prices, and where you can have your hair cut any style you like as long as it is ten years behind the times. There is a gentlemen's outfitters that sells deerstalkers and brogues, night-shirts, woollen vests, suspenders for men and plus-fours; there is a ladies' outfitters that sells tweeds and print frocks, old-fashioned hats, woollen vests, lock-knit bloomers and lisle stockings; there is the garage with its one petrol pump, its cards of spark plugs and fan belts and its repair bay; there is the funeral parlour run by the man who owns the garage, who also drives the hearse; there is a newsagent's and tobacconist's run by the brother of the man who runs the garage, who also helps with the laying out of the corpses; there is a small store selling greengroceries run by the uncle of the wife of the man who runs the garage and another store selling groceries run by the wife of the uncle of the man who runs the garage. There are two butcher's shops that face each other across the square where, each morning, the butchers paint the prices of their meat on their windows in white letters; there is the Royal Hotel where, each lunch-time, gristly meat swims in gravy between generous scoops of mashed potatoes and piles of overcooked greens, and where at New Year there is a dance where people do the Twist and the Dashing White Sergeant, scrap hopelessly and mostly harmlessly, and fall over in the snow outside monumentally drunk. And there is the milk bar.

Run by a family of Glasgow Italians, Nardoni's Ice Cream Parlour was opened in the years just after the Second World War. The milk bar looks out on the square, its large, always steamy, windows surmounted by a fifties façade and a massive, faded plastic ice cream cone covered in pigeon droppings that lights up at night to stand spectrally, the vision of all ice creams that ever were, are or will be, the Platonic ice cream cone burning bright above the Belisha-washed square.

Nardoni's is the gathering-ground for bored teenagers and tired shoppers, for young mothers meeting after play-school or mother and toddler group, who sit smoking and talking about their children and their husbands and their homes over cups of coffee, as their children draw faces in the steam on the windows or cry for more ice cream. It is the meeting-place of home-going schoolchildren who can just afford a Horlicks or a hot Vimto before they make their satchelled way towards homework and the prison of the tea table. It is an island of warmth and light for the young courting couples of the town, who fall in and out of love over countless cups of frothy coffee and endless cigarettes. And occasionally, very occasionally, it will be visited by a passing tourist on his or her way somewhere – always going, never stopping, because the town is a workaday, homespun town.

Dominated by the laird's estate and the chipboard factory above the river on the forest's edge, Ecclemuchty has a mart and a timber yard, two churches and a school. It is overlooked by forests, and looks out on nothing but forests and a bowl of sky. It has no spa, nobody famous died there and no famous writers, poets or artists were born there; although there is a plaque in the public library that declares that James Mungo Cameron, missionary and explorer, who wrote the world-famous hymn *Lead Thy Soldiers, Lord, to Battle* and who converted two hundred heathen before succumbing to blackwater fever close to what is now Mombasa, was the minister there for nine and a half months in 1856. Beyond that it has no famous sons, only the brave and poor whose names are carved on the war memorial where people sit to wait for lifts home. But the poor are never famous, except on Remembrance Sunday, so they do not count, just as they have never counted. And so the town is not, for all these reasons, on any tourist map.

Now it is a Wednesday in February and the air is flushed with a limpid, under-sea light. The mid-afternoon sun falls on the town, burnishing the pinkish grey stone of the walls, the bridge and the buildings in the square, laying a warm wash upon them, a whisper of the spring that is to come. The sun lays its light from its millions of miles of journey through space on the forested valley and the foam-lipped river and the stiff stone finger of the memorial all alike; and it falls through the window of Nardoni's upon an advertisement for Irn Bru, upon a notice for a Young Farmers' Dance that took place three weeks ago, and upon Angus Moffat, who is filling salt cellars behind the counter of the milk bar.

Angus is seventeen, quite tall and slim and pleasant-looking; though he is troubled with bad skin and a vague feeling that though everything seems to be all right, there is something deeply wrong with his life. One of the things that troubles him is his name. He thinks it very twee; it smacks to his way of thinking of kilts and dirks and tam o' shanters, Jimmy Shand and The White Heather Club. He would far rather have been called something more

17

English like John or Peter, or perhaps something really romantic and out of the way altogether like Jason, or Marc with a 'c'. He wondered whether he should change his name? The trouble was, he decided, it wouldn't matter what you called yourself round here, people would still call you by the name you were given. You could call yourself Nebuchadnezzar or Long John Silver or Elvis Sunset Boulevard and they'd still call you Iain or Bruce or Angus.

A blue, single-decker bus skirted the war memorial and groaned out of town, leaving a skein of black diesel smoke behind and little else. It was the Glasgow to Carlisle bus and once a week it left the main road and called in here and occasionally, though not often, somebody got on it or got off. One day, he thought, I'll be on that bus heading south, first to Carlisle and then on to London. People did leave here. A few girls went to university or away to train as nurses. Boys went, too, some to agricultural or forestry college, a few even to university; but most went to the Army and when they came back they were changed, Angus thought. They were distant and sneering, hard and boastful somehow. Angus thought he'd rather stay here for the rest of his life than join the Army and come back with short hair and tattoos, teeth missing from scrapping and a lot of swearwords and a swagger. In any case, when they finally did come back home, as most of them did, they only ended up working in the garage or on the forestry, just the same as they would have done if they hadn't gone away in the first place. Ecclemuchty was like a magnet that drew all its children back eventually. It knew its own.

He screwed the top on the last salt cellar, wiped the aluminium counter down with a warm wet cloth, and looked at the two old ladies sitting in the window. They came every day, winter and summer, and had two cups of frothy coffee each. With their coffee one had a scone and the other a buttered toasted tea-cake, and each day they stayed almost exactly two hours between finishing their shopping and hurrying out for the bus that would take them home. They only came, Mrs Nardoni said, to keep warm and dry in winter and to keep cool and dry in summer. 'If I sell this place,' she used to say, 'I'll have to include them in the inventory as one of the fittings. Thirty-two chairs, eight tables, one espresso machine and two old biddies.' Angus knew the two old women: one of them was the grandmother of a girl he'd been at school with who used to let you feel her tits whenever you wanted. Though Angus hadn't, most of his friends had, and Hamish Bain reckoned he'd gone all the way with her; but he'd lied about a swan's egg he was supposed to have found, so none of the boys believed him. The other old lady was the widow of one of the forestry workers. She lived six miles or so out of town in one of the forestry cottages.

Angus moved over from behind the counter and began filling the sugar bowls. He always tried to look busy when Mrs Nardoni was about because he knew that she 'liked her pound of flesh', as his mother used to say. Mr Nardoni was dead, killed in a car smash coming back from an Italian wedding in Glasgow. He'd been drunk, according to local gossip. Mrs Nardoni had escaped with cuts and bruising and a broken arm, though she had quite a bad scar on her chin which went blue when she was cold. All in all, she wasn't a bad boss – though she was tight with money; and after he'd paid his mother his board and lodging and put in to the endowment policy his father had opened for him, he'd only got three pounds, twelve shillings and sixpence left to last him the week. And with that he had to buy his clothes and petrol for his motorbike, a BSA Bantam, as well as try and get to the cinema or a dance at the youth club. He thought at that rate it would take him a long while before he could save up to go and live in London.

While he was filling the bowl on the old ladies' table the doorbell rang and Angus looked up to see two men come into the café and glance quickly around before moving to one of the tables in the no-smoking area. The no-smoking area had been Liz's idea. Liz only did Saturdays. She was still at school, doing her leaving cert., but she didn't like smoking and had told Mrs Nardoni that the café ought to have a no-smoking area of at least four tables. To everyone's surprise, Mrs Nardoni had agreed.

The men wore tweedy jackets and slacks, but even before they spoke Angus knew they weren't English. It was something in the way they wore their clothes, 'casual-smart' he would have described it.

They sat down at the table and looked at the menu. Angus gave them a few minutes. He guessed that they were American. They weren't French. French people would have been talking at each other loudly and waving their hands. Germans would have been shouting. They could have been Dutch because the younger of the two men had blondish hair grown very long and straight like Mickey Dolantz out of the Monkees, but Angus didn't think they were Dutch, he thought they were American. He knew he was right the moment they opened their mouths.

They asked for a pot of coffee and Angus felt ashamed when he had to tell them that they didn't do pots of coffee, only cups.

'Do we get refills?' asked the older man.

'Well, it's like frothy coffee, you know. From the machine, cappuccino.'

'We'll have a pot of tea, then. You do do pots of tea?'

'Oh yes, and it's real tea, no tea bags. Would you like anything to eat?'

'Two scones with butter.'

'Would you like them hot?'

'No, they'll do fine as they are.'

Angus couldn't stay away from the table. There was something about the men that fascinated him. They weren't father and son, the age difference wasn't that much, but there was some relationship. Brothers, perhaps? Though he didn't think so. He hovered round, keeping an eye out for any other orders, but there were none. The older man brushed some crumbs from his jacket with a handkerchief and looked over at him.

'Nice quiet town you have here. '

'You can say that again – it's too quiet. There's mair life in the graveyard.'

'It's very pretty, though,' said the younger man. 'I half expected deer to come leaping over the hills, and men in kilts to come round the corner playing bagpipes. It looks like something offen a shortbread tin. What was the name of that village in that musical that reappears every year?'

'Brigadoon,' said the older man.

'It's exactly like that. You could imagine that when we drive away the whole lot will disappear again until next year.'

Angus laughed. 'Aye, it probably will. It's no bad in the summer when there's mair folk about, but in the winter it's grim. Are you on holiday?'

'We're just driving through on our way to Lewis and thought we'd take our time and wander round some of the Border towns. We're very interested in stone circles, and there's one not far from here.'

'That'll be King Arthur's Table. We went there with the school.'

'Are you interested in stone circles?' asked the young man.

'No' me! Well, they're all right, I suppose, but I'm mair interested in clothes and music and films; and I've got a motorbike. It's second-hand, like, but it goes well. My faither's a mechanic – he did it up for me. I get out on that. But I like films best, there's a cinema at Drimond – that's twelve miles away. You don't get the new ones, though, you'd have to go to Carlisle or Dumfries for that. I'm saving up to go doon to London. I'd like to find a job doon there.'

'Doing what?'

'I widnae mind. Anythin' wid dae until I found ma feet. I'd work in cafés or whatever until I got my ain place, you know – a flat, like. I'd like tae work in fashion or something like that. Anythin', really, so long as it was different.'

He didn't know why he'd said that about fashion. It had never occurred to him before. It was just something he'd said without thought, in the excitement of the moment. But perhaps it was true?

He *was* interested in clothes and though he hadn't much money he could dress well on what he had. And he kept up with all the new fashions by reading the magazines, particularly fan mags for groups like the Beatles and the Stones. He had a high-collared jacket at home that he'd made himself, by adapting an old double-breasted jacket. He'd asked his mother, and she'd showed him how to do it, though his father had said, 'Lads dinnae sew.'

'Whit aboot you in the Navy? Ye had tae knit yer own socks, so ye did!' his mother had replied, and his father had mumbled something about that being wartime, and had leaned forward to poke the fire.

The young man was looking at him. 'And what about girls? There must be plenty of nice pretty girls around here?'

Angus felt a hole the size of his life opening up in the café floor. 'I'm no' too bothered with girls. They're all right, like, but I've mair important things tae dae than chase the lassies.'

And there was something then, some indefinable shift in the air that happened at that precise moment, that Angus would remember ever after. It was nothing said. It was everything unsaid, and at that split in infinity Angus knew the answer to the puzzle that had been concerning him ever since the men came into the milk bar. They were a couple like any other couple: like his mother and father were a couple, like his older sister and her fiancé were a couple. And he knew also that all those ideas and feelings that had puzzled him for years were not strange or weird, or were something that he alone felt, but that other people felt as he did. That there were other ways of loving, and that in the world outside this Brigadoon there were other ways of living your life.

It didn't all have to be bounded by the forests, the kirk, the Young Farmers, and the Royal Hotel. The universe expanded out beyond Nardoni's and its sugar bowls to the stars; the sun that fell on that dried chip on the floor shone on faraway beaches and snow-covered mountains and palm trees, on busy streets and high buildings, on other hands and faces. He knew then also that, more than anything else, he wanted to be just like that young man, travelling with another older man, who knew the ways of the world, who could take him away, who could show him what there was in the world outside this Brigadoon.

There was a sharp, peevish rapping on a table. One of the old ladies was hitting the Formica with a coin.

'Can we have another two cups of coffee, Angus, when ye've got the time!' she said, quite snotty, looking sharply at the two strangers who had taken so much of his attention.

As he brought the coffees back from the counter the men stood up to go.

'We've left the money on the table.' The older man pointed.

'Good luck with your trip to London,' said the younger man, waving.

Angus's eyes followed them out to their car, a red and cream Vauxhall Victor with whitewall tyres. He'd have loved to have been driven off in a car like that, off down the road going south out into the world. In seconds they had waved good-bye, were in it and were driving off out of the square and his life.

'Did I hear you say you were off to London, Angus?' one of the old ladies asked.

'Och no, I just said I'd like to go there sometime.'

'Jesse McBride's Allan went to London, working. He didnae like it. Said it was awfu' busy and noisy.'

'Too fast,' the other old lady nodded. 'It's aw too fast doon there, wi' they spies and gangsters and suicides and the like. I saw it on the news. It's terrible, so it is!'

Angus went back to the counter and stood frozen in thought. He looked out through the steamy window where a child-drawn face was melting and running in tears and knew that he should have been in that car, too, or one like it, heading out on the tarmac, going south through the forests and over the river, following the deep road through the valley, following the sun as Donovan had done in the song, going anywhere, anywhere at all that would take him out of this pink-grey stone labyrinth of desires, chains and masks that was the town.

He knew that he would never marry a girl called Kirsten or Heather or Helen, that if he stayed here for the rest of his life he would be odd for ever. But where could he go? He knew no one outside the town and the valley, and knew, what was worse, that some people didn't even know there was a town round here.

An ache deeper than any pain he'd ever felt before spread through him like a sudden fever as Mrs Nardoni came in from the store-room and called to him in that rough deep voice of hers, a voice that flew out like a torn bird above the noise of the coffee machine and the school bus passing the window.

'Come on, Angus! Wake up, will ye! When you've finished with your day-dreaming, you can start filling the rest of the sugar bowls and top up the vinegar bottles. And when you've done that, give that cake stand a wipe – and the pilot light's gone out on the boiler again, see if your faither can come round and have a look at it some time. Any time this week will do.'

Strings Attached

Wiping the last traces of make-up from his face, Jimmy Jones screwed the top back on the jar of Leichner removing cream, took a last drag of the cigarette that had been burning down unattended in the ashtray, and screwed it up with thirty or so other fag-ends. He switched off the dressing-table lights, noticing that the three dud ones still hadn't been replaced, and, throwing his coat over his arm and his yellow woollen scarf round his neck, picked up his briefcase and walked down the dimly lit corridor towards the stage door.

The stage doorman sitting slumped down in his armchair was hardly visible through the window of his cream-painted office. He looked up from his sporting paper as Jimmy went past.

'Just a few tonight, Mr Jones,' he said, nodding towards the door. 'The rain's seen most of 'em off.'

'Thanks, Tommy. Here, tell that young berk of a stage manager the lights are still out on my dressing-table, will you? I know he's got his hands full organising his love life, but if he's got time between poking the front line of the chorus will you ask him if he can see his way to finding three bulbs somewhere. Tell him the star can't see to put his slap on.'

Jimmy opened the stage door on to the night. In the yellow cone of light he saw three people huddled in the doorway, sheltering from the wind that whipped inland from the northern sea, bringing with it slicing icy rain. Just the sort of weather you'd expect in August in Blackcombe he thought. Two men and a woman moved towards him, all in their late twenties and all three, Jimmy thought, looked a little slow.

'It's nice – !' he shouted at them, leaving a gap like a hole in the air, as though the wind had torn the last of his words away. They all knew the reply.

'To be nice!' the trio called back in unison into the wind. It was his walk-on line, roared out at the audience as he strutted his way on to the stage to grab the microphone and grin down at them. He used it during the act, too. When a particularly good laugh surged over the footlights at him like a wave, he would punch the line into the darkness like a fisherman lobbing his bait into the surf. It was his pay-off line as well, dropped in just as the last of the exhausted laughter was ebbing on the brass rails of the pit. 'It's nice – !' he would shout into the microphone before leaving the stage with a backwards wave as the audience screamed 'To be nice' at the tops of their voices and he strode into the dark haven of the wings.

'Do you have any photographs, Mr Jones?' asked the girl, pushing her autograph book towards him.

He signed three photographs for the autograph-hunters. For Glynis, Brian and Chuck.

'Can I have a photograph for my brother?' asked Chuck.

He signed another picture to Chuck's brother, Nobby, writing 'It's nice to be – ' and 'Best Wishes, Jimmy Jones' under the photograph.

'We thought you were great tonight, Mr Jones.' Glynis sent the words out in spatters between her chattering teeth. Her glasses were slipping down her wet nose and she had a clear plastic raincoat with a matching hood pulled on over frizzy permed hair. He looked down to her thin legs and her shoes, a pair of tan pumps that had turned dark in the rain.

'You'll catch your death in this rain, love.'

'It's worth it to get your autograph.' She smiled at him, almost flirting. Jimmy was faintly stirred; she was plain but she wasn't ugly, and she looked as though she had a good figure underneath that raincoat and the knitted woollen cardigan he could just see through the plastic. Twenty years ago he would have found some cheap hotel to take her to, and they would have spent the night in bed together. The next morning he would have taken her address and her phone number at work and promised to phone her when he was in town again. Three days later he would have lost the piece of paper and a week later he would have forgotten what she looked like, her name and even what town she came from. Now it was too late, he was too old, and he was too cold, and he wasn't spending the money for a hotel on something he wasn't very good at any more. He wondered if he wasn't getting prostate trouble.

'Will you sign this, Mr Jones?' She pulled a book out from under her plastic mac. It was a *Radio Fun* annual from fifteen years before, and on the cover was a picture of himself in stage trilby and sequined jacket. Wearing a showbiz smile in an unlined face, a stranger looking forward from another country. He signed the book with a scrawl, said goodnight to the three autograph-hunters and walked across the road, his collar up against the wind and rain. A tram rattled its way towards the terminus and a wet dog hurried homewards, its head down, its tail curled up between its legs. A wild buffet of wind slammed into him as he pushed open the engraved glass and mahogany doors and dived into the warm pool of the Oh Be Joyful, the theatre pub.

It was called the Oh Be Joyful because it had originally been a Temperance preaching hall until the brewery bought it at the turn of the century and turned it into a boozer. That was the story the landlord told, and he had a framed and yellowing press cutting from the *Blackcombe Evening Post* to prove it. It was an unspoilt, seaside, back-street ale house used by theatre types, journalists and other serious drinkers who didn't like the more modern pubs where one of those new juke-box things could ruin their drink and chat. It was still gas-lit and even had a small cast-iron gas jet on the bar counter in the shape of a black boy holding a torch for the punters to light their cigarettes from.

In the years he'd been coming to the Gaiety, Jimmy had got to know the pub well. It was a nice, quiet, middle-aged drinkers' pub with never a moment's trouble, even during Glasgow holidays when the town was crowded with drunks. Charlie, the ex-wrestler who ran it, liked nothing better than getting hold of two battlers and cracking their heads together so that they both ended up in the hospital. On fine days in the summer seasons Jimmy played golf with Charlie. It was important that you did something during the day. These seaside towns, he thought, could drive you mad if you didn't watch them.

The lads in the pit orchestra usually made their way to the Joyful immediately after the curtain came down. The tenor player, a notorious lush, would even go across to it during the show if he had a big break. They reckoned he could count his bars of rest as the band were playing in his head. He would walk across the road, drink his two bottles of White Label and a whisky chaser, walk back and take his seat exactly as his next bit was coming up on the score. It was said he'd only failed once, and that was when some drunk had started playing the spoons in the snug and put his count out, so that he'd been four bars late for Joseph Locke singing the Indian Love Call.

The band were normally good for a laugh, he thought – at least musos didn't take themselves too seriously, not like the cowing chorus girls. This lot had been with the tour since Rotherham, and you'd think they were the Tiller Girls the way they kept to themselves. You could usually get your oats off one of the front-line hoofers on the road, but this lot had knickers knitted from steel wool.

He pushed through the crowd to the bar, warmth and smoke and the sea of chatter wrapping their friendly arms around him. Mavis from the circle bar was there. She saw him, waved him over and bought him a drink. He'd had a bit of a fling with her once, seven years ago when he'd played the Gaiety on tour with Frank Randle. Frank had got pissed after the show, as usual, and had thrown an empty Guinness bottle through the bar mirror because Mavis wouldn't serve him after time. Frank had paid for a new mirror and Jimmy had comforted Mavis. The comfort had led him to walk her home and the final few yards of the comforting walk were the top landing and bedroom carpet of Mavis's terraced house behind the roller-coaster.

'Don't wake me mother up. She's deaf, but she's not daft,' she'd said. Then, when she was coming, she'd screamed like a Comanche raiding party and the old woman had shouted from the next bedroom, 'If that's that Reg, you can tell him I know exactly how many slices of ham there are in that cold press!'

The old woman was dead now and Mavis was married to a joiner with a bad chest who led the local Boys Brigade, so there was nothing for him there nowadays, even on Brigade nights.

The ventriloquist, Gordon, was leaning on the bar, staring into the bottles and mirrors before him. Mavis mouthed something about 'Ted' and 'row'. Ted was one of the Tumbling Thompson Twins, and was Gordon's boyfriend. They were always falling out. In the boarding-house in Skegness, Ted had poured a bowl of Brown Windsor soup over Gordon's head because Gordon had been chatting up a young man who worked as a part-time usher. The soup was cold – it always was – so no harm was done and they'd made it up by the matinée in Llandudno.

Jimmy bought Mavis a drink and told her a good one he'd picked up that afternoon from an old bloke in the Winter Gardens about a nun and a parrot, and she laughed until her make-up ran. But he felt tired somehow, and even the warmth and closeness of the bar couldn't disperse the cold fog that was swirling round his soul. The three autograph-hunters had begun to remind him of the three witches in the first scene of *Macbeth*. He didn't know why.

'I'm getting too old for this game,' he told her, lighting their cigarettes from the black boy's jet. 'I'll not be doing many more of these long tours. Had enough.'

'You've been saying that as long as I've known you. You were already talking about that little pub in Devon ten years ago.'

'Well, a couple more tours and I'm out. I mean it.' He always did.

Seven bottles and a couple of Scotches later he made his way back to the boarding-house. Though the rain had stopped, the wind was still gusting off the sea, blowing scraps of paper and ice-cream tubs over the tram-lines and the cobbles and into the shelters where courting couples were clutched together for warmth and comfort for those last few moments before the final tram home.

Jimmy walked into the fish and chip shop and stood in the queue behind a drunk who was doing a very good five-minute act all on his own without the benefit of a pit band. His attempts to find a position of stasis were a wonderful example of mime that could have been rivalled only by the great clown Grock himself. How could he keep his feet so firmly fixed to the floor, and yet manage to gyrate his upper limbs and trunk in so many directions, unsupported by either chip-shop counter or fly-wires? He was pasted into Jimmy's mental scrap-book, and would appear by the Wednesday matinée in Wolverhampton as the Rubber Man in the Chip Shop.

Jimmy slid the bag of fish and chips into the pocket of his raincoat and turned away from the sea front, threading his way down narrow back streets where gift-shop windows were dark and shuttered, and pools of light fell from the street lamps on to the drying pavements. Avoiding a pile of dog mess, he turned into a cul-de-sac and walked to the end of a drab Edwardian terrace. The lights were still on in his home for the week, the Ocean View Theatrical Boarding-House. The title wasn't totally dishonest; if you stood on a chair in one of the attics and peered through the skylight, you could just about see – over the gasometer and the roof of Woolworth's – the grey smudge that was the waters of the Irish Sea. But only if the rain had washed the seagull shit off.

He felt the bottle of brown ale hard against one leg, and the fish and chips hot against his other. At least life held some comforts, he thought. And with luck Mrs Roberts' toothless poodle, Pedro, would be asleep and wouldn't attempt to roger his leg as it usually did.

At the boarding-house some of the other acts were in the parlour watching the new television that the landlady had proudly shown them all when they had checked in earlier that week. It flickered grimly in the darkened room, its black and white images reflecting off the glass-fronted display cabinet with its ranks of trophies won by Mrs Roberts and her Len when they were tango champions of the northern ballrooms.

Kurt, the German strongman act, was staring at the screen entranced, his lips silently mouthing the dialogue. Pauline, a Peggy Lee sound-alike, was knitting yet another sweater for her fiancé, Tommy – a Pat Boone look-alike, who was doing a summer season at Scarborough. Gordon, the ventriloquist, was asleep in the rocking chair, his mouth and flies open. Pedro was asleep in his basket and, though he opened one eye when Jimmy walked past him into the kitchen, he snuffled and closed it again.

Jimmy sat at the kitchen table eating off the newspaper to save using a plate. The cat watched him from its usual position among the sauce bottles and marmalade jars on the sideboard. It was a filthy moggy, Jimmy thought, and it was typical of this dump that she let it sleep near the food. He smoked a cigarette while he read the bits of newspaper the chips had been wrapped in, then, finishing his beer, he crumpled up the paper and threw it into the kitchen grate. He stuck his head round the lounge door to say goodnight and climbed the stairs.

On the landing he paused outside his room and dumped his coat and briefcase before turning towards the bathroom. He eased himself out of his trousers and stood staring ahead at nothing as he passed water. The handle of the cistern dangled from its chain close by his shoulder and for the first time that week, although it could well have been there all the time, Jimmy noticed a length of string tied to the handle hanging loosely down to the level of his waist.

He thought it strange. The Robertses had no children of their own, and as strict theatricals had a sign up in the window: 'No pets, no children.' Jimmy shook the drops off and thought no more about it, either then or next morning at breakfast. When the wobbly egg with the fat running off it and the stringy overcooked bacon and shrivelled sausage were put in front of him, he looked out of the window through the curtains at a man hand-cranking a battered van under grey skies that warned of more rain to come, and the piece of string faded completely out of his mind.

The next week the troupe were in Barnsley at the Civic. The boarding-house there was run by an alcoholic ex-chorus girl with varicose veins and a needle-toothed and aggressive fox terrier called Trixie, which had once bitten a Chinese plate-spinner stupid enough to try and befriend it. Mrs Morgan had hoofed it at the Windmill in her prime, but now she just hoofed it to the off-licence for her 'medicine' and got amazingly and spectacularly drunk. Her husband had run off with a pub landlady some years before, and Mrs Morgan had never got over it. She drank herself into catatonia most nights and lay sprawled on the settee in her housecoat, her legs wide open and everything on show. Once, when they had a seven-card brag school going, the legs akimbo routine had started early; and when one of the girls went to try and straighten Mrs Morgan's clothes out the dog went for her – so they'd thrown a coat over the old lady, and gone on with the game.

After the first show in Barnsley, Jimmy had a few in the George and walked back to the boarding-house under a starry sky. Having a pee before bed, he noticed that there was a piece of string tied to the toilet chain. In York, at Mrs Thompson's very posh and expensive theatrical digs, he saw another piece of string; and the following week, while playing the Liverpool Playhouse, he found another piece hanging from the chain at Nelly Dunn's in Upper Parliament Street.

Jimmy Jones was not a bright man, and he wasn't a great comic either. He was coming to the end of his days as a performer, and the act that had worked for him for the last thirty years was about to be killed off by television and rock and roll. He had a lot on his mind: the bookings weren't coming in as fast as they should have been, and after panto in Hull this winter his agent had found nothing further for him. Week on week of blank pages stretched ahead of him in his diary. He had a good few debts, and a not very good marriage. His daughter was living in sin with a married furniture salesman in Croydon, his son wanted to buy himself out of the Army and they'd discovered subsidence under the house. He had more than enough worries for one man. And now the string was beginning to puzzle him.

It wasn't there at the boarding-house in Glasgow, but by Morecambe it was back. It was there in Derby, Birmingham and Coventry, was missing in Stoke, and back in Cardiff.

One Sunday night towards the end of the tour he was standing in the buffet on Crewe station, waiting for the train to Manchester. The houses had been poor and the run was ending soon. The promoter was pulling out and Jimmy knew that for him, if not for the rest of the company, it was the end of a long line. Nobody wanted variety any more, radio had helped to keep it going for a while. But now they'd rather stay at home with their eyes glued to that glass tube in the corner. Well, that suited him, because he was tired of it too, had enough, chokka, up to here.

He looked at his reflection in the station buffet windows. Years had laid lines and shadows on his face so that now, when he looked at himself out of motley, without the greasepaint and the props, he looked like somebody he didn't know any more, a stranger he ought to feel sorry for.

He ordered another brown ale and looked around him. Outside on the platform were piles of skips, the property of other pros like himself changing at Crewe for weeks in theatres all over the island from Dundee to Torquay, Skegness to Inverness; the whole world of variety and music hall on the move from one tacky theatre to another, one arsehole of a town to another, one run-down boarding-house to another.

Inside the bar the jabber of voices annoyed him. Young pros hardly in the business ten minutes were laughing and shouting, full of themselves; sad old buggers like himself, bleary-eyed and shaky, were wondering whether they'd ever get enough money for that little pub in Devon, that small hotel in Lytham. He ordered a whisky to go with the brown ale.

As he made his way out to the toilet, one of the Tumbling Thompson Twins pushed a copy of *The Stage* towards him. Jimmy sat on the pan and flicked through the pages before him. The same old articles about the same old acts, Max Bygraves in panto at Darlington, Tommy Trinder to play in *Aladdin* in Birmingham, Arthur Askey and Albert Modley in *Babes in the Wood* at Bristol.

A box advertisement at the back of the paper caught his eye: Harry Hamp's Harmonica Dwarves wish to thank Frank McDonald and all the company of *Frank's Pranks* for a great tour, and all our friends at the Civic, Barnsley, the Theatre Royal, York, the Playhouse, Liverpool, the Winter Gardens, Morecambe... and it went on, listing the theatres that Harry Hamp's Harmonica Dwarves had played. They had toured the country, preceding *Jimmy Jones' Fun and Frolics*, by a week at every theatre. Only the Glasgow Empire and the Theatre Royal, Stoke on Trent were missing.

Jimmy Jones thought of all those little hands reaching up to pull on all those strings and started smiling. Then the smile became a snigger, and the snigger became a laugh, and the laughter got louder and louder. He sat there with his trousers round his ankles, laughing hysterically and helplessly, alone.

The rest of the people in the station buffet looked towards the door, wondering why somebody was laughing so madly in the toilet. And Jimmy Jones laughed on, tears drenching his face, his whole body shaking – but whether the tears were tears of laughter or grief, he couldn't himself at that moment have said.

Death Valley Nude

It was unbelievably hot for March, the man on the motel desk had said, and when he'd replied that it was perhaps the greenhouse effect, the man on the desk had said something about the Bible and the end of the world and Revelations – something about the Beast that will come out of the wastelands to signal the end of all. Robinson had smiled and nodded, and as he hurried over to the Howard Johnson's for breakfast he wondered should he perhaps, just for the sake of good manners, have said 'Amen'?

By the time he reached the salt flats at Badwater, they were skimmed by a lagoon of heat haze that pulsed and shifted a foot or so above their billiard-table level wastes; heat was hammering up from the desert floor and there were still two hours to go before noon. Robinson stopped the car on the first piece of level ground he could find, turned off the radio and pushed on the parking brake with his foot. He decided that it would be a long time before he got used to these American cars, the hand brake being another foot brake and that cruise control thing on the steering-wheel. The air conditioning burred, he turned off the ignition and took out the key.

When he opened the door he stepped into another world. Nothing he had read in the books or seen on Bob's home video had really come anywhere near to what he now saw around him. The land all about was gripped in a fist of scorching, crackling heat. At the edge of the flats were dried-up pools that had shrunk to become fields of curled octagonal mud-plates, and lining the pools were boulders that had split and fractured in the desert fires. Beyond the flats the world ran away, liquid and shifting, to the jutting mountains.

Over Zabriskie Point an eagle circled in a drawling glide, dandling on the thermals. Fixing on something in one of the canyons below, it crossed the sky in a skater's curve, slicing northwards in a parabola before dropping, a meteor sinking into the desert hills that stretched to the horizon in folded pleats of weathered stone: saffron, magenta, cerise and purple, so vivid they looked man-made in this intense light, as though some chemical experiment gone wrong had spread this riot of colours on the earth.

His camera bag and tripod were on the back seat. He collected them, locked the car and shouldered the equipment. 'I must look like an old prospector from a distance,' he thought. As usual he had brought too much stuff. 'You always were one for the overkill,' his wife would have said if she had been with him, but she wasn't.

There was a vast boulder field on the edge of the flats, and a massive stone standing above all the others had weathered into the head and shoulders of a giant woman, staring out towards the white salt plain. He found it disturbed him, but he couldn't have said why.

Leaving the levels, he began climbing an arroyo towards a canyon that he thought, as he would later write in his diary, 'might yield some interesting photo-opportunities.' He felt the heat on his back and shoulders as he climbed away from the pull-off and was glad he'd filled two large plastic bottles with water before he left the motel. They were in the cool-box in the car with the rest of his film. He wondered whether he shouldn't go back and get one of them to carry with him just in case, then decided that was stupid because he wasn't going very far, only just along the canyon for a while. He was annoyed with himself for his indecision. It had been happening a lot recently. He often found himself rushing up the stairs only to stop half-way and wonder what it was he was going for. He put it down to all he had been through recently.

He had to stop often to push up the baseball cap he'd bought in Vegas and wipe the sweat out of his eyes. At one halt he noticed a small flower blooming in the desert sand at his feet – a delicate white globe-like head with five petals splayed out like a large white marsh-marigold. On the base of each petal was a crimson-purple roundel. He looked in the guidebook to the flowers of Death Valley he had bought in the information centre: 'Desert Five Spot' the flower was called.

It was very like something Marjory had once grown in the garden. Marjory would have had the guidebook almost off by heart by now, and would have told him the flower's name even before he asked. She had so much energy for those kinds of things: flowers and plants and the names of things and places. She'd always been much more curious and interested in that stuff than he had.

He stared at the slope ahead of him. He hadn't thought of her for two days now; perhaps life really would get better, as everybody kept telling him. He looked up at the hard blue sky, metallic almost. Neutral, like the jungle, he thought, and it would kill you just as quickly.

'Get away,' his son and his two daughters had said. 'You'll destroy yourself thinking about her. You've taken early retirement – use the money for something you'll enjoy.'

He didn't suppose he'd ever understand what had happened. The change, the mid-life crisis, whatever – perhaps a mix of a lot of factors. He was fifty-three now. Had they still been together it would have been nearly thirty years. But out of the blue, completely and absolutely out of the blue, she'd moved half the money out of the joint account into one of her own, told him she was leaving, got a flat and a lover (in that order, he thought) and started wearing clothes ten, fifteen years too young for her. Even their children thought she'd gone a little mad, though they didn't take sides – or, if they did, it was perhaps to see him as more sinned against than sinning.

She'd always been a bit wilder than him. An art teacher who loved her job, she threw herself into everything with what seemed to be limitless energy so that he'd found her exhausting at times. He was older than her; six years must make a bit of difference, he supposed, and being a woman must give you a different view of the world. But he still couldn't work out quite what had happened.

They'd been a normal couple, he thought. Good jobs, nice home, nice friends, nice family; a caravan at Silverdale: a bit boring and safe, maybe – but what was the alternative? You had to eat and live, you had to feed your family and pay the mortgage, no matter what. And luckily they'd both had good careers, managed to bring up the children and get them well educated and settled. They'd not had a bad life. Teaching wasn't such a bad job, and they'd both enjoyed it.

And love? Well, after the first passion you just become good friends and that's it, really, he thought. There's nothing much either of you can do about it, no matter what the women's magazines say. Candle-lit dinners and dressing up in sexy underwear is all right, but it's still the same old two of you when all the fantasy's gone.

He had been quite happy for them to trundle along into old age together, gardening and visiting the grandchildren. She obviously hadn't. He'd gone through it over and over again in his head on those teems of sleepless nights since she left, and the only thought that came to him, time and again, was that it was probably something to do with her hormones. As a science teacher he knew enough about the chemical make-up of the body to have reached his own conclusions about illnesses such as schizophrenia and post-natal depression. He'd talked to other women about it since, and they had all seemed to agree that it was probably her hormones as much as anything else. And you can't do much about hormones.

'Come on over,' Bob had said, 'spend as long as you like.' But although the two couples had been really close when they lived next door on the new estate where their children had grown up and fallen in and out of trees and love with each other, and although they had written and done their best to keep in touch in the five years since Bob and Hazel had emigrated to Los Angeles, they were a million light-years apart now. And even while they made him welcome in their big house with its pool, its sit-on lawn-mower and fridge the size of a garden shed, he felt out of it all – detached somehow, unreal.

Bob and Hazel were nice people and had done their best to give him a good time to make him feel relaxed, but there was something very strained about it all. Much of it, he supposed, was because they had been used to seeing him and Marjory together as a couple. Now he was on his own, and there was a new set of roles and rules to get used to.

He and Bob had always got on well together. They liked the same things: cameras, classic cars, boats – anything, really, that had gadgets. They'd always had something to talk about. Bob was doing really well in America. His firm made tapes for the recording and computer industries and Bob, who'd been the head of their English sales force, had been moved over to the States as export manager. He was a lot fatter than he had been and Hazel looked as though perhaps she'd had a face-lift. Back home she'd worked in the Town Hall as the head of some department or other. Here she'd got herself well in with a firm of insurance brokers and was now a partner. They must be worth a fortune, Robinson thought.

But they'd done their very best to make him feel comfortable. They'd even tried to fix him up with a divorcee at one of the local parties thrown in his honour; it had been a disaster. He'd ended up in bed with her, but had been too drunk to do anything that night, then in the morning (when he'd put on a condom for the first time in thirty years: 'It's the age of Aids, honey – I hope you don't mind?') they'd gone through what they both knew were the lonely motions almost expected of two people like themselves, in that kind of situation. It had been disaster that his face still burned to think of.

At another dinner party, towards the end of his stay, he'd found himself next to a plastic surgeon who'd moved to California from England a few years before Bob and Hazel. He'd made a fortune treating rich old people who wanted to look like rich young people, but who merely succeeded in looking like partly finished models of human beings. There were only English people at the party, and the surgeon had sounded off at some length about Americans. 'Their problem is that they think death is optional. They don't realise that after you're forty the planet has no more use for you, and basically you're a drain on its resources.'

'How do you mean?' Hazel asked. 'I'm over forty, and I sure as hell don't feel like I'm finished!' Robinson had noticed how both she and Bob had developed Americanised ways of speaking.

'You might not think you're finished, I might not think you're finished, Bob almost certainly doesn't think you're finished – but Mother Nature does. You're past the best breeding age, so is Bob, and as far as the planet is concerned you've fulfilled your function and you're now just a couple of freeloaders.'

Bob laughed and said something about getting his sperm counted, and a man called Alan, who came from the Midlands originally and now sold classic cars in LA, said, 'What about the wisdom of the elderly? Even African tribes sort of revere the ancients and look after their old people, if you see what I mean.'

'That's only because we've developed that way. In the animal kingdom, after you've bred and reared all the young you're going to have, you usually get taken care of by predators.'

'So in the normal course of events we'd have been left out for the hyenas?' Robinson asked, and the rest of the guests at the dinner-table laughed.

'Take no notice of Greg,' the surgeon's wife told him. 'He's always trying to stir it. He just likes to be controversial and get things going.' She put her hand over her husband's wine glass. 'And you're not having any more of this – you're driving home.'

After two weeks with Bob and Hazel he'd been glad to get away on the rest of his trip. No schedule, no time-base, freewheeling across the Southern States for as long as the money held out, something he'd been wanting to do for twenty years. He'd always wanted to see the great National Parks, the Grand Canyon, Zion, Death Valley, Arches. Now there was nothing to stop him. No one else to worry about, free and easy, all by himself. He'd budgeted wisely, he thought; staying in motels was cheap and he'd got a good deal on the rental car. By eating in the IHOPs and Wendys next to the motels he'd been able to keep his costs right down, and doing it this way, travelling alone, also meant that he'd nobody else to spend the money on. He liked it better that way.

He'd always been careful with money. Too careful, she would have said. But she was a bit of a spender. 'You can't take it with you,' she'd often remarked, but he'd been brought up to believe in saving so that you were never in debt and could leave a little something to your children when you went.

The heat pulsed down on him from an iron sky and up at him from the white desert floor as he climbed further into the canyon. He stumbled a couple of times and his camera bags were chafing his shoulder. He wondered whether he shouldn't have got a good pair of boots instead of the cheap Taiwan trainers he'd bought from the K-Mart. People got lost and died in Death Valley every year, the poster at the information centre said. He kept his car in view until the arroyo twisted into the canyon, then he put a stone on top of a boulder as a marker, doing this every fifty yards or so. He'd read the Death Valley journals of some people who'd been lost there in 1849 and had drunk salt water and gone half-mad, eventually killing their oxen so that they could drink the blood from their veins. He felt a not unpleasant twinge of fear as he walked further into the deepening canyon.

Alone, and some distance from his car, he felt out on the edge. What if he were to fall and break a leg here? It would be days before anybody came looking for him and by then he would be long dead. The canyon deepened around him.

A sudden flick of life in some boulders at the base of the high wall made him turn and fumble for his long lens. A lizard with olive and bronze skin had raised its head, and was looking at him from the top of one of the boulders. But by the time he had fitted the telephoto lens on the camera body it had skittered into a crack between the rocks and only its snout and eyes were visible, poking out of the darkness. He stood perfectly still, watching it for a while, then began to move towards it little by little, hoping it wouldn't run and hide, but when he was no more than four feet away it backed into its hole and didn't come out again.

Robinson took some pictures of the vividly coloured rocks and sands in the canyon and walked on slowly, curious at how little he was sweating, until he realised that the desiccated air was sucking the moisture from his body. After he'd walked for another half-hour, the canyon kinked. Instead of cutting further into the mountain, as he'd expected, it turned and opened out into a hanging valley that looked out over an arid sulphur-tinged flat far below. The valley had cut been cut through the shoulder of the mountain like a gash by millennia of grit-bearing winds. A steep track came up from the valley floor towards a ruin that lay just before and below him, on the lip of the gully. It was two-storeyed, stone-built, ruinous and carious. An ore wagon was falling to decay before it and the remains of a cable-way snaked down to the valley floor below.

He took some shots of the whole of the valley twisting and shaking in the glassy light, using the ruin as a foreground to draw the eye out to the distance. He could imagine the shot printed up and framed at the next camera club exhibition, underneath the title *Deserted Mine, Death Valley, California*. He tried a range of filters and lenses and then scrambled down towards the ruin. A sudden snake slipped away before him and a flush of fear stopped his breath. He watched for a few moments as the snake arrowed under a pile of rocks. He was sure that if he'd trodden on it, he would have been dead. He waited until his heart stopped hammering and then, taking care to breathe slowly and gently, he walked the last few yards to the ruin. Its roofless husk would make a perfect frame. He remembered one of the classic shots by Edward Weston (or was it Ansel Adams?) of a desert ruin filling the frame – and yet framing the desert itself, which was seen through a gap in the fallen walls.

He set up his tripod and snapped his camera on to the shoe. He used an old twin lens Rolleiflex for most of his landscape shots. He liked looking down on to the ground glass screen and framing his shots precisely. He moved the tripod to one side to line up the mudstone hills with a ruined window-frame, and looked down again at the screen.

As he focused the lens, a figure stepped into the edge of the viewfinder and started to undress. Startled, he looked up. No more than ten or so yards away was a young woman, her skirt and top already on the floor. She flicked her bra off in one movement and quickly slipped her pants down and flung them on the small pile some yards away in the dust. She turned to face Robinson and stood, legs open, her hands behind her neck, her face tilted up towards the sun, eyes closed tightly.

She held that pose for a long time before breaking and turning to the wall, leaning her back against the edge of the building and looking out off into the far distance where the mountains shook in the heat. She was very beautiful, Spanish-looking, with long black hair and a long, slim, tanned body. Her breasts were quite small, with dark nipples that pointed out to the blue sky over the hills. All this Robinson took in speechlessly and achingly, without moving, staring at her.

She began to circle around in a kind of dance, as though she were celebrating her own youth and beauty and yet mocking him with them at the same time. She spun calmly around the dusty ruin in a saraband, finally coming to rest facing him again with her legs

43

spread and her arms extended, a perfect X, framed in the mine ruins; and at the same time framing the desert and the sky herself with the twin vees of her legs and arms. Robinson, dry-mouthed and shaking, clicked the shutter.

It was only then that she looked up into the ruin and said in a languid voice, 'Will you get it together, André, before any more pervs arrive? We've got a visitor already, and if you don't get your shit together we'll have every weirdo in California out here jerking off!'

Robinson followed her line of sight. Almost completely hidden in the ruined wall, half-way up the building in what had been a cupboard or alcove, was a young foreign-looking man with long, thick, black curly hair pulled back in a pony-tail. He was very brown and was wearing a singlet, shorts and thong sandals. He looked down from his camera and rig to Robinson, seeing him for the first time, and at his side was a woman, obviously his assistant, also in shorts and singlet, her hair up in a scarf and her hands full of films and lens shades.

André looked down at Robinson and in a voice larded with French tones said, 'We are making a shoot here. Okay? Why don't you go and jack off somewhere else, mister, eh?' And his assistant looked at Robinson from her roost as though some low kind of desert life had crawled from under a stone.

'I beg your pardon. I'm really very, very sorry. I'd no idea you were here. I can explain everything. Honestly, it's very simple...' – and he smiled.

But, before he could explain anything at all, André had spat at him from the ruin above and was throwing his words back at him in mockery. 'Ah beg yer pardon, ah am very very sorry. Oh ah do beg yer pardon! Very much! Oh ah do beg yer pardon! Oh yes!'

Robinson turned, threw his gear into his bag in a jumble and hurry, and climbed quickly back towards the canyon, scrabbling up the scree slope, oblivious of snakes or lizards, his face blazing with a heat that had nothing to do with the Death Valley sun. He ran into the shadow of the canyon and leaned against the wall. The best thing was to get back to the car and drive away.

It wasn't his fault, but nobody would believe that. They wouldn't see it as a blunder, a piece of innocent stupidity. They would just see a dirty old man with a camera. What was he supposed to have done? Turned away immediately he saw her? He supposed the answer was yes.

He walked quickly along the canyon and gradually the sense of shame and embarrassment changed to one of unease. Where were the stones he'd placed on the boulders on his way in? Perhaps they were further in. But as he went deeper into the canyon, he noticed that not only were there no stones on any of the boulders, but that the canyon was very different now. It was steeper, climbing into the mountain and not down away from it. If he went further he might get lost. He should go back. But if he went back then they would think he'd come back to get another look.

This was crazy. He could explain everything. This was all very stupid, they were all intelligent people. Surely they'd understand that he'd stumbled on them by mistake? He ought to go back. But he knew that he wouldn't.

If he went on, perhaps he could climb up high enough to find his way back in to the first canyon. He looked ahead to where the horizon crackled a mile away. It would only take him twenty minutes or so to climb on to the shoulder ahead, and he would be able to get his bearings from there.

The camera bag and tripod unsteadied him as he scrambled the last few yards to the ridge. It was steeper than he had thought and at one point he had to get on his knees and crawl. At another he had to do a bit of real rock-climbing to get out of a gully. Distances, heights and contours were all false in this melting light. He was thirsty now, and dizzy from the climb.

He moved across the shoulder to get his bearings and found that he could see clear across a succession of pleats and folds in the coloured rocks of the landscape to Badwater and the mountains. Behind him another violet and orange range led towards the nothingness of the wastelands. The ridge he was on rose on his left to the summit of the mountain, a sugar-pink and yellow fairytale castle of a stump rising sheer from all the ridges that led to it. To his right the shoulder led back the way he had come, above the canyon he'd come along; in front of and beneath him it fell in a slope before dropping away into blackness. He walked to the edge. Below him, under five or more hundred feet of sheer cliff wall, was the canyon he'd come through. There was no way down. He'd have to go back and face them again. Anything else would be stupid.

He was sliding on his backside over the bad step of rock he'd scrambled up when his bag unbalanced him and he slid to the rocks below – only ten feet or so, but enough to hurt him. He fell feet forward into a jumbled mass of boulders and felt the ankle of his left foot go over. There was a crack of pain that started at his foot and went jabbering up his leg. He felt sick, and watery flowing lights before his eyes shifted the horizons.

Holding on to the rock he checked his cameras. They weren't broken, neither was his ankle. He knew that. He'd broken one before at Llandudno, playing cricket with the children. He'd jumped off a breakwater and there'd been a snap and he'd been unable to move. He could move now but it hurt. He had to go. What he needed was cold water for his ankle. He couldn't put his weight full on it without it hurting enough to make him want to shout. He needed to get back to the car as soon as he could.

He used the tripod as a support and that helped, but it made the steep descent slower and more awkward because now, with the bag on one side and without the counterweight of the tripod, he was unbalanced. He decided that, rather than go all the way back out of this canyon, he would follow the ridge down almost to the level of the mouth and cross over there into the first canyon where it was lower and safer.

He took another fall on the ridge and grazed his hand as he tried to stop himself sliding any further. The skin was torn and there was plenty of blood coming out from under the flap, but the wound wasn't deep. After an hour of descent he found a short gully that led down into the canyon he wanted. The sun was now moving beyond its zenith, but it was hotter than it had been all morning.

He sat down to get his breath. His tongue was dry and sore from the heat and the alkali dust, and his lips were cracking. Looking down a hundred feet or so to the canyon floor, he could see how he'd been wrong-footed. The canyon he had come by took a dog's leg that presented a blind opening to the ruin; he'd scrambled past the opening of that canyon into this one. He looked down at the slope before him. It was a scramble with a couple of bad steps that would need a bit of rock-climbing, but it would be better than facing those people again. If he took it easy and faced into the rock at one or two points he could be down in minutes.

It was on one of the bad steps that he saw the snake. He had hooked the tripod into his bag strap and, turning into the rock, had got a handhold and had begun to hop slowly down a twelve-foot slab with plenty of good holds. There was a ledge off slightly to one side of the slab, an arm-stretch away, and as he pulled himself across level with it he saw the gold-green coils and the sleeping head. Nothing moved: not he, nor the snake, nor the air.

Then the snake reared up and at the same instant he let go, sliding down the slab and falling again into a cluster of boulders. This time he fell backwards and rolled down to a scree slope where he was able to dig his feet into the loose mudstone chips and stop himself sliding any further. He ran, lurching on his bad ankle, down the last of the slope until he made the canyon floor.

There was blood on his shirt and more was running down his face. When he wiped himself with his sleeve he saw that he was bleeding from his head somewhere. His ankle felt even worse, and there was a sharp and cutting pain in his left knee now. He looked in his camera bag. One of the filters on a lens was smashed and he'd lost a cable release and a blower-brush; otherwise there was no harm, beyond dust having got in everywhere. The tripod had one leg bent almost at right angles, which meant that it was finished, but beyond that there wasn't much that a wash, some antiseptic and a few dollars wouldn't sort out. He supposed his holiday insurance would cover the breakages.

He limped along the canyon following his pebble trail and hobbled down the arroyo back towards the road, where he could see his car shining maroon against the white salt flats. There was another vehicle parked close by and somebody was walking round his car, looking in the windows. When he got closer he saw that it was a man in uniform – a State trooper or a National Park ranger perhaps.

The man looked up and saw Robinson coming awkwardly towards him, leaning on the bent tripod. 'Shit, mister, are you okay? You look a mess!'

'I'm fine. I just took a bit of a fall, that's all. I've just a few cuts and grazes. I saw a snake up there – it gave me a shock, and I fell. All I need now is a drink of water, a bath and some clean clothes.'

Robinson realised he was gibbering. Probably the shock. The man went to his own car and came back with a plastic bottle of ice-cold water. Robinson took a long drink from it.

'Snake didn't bite you, did it?' Robinson shook his head. 'You sure you ain't broke something? You can't hardly walk there.'

'No, I've just wrenched my ankle a bit. I'm on my way out of the valley, by Scotty's Castle. I'll be okay, honestly. It's good of you to take all this trouble.' *What trouble?* he thought. *It's the man's job, probably.*

'You from Australia?'

'No, I'm from England.'

'I bin to England. I went to London once. I liked your English pubs, but you couldn't get real ice cream there. Not then, anyway.'

'Yes, you can probably get it there now. We've even got McDonalds now. They're all over the place.' Robinson groped for his car keys.

'Yep, those guys get everywhere. They reckon they're gonna open one in Moscow sometime soon. Ain't that sumthin'? A McDonalds in Moscow!' He watched Robinson struggling to get his cameras on the back seat and gave him a hand. 'Listen, there's a washroom at the visitor centre up at Furnace Creek. You can wash up there. If you still feel bad, then they can probably get a paramedic to look at you. Just ask one of the people in the visitor centre. There's usually two or three rangers there. Maybe you should do that anyway?'

'Thanks very much. I'll see how I feel when I get there. Thanks again for the water.'

'You're welcome. You can keep it. I got plenty more in the ice-box. I just stopped to look at your car when I saw it parked empty here. Just making sure. Last year we found three people dead up there in them canyons. Three people takin' photographs just like yourself, got themselves lost and wandered round up there till the heat and the thirst got them. First we knew of it was an empty car and a sky full of buzzards. They was mighty near picked clean by the time we found 'em. You got any water? You can take some more if you like. Like I say, I got plenty.'

'I've got a couple of bottles that should see me through. Thanks anyway.'

'You're welcome. Straight on up to Furnace Creek, now, and get yourself washed up. You look like an old prospector.' And Robinson laughed.

Robinson washed up at Furnace Creek, and changed his torn and dirty clothes. Nobody even looked at him as he limped into the restroom covered in blood and dust and came out again clean but still limping. There was a gash under the hairline that had congealed in a lump just covered by his hair and his hand had stopped bleeding now. His knee hurt as though something bad had happened to the joint but not enough to stop him walking. His ankle was the worst but luckily it was his left ankle and the car was automatic.

He thought about driving back to Bob and Hazel's and resting up there a few days but decided to carry on instead. He'd be all right by morning. He'd get a walking stick from somewhere, perhaps see a doctor – his insurance would cover that. He'd find somewhere nice to rest for a few days. Flagstaff, perhaps?

A Cherokee jeep with an Airstream trailer turned into the car-park and pulled up close by the visitor centre. As Robinson walked towards his car the photographers climbed out.

'It's Mr Jerkoff!' the model called at him. 'Hello, Mr Jerkoff!'

The other woman looked at him in silence, cold eyes freezing him out behind her glasses. André stood on the sidebar of the jeep and sneered down, making a masturbatory gesture at him.

He climbed into his hired car and, slamming it into drive, he raced out of the car-park, almost crashing into a camper-van that was turning in. Shaking and on the edge of crying, he drove on through the dust with the air conditioning full on to try and cool his throbbing burning head. His trembling fingers punched the buttons on the radio, searching for something that would still the jabbering voices in his mind. He found a country station and turned it up as loud as he could bear until the car was filled with the slither of pedal-steel guitars and the throaty wails of voices lamenting lost loves and troubled lives.

All that afternoon, on his long drive along those wide south-western roads, the twisted rock forms and strata in the hills and canyons around took on the shape of female limbs and breasts. That night in his room in the almost vacant motel, as the neon sign flashed through the curtains and the air conditioning hummed under the window, the ceiling was patterned by the headlights of passing cars; and yet he saw, instead of splashes of coloured light, a tangle of legs, arms, dark hair and breasts. The snake, his terror and his embarrassment had all slid to some corner of his mind now, to be replaced by a sense of wonder and terrible loss. His body hurt but not nearly as much as his soul, which felt dryer and deader than any salt flats or dusty arroyo.

A lost world of infinite possibilities of which he was no longer a part, and which he realised he had never really understood, ran before him: a masque in which he saw the dancing girl in the dusty copper-mine ruins; his wife running naked into the moonlit sea in Crete, laughing at him because he wouldn't join her; and he saw himself back in the canyon, as though he were looking through the eyes of the eagle over Zabriskie Point, scrabbling for safety like the lizard on the rock.

He remembered then the words of the plastic surgeon at the party: 'after you're forty the planet has no more use for you.' And he saw himself as someone infinitely sad and infinitely ineffectual and saw, too, that all the years and the work and the scrimping and money and the ambitions really meant nothing, were nothing but dry dust and arid salt-pans. None of it was permanent, none of it really significant, all of it transitory.

And he lay very still, watching the lights of passing trucks moving across the ceiling, crossing the pulsing flushes of red and violet from the neon sign, and he lay that way without moving until the ice-blue desert dawn came seeping through the slit in the curtains and only then did he finally close his eyes in sleep.

Guy Fawkes and the Fat Lady on the Beach

A fter less than six days of her Greek holiday, Rachel Harrison realised that the whole idea had been a miserable mistake, and half an hour after the Fat Lady got stung on her left breast by a hornet most of the people on the beach knew this, too.

Rachel met Jason McCalman at a party given by a friend of a friend of a friend, the sort of party that often takes place in those large old houses in the inner suburbs of the larger cities of England, where nurses, teachers, social workers and 'alternative theatre' actors live in little cells that were once the bedrooms, master bedrooms, maids' parlours, nurseries and butlers' pantries of the one-time rich. It is a world of crumbling gateposts and of leaning sycamores whose unlopped limbs stretch over numbered dustbins, the lids of which are forever being stolen in a game of Chinese whispers by other people whose dustbin lids have been stolen. It is a world of damp overgrown gardens, of individual meters, Habitat and Ikea, of New Age music and heavy bread.

Where once carriages rolled up villa drives to take the master to his work on the floor of the cotton exchange or wool exchange or cutlers' hall or haberdashers' hall in the city, now the Citroën Deux Cheveaux and Volkswagen Golfs with their 'Atomkraft Nein Danke' stickers are ranked in lines, and the Suzuki four-wheel-drives of photographers' assistants and television researchers jostle each evening for a parking spot. Where once the scent of night stock and sweet pea lay heavy on the air as news of the

Somme was passed from garden to garden, and tennis was played on the long back lawns by bright young things who would, in a few years' time, be packing parachutes and flying Wellingtons, now the evening air is thick with the scents of chilli con carne, spaghetti bolognese and vegetarian curry, and the dustbin bags jangle on the binmen's shoulders to the tune of empty Beaujolais Nouveau, Hunter Valley Chardonnay and Vinho Verdi bottles. Gardens that once knew only Leonards and Virginias and the footsteps of boys delivering *The Times* and the *Telegraph* now echo to the cries of children called Tamsin or Timon and of a morning the hallways of the villas are espadrille-deep in copies of the *Guardian*, *New Society*, *Viz*, *The Face*, *Cosmopolitan* and *Nursing Mirror*.

The party at which Rachel met Jason and which brought about the affair that was, much later, to result in the embarrassment of some and the amusement of many on that far-off beach, was a joint bonfire party arranged by the tenants of The Laurels, Ruskin Crescent. The three teachers, two nurses and the sociology lecturer who lived on the first and second floors and the musician, the television researcher and the Nigerian post-graduate student researching into strains and stresses in pre-cast concrete at sub-zero temperatures, who lived on the ground floor, had come together as a kind of ad-hoc entertainments committee to sling light bulbs from the trees around the overgrown garden, to buy fireworks and garden candles and to gather as much junk furniture, old wood and rubbish as they could lay their hands on for Guy Fawkes Day. Couples with children came from neighbouring houses re-converted from flats, and friends brought friends of friends and home-made toffee, cakes and safe fireworks.

The bonfire sent sparks pouring up into the inky night, children ran squealing about the shadowy garden, safely watched by Barbour-jacketed parents. The roast potatoes were excellent, the vegetarian quiche and the kofta curry were wonderful and the night was so full of stars and the paper cups of wine so plentiful that

Rachel, who had just finished a week of nights on the neo-natal unit where stress was a way of life, found herself, as the fire became a mound of pulsing embers, leaning her head on the shoulder of a man called Jason who had been nice to her for the last four hours.

Rachel was thirty-three, and though she had been in several relationships none of them had got as far as the door of either church or registry office. As her friends paired off to get married and have children like Spitfires leaving formation, she found herself going to more weddings and christenings than parties. During the summer months she would hardly be out of her big hat and nice frock, usually ending up in the kitchen with the washing-up, fending off the advances of some wet-eyed uncle who was politely but determinedly following her round the kitchen table.

It was funny, she thought later, how at parties everybody seemed to gravitate towards the kitchen. She'd gone into the house to fill her paper cup again with Hunter Valley Chardonnay and Jason had been standing near the drinks in the crowded kitchen. 'I'm the unofficial barman,' he had said. 'What can I get you? You look thirsty.' They had started talking, which had led to them walking out again to the fire where they had sat, drinking and talking, then holding hands, then cuddling and then kissing as the children were bundled off and the guests went in and the fire died down to a mat of coals throbbing in the night breezes.

'Happy?' he asked, stroking her hair as they sipped their wine on the cast-aluminium imitation wrought-iron bench.

'Very,' she answered, in complete truth.

Later, as the stars were dulled by a moon that painted the slate roofs milky white, they walked along the Crescent to the friends' house where he was staying the night, climbed the stairs to his room and made love. His body was hard and slim and it was so long since Rachel had had sex with anybody that her hunger made her especially sensitive and, loosened by drink and the romance of the moonlit room, she took Jason in a rough and urgent manner that surprised her slightly.

He made love in a quiet, undemanding, almost detached way, whereas she felt her body was more open and hungry than she had ever noticed before. Straddling him for the second time, she saw him staring at the silvered window with a distant look on his face and began to wonder whether she wasn't enjoying herself more than he was.

They met as often as they could for the next few weeks. Her friends at work noticed a definite change in Rachel and in conversation decided that they were all happy for her. 'Rachel's got a new bloke,' someone said at coffee and the affair became a talking-point. Even the consultants found her chirpier than usual.

I suppose if we were all honest, we'd own up that a good half of being in love is wanting to be in love; and in Rachel's case it was so long since she had been in love that now she was in love she was enjoying everything about it. Her stomach tingled, she lost weight, her skin looked better and she stopped smoking because Jason couldn't stand the smell of tobacco; even though the other nurses all went at it like pyromaniacs and there were times when she'd have murdered for a cigarette, because her nerves were frayed with trying to keep alive the tiny rags of mortality who lay panting like spent marathon runners in their glass and wire wombs. But in spite of all the temptations and the offers of cigarettes from the other nurses, she stuck it out and chewed gum and mints to curb what was at times an almost delirious lust for tobacco.

Physically Jason was exactly the type of man she liked: quite tall, with thick brown hair well cut in forties fashion and gelled back, clear fair skin and a small neat moustache. She liked moustaches on men. She said that to him once and he replied, 'Yes, they don't look too good on women.' He was witty like that. He had nice brown eyes, but she wasn't sure if they weren't a bit too close together; his nose was quite long and his mouth a little thin-lipped, but when he smiled he did show a good set of teeth. She thought that, despite seeming very confident, he blinked a lot – as if he was nervous deep inside, something she found touching. That small sign of weakness drew affection out of her. She'd been used to men who were often nothing more than big, silly boys with little sensibility and less sensitivity. Jason wasn't like that.

He dressed well; but curiously, even though his clothes were modern, they looked somehow old-fashioned on him – a little too precise, a touch conservative. For work he wore good but not expensive suits, always with a tie, and his shirts were always well ironed. For casual wear he favoured slacks and sweaters in muted colours, usually from Top Shop or Next. He lived on his own in a large flat on the other side of town; a married sister did his laundry and he had a cleaner who came to his flat once a week. His shoes, Rachel noticed, were never quite as clean as they should be. This disturbed her, since her father, when he was alive, had always told her that you could tell a man's character by the kind of shoes he wore and the way he looked after them.

As the months went by their relationship became more established and Rachel began to see it as something that would stretch ahead into the future. She was not so stupid as to talk of wedding bells yet but, as she said to one of her friends, 'You never know. And I did catch the bouquet at Rowena's wedding.'

They went to the cinema with some friends a handful of times and once to the theatre, where they sat through a touring production of a West End success that looked over-dressed, tatty and road-weary; though when Jason expressed his opinion on the way home he seemed more concerned that it had cost them almost eighteen pounds each to sit through it than he was by the standard of the production. They went bowling a couple or three times with the people who had given the Guy Fawkes party, baby-sat for Rachel's sister twice and, when her shifts allowed, went for Indian and Italian meals with other friends. They went sailing twice on a boat belonging to another couple and to the Lake District for a walking weekend with a couple who had a holiday cottage there. But when she thought about it later she realised they had spent little time actually getting to know one another. Most of the time they were with other people.

She enjoyed the few times she was alone with Jason, though he was often very quiet and went into a kind of closed-off mood, which she thought was a sign that he was not flighty or comic-cocky like other men she'd gone out with, but that instead he was deep and dependable. In company he was quite different: then he could be very witty and confident, though much of his wit had a tinge of sarcasm to it. In the pub and at dinner parties he would make people laugh; most people he met thought he was a bit of a card and she knew that more than one of her women friends thought he was quite fanciable.

As a lover he was adequate, though his love-making was a little short-lived and unadventurous. Sex tended to be passionate but somehow distant, and foreplay to him seemed largely a case of undressing, grabbing bits and putting them together. She believed it would improve, given time.

Her figure, she knew, was good: she had a good bust, and her legs were well shaped, though her thighs, she thought, were getting a bit flabby. Perhaps she ought to take up swimming again – she'd been quite a strong swimmer at school. She thought her hair was her best point. Thick and almost jet black, it was trimmed close around her face, making her look a great deal younger than she was. In certain lights she looked almost like a child, for she was quite short – only five foot three and a bit inches – and she rarely wore high heels, because they crippled her after a day on her feet.

Occasionally he met her straight from work while she was still wearing her flat shoes and nurse's raincoat – he said they made her look like a schoolgirl. 'My little schoolie,' he called her. It seemed to get him very excited and often when she was dressed like that he would be in a hurry to make love – such a hurry once, when he had collected her after an early shift, that they made love on the floor of his flat and the window cleaner almost caught them at it.

They were already beginning to be thought of as a couple when he went away for six months to Australia. He worked for a big construction company in middle management, something to do with the finance of building roads and bridges. He had trained as a quantity surveyor but had taken a sabbatical to study for a diploma in business studies. After that he'd moved into management. The trip to Australia was connected with a sister company in Perth that was building a road across the desert to a mining camp. He had talked about it at great length when they were having dinner one night but it had either been too complicated or he had explained himself very badly – she couldn't decide which – and she hadn't in the end understood much about it except that there was an enormous amount of money involved and that a man called Higgins who was looking after the Australian end of the investment had made some big mistakes about plant hire. These were costing the company thousands per day and he, Jason, would have to go and sort it all out.

He was to leave England just before Christmas and would be away until the Whitsun holidays. She saw him off at the airport and was so upset that she cried all the way back to town and had to go to a girlfriend's flat for comfort. There she cried again, drank a bottle of wine and woke up on the futon the next morning with a murderous hangover.

He phoned her once a week, staying on the line for ages, telling her not to worry about the cost because it was a company phone. They also wrote once a week but though she'd always enjoyed writing letters and filled hers with gossip and news, his were short notes of places and jobs and always finished: 'Must dash to get this to the post.'

Over the phone, towards the end of his trip, he told her that he'd a long leave due to him and planned to take it as soon as he arrived back. He suggested that they might go to Greece together for two weeks. She booked a package holiday on one of the Greek islands; it was out of season and therefore cheaper than usual, though it would be cooler than in the summer. He said that sounded fine, and that he would send her the money for his share. She was a little puzzled by this and laughed and said it would keep until he returned but he insisted, and in fact a few days later a cheque for exactly half the cost arrived by air mail. She remembered then how he had always checked carefully the cost of things before going into a cinema or a restaurant and how, on the times she'd insisted on going Dutch, he hadn't made any more than a token refusal. Still, she thought, it was better to be careful than a spendthrift.

She was really happy in the weeks before the holiday, rushing to town after work and on her days off to buy new clothes and sun things. She even enrolled in a health club where she spent an hour a day lying on a sun-bed to get the beginnings of a tan. 'I don't want to lie there in the middle of all those wonderful bronzed bodies looking like a beached white whale,' she told her friends, who laughed.

She met him at the airport and cried on his jacket as he hugged her. They had that night together before he drove to head office in Birmingham for a debriefing. Three days later they met again at the airport and flew Sun Club Air to Portos. The plane was full, many of the other passengers couples in their thirties to fifties, wearing matching lime and avocado shell-suits which made them look like some sort of team, though they weren't. He fell asleep shortly after the meal so she started reading her novel.

She woke him up as the plane circled over the clear green seas that washed the rocky bays of the island. He was a bit grumpy – probably due to delayed jet-lag from Australia, she thought. By now many of the shell-suits were tipsy and excited and were singing, 'Here we go, here we go, here we go,' as the plane banked for its landing approach.

He grunted towards them. 'Bloody marvellous! The lunatics have taken over the asylum. Ten years ago they would've been going to Blackpool on a coach – now they're going looking for fish and chips on a Greek island.'

She was puzzled by the bite in his words. 'They're all right. They're only out to enjoy themselves, just like we are.'

'Well, I hope they're not staying in the same villa as us,' was all he said. She decided it was definitely jet-lag.

He wasn't too pleased about the villa, either. Though it looked exactly as she'd seen it in the brochure, it was surrounded by building sites, concrete mixers and scaffolding.

'Just what we needed,' he moaned. 'We'll be woken at six every morning by some Greek pillock kick-starting a cement mixer!'

'It won't matter,' she said, 'we'll be on the beach most of the time.'

'True,' he said, and kissed her.

They made love quickly before changing for the beach. She wore shorts and a halter top with her bikini underneath. He wore swimming trunks under baggy khaki shorts and an imitation Lacoste tee-shirt he had bought in Hong Kong on his way back from Perth. At the beach he paid for two sun-loungers and in minutes was sprawled out under his umbrella. All about them were brown bodies toasting in the searing sun which by now was almost overhead. They could hear excited voices mingling with the constant mutter of waves on the sandy beach, while from a Tannoy on one of the beach bars there came a voice which she recognised as Max Bygraves', singing something about a pink toothbrush.

He groaned. 'Oh no, not Max bloody Bygraves! We might as well be at bloody Brighton!'

She looked about her at the people on the beach. From the look and the sound of them she decided that they were mostly English.

A man walked along the wet sand close to the sea-shore with a tray around his neck and as he came closer she saw that he was a pot-bellied smiling Greek with a thick black moustache selling doughnuts. In a loud rusty cigarette-stained voice he was barking out, 'Donuts ver' fresh, all make today! Donuts ver' fresh, all make today!'

He winked at her as he passed, and waved. She decided she was going to enjoy this holiday. After a year of saving and losing dying babies, mindless fun was just what she needed. She looked at the women around her, most of them sunbathing topless, took off her own bikini top and began to spread cream on her breasts, laying it thickly on the nipples.

He opened one eye. 'What are you doing?' The tone seemed to be slightly accusing as well as questioning.

She laughed. 'What do you think I'm doing?'

'You're not going topless, are you?' There was a hint of schoolmarm in his voice.

'Don't be silly! Everybody is.'

'That doesn't mean you have to.'

'Does it offend you?'

'Not particularly. I just didn't think you'd want everybody looking at your tits.'

'But everybody isn't looking! Nobody's taking the slightest bit of notice! You are silly,' and she laughed, but she also felt a flush like a cloud pass across her face.

'That's all right then,' he said, and turned over.

She looked around her and in truth nobody was looking at her, but what he said had made her feel self-conscious and so she lay on her belly for a while. Soon she fell asleep and when she woke she had a headache and a dry mouth and didn't feel as happy as she had. He obviously felt the same, because he suggested that they should go to one of the beach bars for a drink in the shade, and they packed their things, pulled on their shorts and tops and walked barefoot as fast as possible across the hot sand.

At the bar they started chatting to two other English couples, Terry and Wendy and Dave and Sarah. He brightened up and soon had them laughing with him. Her mood changed with his and the slight grey cloud she had felt slipped away like the tide running from the beach. It was nice, she thought, that they were making friends already; though Jason told her afterwards that he thought they were a bit common because they came from the Black Country and had strong accents.

For the next few days the three couples met up on the beach in the morning and sunbathed until the sun got too hot, when they went for lunch together. In the afternoons they would sunbathe and swim again for a couple of hours and then go off to shower and get ready for the evening when they would meet for drinks before eating at one of the tavernas on the harbour front. After dinner they would go on to one of the island's many discos, though Jason didn't like dancing very much and would stay at the bar drinking with the other lads while she danced with the girls. So they would drink and laugh and dance and sing into the early hours, walking back, three young couples arm in arm, talking and laughing under the wonderful Greek night skies as the waves rushed up the beach and the smell of charcoal and cooking filled the air. She thought that she had probably never, ever been so happy.

On the morning of the fifth day he said he thought they'd had enough of lying on the beach and suggested they went to a temple in the hills that he'd read was very interesting. He was wearing a straw hat, sandals, baggy shorts and another aertex sports shirt with the Lacoste symbol. He was also wearing a money belt with his money and passport in it, because, he said, the Greeks were basically an honest people but you couldn't be too careful. She wore shorts and a tee-shirt and he advised her to put a bra on because he said that Greek men stared at women who didn't wear bras.

They waited by the roadside before their villa to board a bus full of locals. There were old women with baskets, and young women with small staring children, and men who all seemed to be carrying string bags and smoking strong tarry cigarettes. They sat for two hours in the dripping heat as the bus wound its way into the hills, lurching along terrifying mountain roads, pumping out thick oily smoke, scattering goats and stopping for anyone who waved it down. At each change in the gears, the noise of cicadas rose above the sound of the engine as they chanted in their trillions in the roadside thorns and thyme.

The bus seemed to stop every few hundred yards, dropping people at tiny villages that were little more than a cluster of dusty houses, a taverna with tables and chairs in the shade, the men already playing tric-trac, and on the outskirts of each a blindingly white church with a shimmering blue roof. She found it all very exciting and felt that after the 'Brighton with sun' of the beach she was seeing something of the real Greece. But Jason complained all the way about the smell and the heat, though he'd been the one to suggest that the bus was cheaper than hiring a car. When she'd suggested that they hire a car next week, he'd said it seemed a good idea; the way he said it made her think that he had no intention of spending two hundred pounds on a Suzuki jeep, though she wouldn't have minded going her share at all.

He unzipped his money belt and took out a small notebook. Pasted inside the cover was a page he'd photocopied from a book he'd borrowed from the library. On other pages notes had been made in writing that was small and bunched, more like printing than curved lettering. She had noticed that when he wrote, he used a ruler to form the bottom of his letters.

'Why didn't you copy the whole article?' she asked, noticing that the last three or four lines were missing from the photocopy and had been added in his midget printing.

'At ten pee a sheet?' he asked, and the question sailing out into the dust and cicada song implied that it needed no answer.

She'd begun to notice a closeness about him, a concern with money and things that bordered on meanness. What she had taken before as signs of a careful and serious nature were now starting to seem more base. She'd noticed that when they were in the bar with Wendy and Sarah and the other blokes, he often managed to be in the toilet when it was his turn to buy a round. Two or three times she'd actually bought a round herself, which she didn't mind of course. It was just that he seemed to be missing more when it was his turn to pay than at any other time. He had what she would later describe as 'a convenient bladder'. And he didn't like kitties, he had told her that on the first night.

'I don't see any sense in them if you don't drink as much as the others, you're just subsidising them getting drunk.'

'I don't think it matters when you're on holiday,' she'd replied.

He pulled back a little. 'Fair enough. I mean I'm not going to make an issue of it or anything, you know what I mean. I mean I'll go along with whatever anybody else does. But I just have this thing about it, that's all.'

They left the bus on a pass, standing in the roadside dust as it rumbled off down into another valley and further villages. When it had gone there was no noise but the sound of insects and nothing moved but the breeze. The air was cool, even though the sun was right overhead. They must, she decided, be quite high up. Many miles away, reduced to a blue smear, the sea softened into the sky. Beneath them the island fell away down towards the coast, the detailed groves and terraces lost in a blur of sand and olive. They left the road and, following his reading of the guide, climbed into a thicket of thorns and shrubs looking for the way to the hill-top temple site. They thrashed and leaped about searching for the path or goat-track that the guide claimed was there. They didn't find it, and soon it was obvious that they were lost. They had strayed into a gully choked with thorny bushes and clearly they could climb no higher. Her legs were badly scratched and she was cross and sweaty and in pain from insect bites and scratches.

The air suddenly grew even cooler and, almost as they watched, clouds rolled from the coast towards them. In less than half an hour a frightening black thunderstorm had burst on the mountain, drenched and battered them and rolled on as they sat silently under a twisted olive tree. They found what looked like a goat-track among the shrubs and followed it down as the last of the clouds trailed across the sun and the day brightened again, warming the steaming earth. After an hour of descent they came on a goatherd wearing thick trousers and knee-length boots; he stroked his long moustache and looked first at Rachel's bleeding legs and then up at her, as though she had just landed from the sky.

Jason pulled out a Greek phrase-book.

'Ey-faristo polly, el taverna?' he droned in a crabbed voice.

The goatherd waved his arm and pointed back up the mountain, speaking very fast. Rachel sighed and started climbing back up the gully. The man immediately rushed to her and, before she could say anything, picked her up in his arms and carried her over the thorn bushes to a clear broad path that they had missed a few yards away. The sun came out fully as they shouldered the hill and saw a small village below them where they could wait for the bus back to the harbour, all thought of the temple now abandoned.

Jason had been silent since the goatherd had put her down and they had thanked him and waved goodbye. 'I bet he tried for a feel, didn't he?' he asked in a low peevish voice.

'What on earth do you mean?'

'These Greeks think all English girls are easy meat. They'll try anything.'

'Well, he didn't try anything with me,' and she started crying, but whether it was because of his words or the pain of the scratches or because she was wet through, she didn't really know.

They rode the bus back to the villa in silence, though later that night after a bottle of retsina, when they told Dave and Sarah and the others about their silly adventure, it all seemed funny rather than miserable and they laughed about it and Rachel almost forgot the scratches that she'd tried to cover with make-up. They both got quite drunk and at one point they all started doing silly toasts, to each other and the waiter and Thomas the Tank Engine and Postman Pat. Rachel proposed a toast to Guy Fawkes.

'Guy Fawkes?' said David.

'If it hadn't been for Guy Fawkes, we'd never have met,' said Rachel.

'Eeent that rowmantic!' said Sarah, and Jason leant over and, taking Rachel's hand, kissed her fingertips; the men groaned and called Jason a creep and the women sighed and said that the men were an unromantic lot.

Next morning they decided to lie on the beach all day. They were both a little hungover, and the trip up the mountain had left Rachel feeling that all she wanted to do was bake in the sun and swim and drink lots of cold liquids. Jason sat up on the lounger reading a Jeffrey Archer, his straw hat on his head.

They'd moved down the beach almost to the end of the cove to get away from the bar speakers that blared out 'Una Paloma Blanca' every few moments, and to avoid the shell-suits who seemed to have formed a gang and who smoked and fooled about a lot – both of which annoyed Jason.

There was just a handful of people around them. A fat lady on her own, two other couples and two girls who Jason said were lesbians because they rubbed sun-cream on each other's backs and seemed to be having a good time together. They'd seen them drinking in one of the bars last night, and they seemed to be quite happy on their own though every so often they would have to fend off the trendy young Greek boys – those Jason called the beach rats. They did it quite simply and effectively either by ignoring them completely or by killing them stone dead with their eyes, at which the boys would shrug their shoulders, laugh to each other and move on, looking for easier game.

The only other people on their sector of the beach were a few young men in their early twenties grouped around some loungers a little way off. They were kicking a ball about, drinking cans of lager and running to the sea every so often to dive headlong from a rock that jutted out a little way into deeper water. Some of the dives were belly-flops but one or two of the divers were quite graceful and arced into the water, slicing it cleanly and coming up on their backs spouting water to the hot sky.

Jason watched them for a while then, muttering 'Noisy show-off yobs,' he tilted his hat down and carried on with his book.

The Fat Lady stood up and walked towards the sea. She wore a brightly coloured kaftan that floated around her as she walked and after paddling about for a few minutes she came walking up the beach towards them quite alone, a large beach bag on her arm. She must have weighed almost twenty stone, Rachel thought. She was quite light-boned, with hands and feet that looked far too tiny for her body; but still there was something appealing about her. She had long dark wavy hair and moved, like many overweight people, quite gently and gracefully.

Rachel remembered a phrase she'd read somewhere that described a woman like that as approaching like 'a ship in full sail', which she thought was quite a fair description. The Fat Lady picked out one of the loungers fairly close to their spot and began to set out her books, sunglasses and oils. She stood to take off her kaftan and underneath she wore nothing but a small pair of bikini bottoms, which seemed to disappear under the overhang of her stomach. Her breasts were enormous. Despite her years of nursing, Rachel didn't remember seeing many breasts as large.

'Jesus, that's disgusting,' Jason whispered, and turned his back away.

'D'you think it really matters?' said Rachel. 'They're only bodies after all and if we weren't so hung up about them we'd all probably be a lot better off.' And she laughed at a thought that had just struck her. 'Thin people die too, you know! She's probably quite happy and content as she is, getting on with her life in her own sweet way, while half this lot will be down the gym every day trying to conform to some idea of beauty, whatever that may be. I think we worry too much about appearances and what other people think.'

'I don't care what you think! I think that's the ugliest, most disgusting thing I've ever seen,' he threw back in a mutter over his shoulder.

Rachel looked at the woman again. It was only the ideas that magazines gave us about our bodies, she decided, that made some things 'beautiful' and others 'ugly'. The Fat Lady had a kind, warm face and gentle eyes. She looked towards Rachel and, seeing her smile at her, moved across the sand and sat down on a neighbouring sun lounger. She was English, from Hereford, she said. Her husband had gone off sea-fishing.

'Dear, I don't know how much I can stand today. I took a lot of sun yesterday. Got proper frazzled I did, I got quite dizzy with it.'

'You shouldn't take too much sun, particularly with fair skin like yours. You might get sun-stroke.'

'Well, I'm just going to let a bit more sun at me for an hour and then I'm going for a swim. 'Tis lovely here, the water's ever so clean and clear. You can see right to the bottom, way out. You enjoying your holiday, then?'

Jason didn't even acknowledge her, but turned on to his back and covered his face with his straw hat. The Fat Lady nodded towards him. 'Looks like he's sleeping off a good night.'

Rachel laughed. 'We both are. We'll probably need a good holiday when we get back, to recover.'

The Lady smiled. 'You enjoy yourselves while you can, my dear. Me and Herb, my hubby, have just started enjoyin' ourselves. We had a garage for thirty years, then we took early retirement. "Come on gel," he says, "they don't make pockets in shrouds." So we sold up last year, fifty-five we both are, and we've got enough to live on fairly comfortable, like. Kids 'ave growed up and gone off, they got their own lives to lead. I got a couple of lovely grandchildren and now we're enjoyin' ourselves.'

'Good on you,' said Rachel, smiling.

'This is our second holiday this year. Herb loves his fishin', so we went to Ireland at Easter to Kerry. Oh, I love Ireland – I do, they'm ever so friendly the Irish people, and 'tis bootiful countryside.'

The Fat Lady chatted on in this way for a while until within an hour she'd told Rachel her life story, and Rachel had told her hers.

'I'm ever so glad to have met you,' she said. 'Herb'll like to meet you, too. He likes people, does Herb, he's like me. He loves his fishing, too. Fishing mad he is nowadays. I watch him for a minute or two, but I get bored. I'd rather be with people. People are ever so interestin'.' She wiped her face with her towel. 'Lord, I'm hot now. I think I'd better go and cool meself off a bit, before me brains melt.' She laughed. 'Not that I've got many to melt!' and she stood and tiptoed over the burning sand to the sea.

'Christ! She's a nosy old bitch,' said Jason when she was out of earshot. Rachel suddenly filled with anger and was about to say something when she heard a scream. The Fat Lady was at the water's edge, flapping and writhing and flinging her arms around as though she were being attacked by an invisible mugger.

'Listen to that bloody row,' said Jason, turning round.

'She's hurt.' Rachel stood up to see better.

'She's a looney. Stupid old cow!'

Rachel ran towards the woman, forgetting about the heat of the sand. Two other people, a man and a woman, were already there. Jason put down his book and watched.

'I'm a nurse, is there anything I can do?' Rachel saw that the Fat Lady looked very faint and waxy.

'She's been stung by a big wasp,' said the other woman.

'I think it was a hornet,' said the man.

'Where?' asked Rachel, and the woman pointed at the Fat Lady's breast.

'It's underneath, I think.'

With professional detachment Rachel lifted the heavy breast and pulled out the dead insect. There on the underneath of the breast, and already swelling with the poison, was an angry red lump.

'I've got some antihistamine in my bag,' said the woman, pulling out a tube and while the man helped to support the Fat Lady and his wife held up her breast Rachel smeared the cream on the sting. She glanced across and caught Jason watching what she was doing with a strange look on his face. He looked away.

The Fat Lady came round from her faint after a moment so they brought her a glass of mineral water and helped her back to her lounger where she lay in the shade for a while, recovering.

When she felt strong enough she collected her things and set off to walk slowly back towards the town and her villa.

'I'll lie down in the cool,' she said as she left them. 'Herb'll know I've gone there. He'll come and find me. If it gets any worse I'll do as you say and find a doctor, but I think it'll be all right. Thanks for lookin' after me. I couldn't 'ave been in better 'ands. Lucky you bein' a nurse, though. My Herb always says I got the luck of the Irish. I did feel proper daft. 'Spect I looked a show, dancing and screaming away there.' And she laughed and made her way slowly off the beach.

'Well done, Florence Nightingale,' Jason said, and his voice was larded with sarcasm. 'It's a good job one of those tits didn't fall on your head. It'd have fractured your skull.'

The smallness and meanness of this man's mind, the fact that she hadn't really understood until now how little she knew him and how much she had fooled herself into thinking she was in love with him, his cold cheapness and his selfishness – all of this suddenly welled up in her and immediately the day took on another dimension. As though she had shifted into another universe she leaped up, and tipped his lounger over, and with possessed fury screamed at his surprised and blanching face.

'You stupid, bigoted, mean-mouthed, prudish, self-centered…' her brain searched for the worst word she knew '…wanker! Fuck you! Fuck you!' and lastly, in a sob through tears of anger, 'Double fuck you!'

A German family who had just settled close by looked up, smiling at the sudden crumbling of English *sang froid*, and as Jason, ice-faced, stalked off through the sand, towel and sun oil in one hand, sandals and Jeffrey Archer in the other, the group of young lads on loungers raised their cans of lager and cheered and clapped the scene. And the tubby smiling Greek man who sold doughnuts from a tray round his neck grinned and shouted, 'Donut ver' fresh,' at Jason as he strode past, while Max Bygraves crooned from one of the distant café speakers some lines of nonsense about mice in windmills in old Amsterdam.

The Fête

It was a fête, his mother had said that morning. And his grandfather, polishing his glasses on a corner of the tablecloth before reading the paper, had laughed and said, 'Huh! A fate worse than death!'

'Don't start!' his mother had said in that voice of hers, and his grandfather had winked at him and stirred his mug of tea.

His mother was a widow, which he knew was spelt like window without the 'n'. He could spell very well. Miss Halliwell had told his mother it was because of all the reading he did.

'He never has a book out of his hands,' his mother had said.

He had read a lot of *The Wind in the Willows* and *A Child's Garden of Verses* by himself. He liked the poem about the lamplighter best; and he saw himself as the Mole in *The Wind in the Willows*, not Ratty or Badger, definitely the Mole. They had a gas lamp outside the house, but it didn't need a lamplighter. It came on all on its own. It had mantles. Mantle was another word for dress. His mother made mantles for a Jewish man in Hightown near the jail and his aunty made gaberdines, which was another word for raincoats.

Some Jews killed Our Lord. But that was a long time ago, and they weren't like the ones he played with – Ian and Jeffrey. Their mothers gave him matzos that were like thin crackers and sometimes, on Saturdays in winter, he would light the fire for them because they weren't supposed to.

He leaned against the table, his bare elbow sensing the grains of sugar on the cloth, his head on his hand. His finger stirred the sugar in the bowl. He licked some off the end of his thumb.

'Can I go, mam?'

'I don't know. And stop eating that sugar, you'll get worms!'

'Anyway. When will you know?'

'How do I know when I'll know? Did you ever hear such rubbish from a child in your life! How old are you?'

'Eight.'

'Well, "don't know" means *don't know*, and get your elbow off the table!'

'Oh, mam, please can I...' he intoned, at just the very pitch that he knew, musician of the nerve endings that he was, would either win her over or make her even madder.

'Don't "Oh, mam" me like that, and look at the state of that shirt you've put on. How many days have you had it on?'

'I don't know.'

'Well, you can just get upstairs and change it – now. I'm not having people say I turn you out like a rag-bag.' She went into the scullery to put the pots in the sink –'slopstone', his grandad called it.

When he came downstairs again he went to the window and stuck his nose on the net curtains, pressing them against the glass. They smelt sooty. They always smelt sooty, especially on rainy days, and if you sucked them they were sour, like the leaves of the privet tree in the yard. It was all the factories, his grandad used to say. 'It's a wonder any of us have got any lungs left, breathing all that muck.'

If it was foggy in winter his grandad made him wear a handkerchief around his mouth and when he got home it had a round black mark where his mouth went. That would have gone in his lungs, his grandad said. He wondered how long he could hold his breath. Probably not all the way home. Jeffrey Cohen could do a whole length of the baths under water but you'd have to hold it a lot longer than that to walk home. You'd probably be dead by the time you got home. They'd just open the door and you'd go 'dunk' on the doorstep with your face all purple. A boy drowned at the baths once, when his finger got stuck in the grid that the water went down at the deep end. He hadn't seen it, but Jeffrey said the kid was all purple with his tongue all sticking out all black.

He looked across the yard at the back of the house across the way. Mr Simpson was painting the gutters. Mr Simpson was a signalman on the railway and put the oil in the signals. He said he had three different colours of oil – red, yellow and green – for the different coloured lamps, and you had to be careful not to get them all mixed up. He had told his grandad this, and his grandad had said that he'd forgotten about the black oil for when the lamps were out during the day. He thought his grandad had made that one up.

It was warm and sunny outside, even though it was still morning. It was going to be a hot day. Perhaps the pitch would melt in between the cobbles again and he could get a stick and play with it. If you got it on you, you got into trouble and your mother had to get it off with butter. If you got it in your hair it really hurt, 'cos you had to pull it out. He watched the cat walk along the wall between his yard and next door's; he could hear the shouts of boys kicking a ball in the back entry. The cat leapt delicately on to the tarred felt on the coalshed roof and begin washing herself in the sun.

'Cats can't wash the backs of their necks,' he told his grandad.

'No more can you,' his grandad laughed, 'you could grow potatoes in the back of your ears,' and he laughed again. 'Do you know why cats stick up their tails when you're stroking them?'

He knew that this was going to be one of his grandad's jokes.

'No.'

'It's to stop your hand falling off the end,' and they both laughed at that.

His mother came in from the scullery, carrying an oil-cloth bag. It rattled.

'Here,' she said in a rough voice, though he knew she wasn't angry but that it was her way of showing him that she was giving in and not giving in at the same time. 'There's some empty bottles for you to take back to Mrs Hughes', you can have the money back on them. There'll be enough for you to spend in that lot.'

'Oh thanks, mam!' He felt a deep, almost delirious, delight.

His grandad reached in his waistcoat pocket and winked at him. He pretended the pocket was empty, and fiddled in all the others, before going back to the first one. It took a long time and he kept winking and sighing and blowing through his nose and saying, 'Now where is it? Where did I put it? I had a million pounds somewhere. I'm sure it was in one of these pockets.' Then he said, 'Here's a shilling for you. But you can only have it if you'll promise to clean my shoes before Mass tomorrow,' and he gave him a sixpence, a threepenny bit and three pennies.

He pointed at one of the pennies. 'D'you see that? That's Britannia, the symbol of the British Empire. Do you know why the sun never sets on the British Empire?'

'No.'

'It's because God doesn't trust the beggars in the dark.'

'Dad! What are you trying to teach the child?'

His grandad often made jokes about the English. He sometimes came home from the pub with Uncle Aidan and they would sit up until really late and talk about people called Michael Davitt and Collins and a man called Parnell. They wouldn't come to the house, he thought, because they talked about them as though they were dead. His grandfather would sing songs sometimes and Uncle Aidan would shout, 'Fair play to you Henry!' and bang the table and his mother would tell them both to shut up. He could hear all that from his bed.

One of the songs was about a boy called Kevin Barry who was hanged though he was only 'of eighteen summers', and his grandad would sing it in such a voice that it would make him cry, even though he was in bed and couldn't hear all the words.

There were no other customers in the corner shop. Mrs Hughes took the bottles and gave him the money, pushing a shilling and two pennies over the counter. She looked at him over her glasses.

'I suppose you'll want the penny tray now, Barry?'

'No thanks, I'm saving all my money for the garden party.'

'So you're going to the fête, are you? I didn't think your mam would have let you go, you being Labour.'

Then he remembered that at election time Mrs Hughes had a blue poster up in her shop window, and they had a red and yellow one in theirs; and that the red and yellow one won most times round their streets, but that where the garden party was was near the big houses with gardens where the blue posters always won.

'She doesn't know,' was all he said and he ran from the shop, the money safe in his pocket.

There was a lady just inside the gates dressed like the woman on the penny, with a shield and a spear and a helmet. She had a scraggy neck with flops of skin that waggled like the skin on the turkey his grandad took the insides out of every Christmas. She asked him for threepence for admission.

'What do I get for that?' he asked, in surprised innocence.

'You get to go in,' she snapped back, 'and you get a free raffle ticket. The prizes are a hamper of fruit, a bottle of sherry and a box of chocolates. Now, are you going in or not? Because there are people who want to go in if you don't.'

He paid and went in. He was a bit disappointed. He'd expected a fair with rides and shooting galleries and candy floss, but instead there were just stalls selling things like cakes and home-made jam and stuff; a Punch and Judy show that wasn't open yet; and a wind-up ride with an old man in a cap and a moustache turning the handle, and four wooden aeroplanes you could sit in. Barry decided it was too much of a baby ride for him. It was getting very hot. He had a go on the 'Roll-a-Penny' but didn't win anything and nearly lost sixpence. Then he watched a man blowing up hot water bottles with his mouth until they were huge. But he got fed up of that and wandered to the end of the field where there was a stage with bunting round it.

A lot of people sat on chairs in front of the stage and a man in a striped blazer and a straw hat stood at a microphone, shouting something about everybody sitting down soon because the show was just about to begin. Barry read a sign at the side of the stage: 'Children's Grand Talent Competition. First prize £5', and somebody had drawn a five-pound note on the cardboard.

Two small girls got on stage wearing ballet clothes. They looked like sisters. A man put a record on a record player and held the microphone near it and the music came out over the speakers, crackling and hissing through the hot air of the afternoon as the little girls pranced and spun on their tiny silk shoes. Barry decided that the elder one was lovely and that he would like to marry someone like that. Perhaps he would marry her. The little one missed her step and made a mess of the dance and the other one gave her a look. The little one started crying and ran off, the other one took a bow and stamped and strutted off to where their mother was comforting the little one saying, 'Never mind, Penny, it doesn't matter.'

The man came to the front of the stage. 'Now come along, boys and girls, there's a first prize of five pounds, a second of one pound, and a third and fourth of ten shillings each to be won. Now how about having a go?'

A fat boy with bright red curly hair wearing short trousers that showed an amazing pair of pink knees got up with a violin and played something horrible and everybody was embarrassed but clapped at the end because, as someone said, 'the lad tried'. Next a girl of about twelve got up and sang 'On the Good Ship *Lollipop*' not very well and she danced about while singing. But she didn't realise that when she danced away from the microphone no one could hear her, so the words kept coming and going. Still, she got a good clap.

By now there were a lot more people sitting down to watch and
Barry noticed for the first time the judges sitting at a table at the
side of the stage. One of them was the Bacon Man who came to Mrs
Hughes' with the bacon. He recognised Barry and waved to him.

The idea that he might get up and do something that would win
the five pounds crept over Barry like a fever and he found himself,
on that hot August afternoon, getting cold and hot as fear and
longing and excitement washed through him like the incoming
tides rolling up an estuary. Something pushed him to the edge of
the stage. A man was writing down the names of two boys in front
of him.

'What are you going to do, boys?'

'Tell some jokes,' they said, and they went on stage.

Barry gave his name, Barry Aidan Riley, and said he was nine
years old and would sing a song.

'What school do you go to, Barry?'

'St Malachy's.'

The man looked up, then wrote it down on a slip of paper.
Barry sat at the edge of the stage to watch the two boys and wait his
turn, his stomach all jumpy and jelly. The boys were about ten.
One was tall with bright red hair sticking up like a brush and the
other was fat with greasy hair that lay on his head like Oliver
Hardy's. They got the giggles and every time they tried to say
something they spluttered and tittered and in the end the man
came and led them off stage. His face looked really mean and
angry.

'If you think you can act sensible, then you can have another go
later,' he muttered at them between his teeth, 'otherwise don't
bother. Next?' and he nodded at the man who was taking names.

'Barry Riley, nine years old, from St Malachy's and he's going
to sing a song, aren't you, Barry?'

Barry nodded, his tongue glued to the roof of his mouth. Like
when the Holy Communion wafer got stuck there and you couldn't
get it off.

'Well, ladies and gentlemen,' the man shouted into the microphone, 'Barry Riley from St Malachy's school is going to sing us a song. He's nine years old. Give him a big hand.' Everybody clapped as he walked to the front of the stage.

Barry had only sung this song at home at family parties with the wooden spoon his mother used to make cakes with as a microphone, but in front of the crowd something happened to him and he sang it as though he really meant it. It was like electricity going up and down him.

'I was born one morning when the sun didn't shine,
I picked up my shovel and I went to the mine.
Loaded sixteen tons of number nine ore,
Till my hands were busted and my back was sore.
You load sixteen tons, and what do you get?
Another day older and deeper in debt.
St Peter, don't you call me 'cos I can't go –
I owe my soul to the company store.'

People were clapping along in time to the music, and he felt that sudden flow of empathy that happens when an audience loves a performer and wants him to be good; and as he sang the song he wiggled and moved his hands and got better and better until when he finished and bowed there was a huge roar, and people cheered and whistled, and the man in the blazer came on with a grin on his face.

'Well, that was lovely, ladies and gentlemen, boys and girls, wasn't it? Really lovely. Nine years old, but what a little performer. Watch out, Frankie Lane.'

'More! More! Encore!' the crowd shouted, and the man leaned down to whisper into his ear, 'D'you know any more?'

By now he was possessed by Fame's demon and felt he could do anything: swim three lengths under water, kill the Emperor Ming and save Flash Gordon – anything, anything at all. The elder ballet dancer was looking at him and smiling shyly.

'I don't know any more songs, but I know a joke,' he said.

'Ladies and gentlemen, Barry's going to tell us a joke!' The man stood at his side.

'Why does a cat stick its tail up when you're stroking it?' A few in the crowd shouted, 'Don't know!'

'It's so your hand doesn't fall off the end.'

There was a good belly laugh at this and now, having dropped his role as country-and-western, coal-mining, hard-done-to singer, he assumed the mantle of comic and all-round entertainer and asked the crowd why the sun never set on the British Empire.

'Hear, hear!' said a half-drunk voice but when he told them the answer, substituting 'buggers' for 'beggars' in a sudden act of extemporisation, because he knew that was what his grandad would have said if his mother hadn't been there, there was a very different reaction.

A few people laughed or snorted into their hands, but most of them shouted things like 'Get off!' and 'Shame!' and 'Give him a good belt!' and the man in the blazer pushed him off the stage, hissing, 'Get out of here as fast as you bloody well can, sonny!'

Suddenly realising what a terribly fickle friend Fame is, he ran a gauntlet of shouts and scowls all the way back to the gate, feeling cold beyond belief on this hottest of days, and he didn't stop running until he got back to their street and the corner shop.

He still had almost a shilling left so he bought an ice-lolly and some sweets and went off to find some of the gang. But when he knocked and asked, their mothers told him they'd all gone off to the swimming baths, so he went home.

'How was the fête?' asked his grandad.

'Worse than death,' he answered, and though both his grandad and his mother questioned him he just said it was 'all right' and 'not much' and hoped it would be left at that.

Of course the Bacon Man thought it was very funny and told Mrs Hughes, and Mrs Hughes told his mother and she smacked him for saying 'bugger' and showing them up in public, and someone from the garden party organisers made a complaint to Miss Higgins, his headmistress, and he got strapped for it, but secretly he didn't care.

He was already learning 'Tom Dooley', and his grandad had laughed for days when he heard the story, and given him ten shillings when his mother wasn't looking; and Uncle Aidan had laughed so much he'd got the hiccups and he'd given him half a crown, too.

The Cowardly Barber
- a Pardoner's Tale -

It's not often that you meet an ordinary man in the street who with one stroke could quite literally have changed the face of history, and it's not often that that man is an Irishman – but I did meet a character exactly like that once. It was in Spain, twenty-five or so years ago, that I bumped into him. And to look at the bloke you would hardly imagine that he had any place in history at all.

A little stocky fellow he was, bandy like a jockey, with a funny small round face covered in lines, a face like a polished walnut. He had a bald, red-brown, sunburnt, freckly head and big sticky-out ears with little tufts of white hair over them. He was just like one of those leprechauns you see in the films.

I was a student at the time I met him. Or rather I should say that I'd been a student. I'd just got my degree, an upper second – which wasn't bad, considering I'd spent most of my time at Uni screwing round, smoking dope and running the Entertainments in the Union.

That's where I first learned how to make money: booking groups from London promoters for our Uni, then taking a cut for promoting them on to other colleges. One of the lads I worked with on the Ents committee went on to found one of the biggest record labels in the world, so you get some idea of the class of people I was in with. We booked the Kinks, Status Quo, Roy Wood, Elton John – you name them, and I've done drugs with them. I even booked Paul Simon for twenty-five quid once. I picked him up at the station and he told me about this song he'd written while he was waiting for the train. 'Homeward Bound' it was called, he sang it that night. I didn't think much of it, to tell you the truth.

Mind you, I didn't know much about music. I was more into figures. My degree was in Economics and Politics and I've a pretty good memory for facts, so I was able to learn quick and run my little business on the side and still sling in my work with the minimum of effort. Beyond a couple of earnest, bearded, weirdo, Marxist-Trotskyites, most of my lecturers were too busy trying to screw their students or work their way up the departmental ladders to worry too much about somebody like me who was working the system to his own advantage.

I learned then a very important lesson: that if you've got a reasonable amount of intelligence (not too much, clever people never make it – they get side-tracked), if you've got a lot of good common sense and a lot more ambition – particularly if you don't give a shit about anybody – you can be a great success in this world. A bit of common sense and a lot of ambition is a winning combination. I've found that this philosophy has stood me in good stead over the last few years.

Another thing I've discovered is that the one thing that unites us all is greed. If you want something doing then don't appeal to someone's good nature or their sense of fair play, offer them a cut, a deal, a piece of the action. The sponduliks, the greens, the mazuma – whatever you like to call it – is mightier than the sword. There's only one thing money can't buy and that's poverty.

Almost straight after Uni, I formed my own agency and did so well that I started buying up property for venues for bands; that got me involved in the property market, and that showed me where the *real* money was. The real money wasn't in working or doing or making or creating, it was in manipulating money. So I bought my way into a firm of brokers in the Midlands and while I was there I got poached by a City firm before poaching was even called poaching. They didn't like my Black Country accent at first but it was the Swinging Sixties, and at that time it was still hip to be working-class so it wasn't long before I became quite a minor celebrity. The other point was that I was bloody good at my job. They kept telling themselves I was a rough diamond and chortling over their port at my after-dinner performances. I was also making a fortune and pissing up their backs at the same time.

I suppose you could say I was a Yuppie before the word had even been coined. It was a time when young blokes like myself, from the provinces, were really beginning to make their mark on the world. Hairdressers, footballers, rock stars, writers, photographers, we slid across the pages of the new Sunday colour supplements like a wave of freshly oiled barbarians. Me and Georgie at Old Trafford, me and Ringo in Mustique, me and Britt dining at Chows. I lost count of the number of lords' and viscounts' daughters I shafted. I must have had more right honourable hole than Eton College golf course.

From asset stripping I moved into offshore insurance and then I got into the pension fund scam. I formed my own company specialising in self-administered pension funds. I bought a load of mountains with acres and acres of rough bog-land from some skint farmers in Scotland, and paid next to nothing for them. Then with the help of a few tame local councillors, who chuntered on about jobs and employment in the area, I got planning permission from the local authority for a big forestry development. I set up an offshore company, hired an ex-National Park planner who'd turned himself into a 'planning consultant' (your classic case of a gamekeeper turned poacher) and sorted out the opposition. I got a fortune in government forestry grants and by offering big tax incentives we were able to draw in a mass of investment.

After ten years I sold off several hundred thousand acres of boggy Scottish moorland that trees would never grow on properly in a month of Sundays, Mondays and Tuesdays, sold off a few other bits and pieces I had my fingers in, and I moved to Spain worth six and a half million when I was thirty-five.

Which is where this story comes in, actually, since it was in Spain that I met the little Paddy when I was a student all those years ago. I'd spent a couple of weeks hitch-hiking across France with two girls from Uni and, after making our way south, we crossed the Pyrenees and travelled on down into Spain. I've always been a bit of a silver-tongued devil, never had any trouble with the ladies – I suppose you could say it was a gift, really – and I'd charmed them each into thinking she was the only one for me. Since they both had lots of lolly, they were payrolling my holiday. As far as Malaga anyway, then one of the girls got fed up of waiting for me to make my mind up and clicked with a rich German in a bar and went off to live with him for a while on his yacht. The other, a blonde Mia Farrow type with a first in French and a lovely tight little arse, suddenly got the Aztec two-step pretty badly and wired mummy for a plane ticket to fly her back home.

So off Wendy flew, leaving me all on my own without visible or invisible means of support, apart from my wits. I scouted round and got myself a job as a barman in an English tourist bar called El Capitano's. It used to get full of fat couples from South Shields and Birmingham who got pissed out of their brains every night and sang 'Black is Black' and 'The Blaydon Races' for hours on end. I still can't hear those songs without thinking of those days.

Anyway, one evening I'm working in the bar and this real cute chick comes in all on her own. A real Spanish doll – fabulous figure, thick black hair, lovely eyes, flashing teeth… You name it, she's got it. Thelitta, she was called. Well dressed, too, in an expensive but really classy way. I knew I was into money here, but not how much. And the thing is, she turns out to be very attracted to me.

I forgot to mention that in the sixties I looked a lot like Georgie Best. I was really fit from swimming every day and football on the beach – 'English barmen and couriers versus the Spanish waiters' – all that sort of thing. I had less belly and more hair then. Anyway, I was telling you about Thelitta.

She orders a drink and there's nobody in the place so I start talking to her and she turns out to be a Spanish contessa – straight up! A real, live, walking, talking contessa with her own castle! She's married to a real old count, one of the local big noises: lots of bread, a town house in Madrid, another in Seville, flats in London and New York, and a big castle about fifty miles up the coast, overlooking the sea. Thelitta speaks excellent English and she tells me that the old count is always going away to South America and other places on family business, and without her saying it and reading between the lines, it seems he isn't looking after her – in more ways than one, if you see what I'm getting at.

So she sits in the bar all evening, talking to some other girls she's been waiting for, then off they all go to paint the town red. But at the end of the night when I go outside, she's waiting in her car for me and we drive off to a quiet cove and we end up walking on the beach by moonlight and all the rest of it.

I don't get my end away that night but it seems that there's every possibility I will another night. We start walking back to the car and she asks me when I've got some time off. I say Wednesday and Thursday next week are my days off and I finish lunch-time Tuesday. She says I must come and stay at her house. I say how do I get there and she says I will send the car for you. Where do you live? she asks. I say above the bar and she says, next Tuesday my car will come for you at five, be ready to come. I say is the duck a Catholic, does the Pope crap in the woods and can a bear swim? And that's that.

So the next Tuesday a whacking big Merc rolls up outside the bar and it's being driven by a little chauffeur, complete with shiny boots, cap and full olive-green uniform. He picks up my bag and puts it in the boot and then opens the back door for me. So I tell him no, that's all right – I'll get in the front with him. Only I say it in my not too good Spanish, because he's so brown that I think he's a local.

He says that's fine, but would I mind if we speak English because it's not often he gets the chance to speak anything but

Spanish. I get in the car and ask him where he's from, because I've noticed a tinge of an accent there and I can't place it, and he tells me he's from near Galway originally.

'But you could say I'm a bit of a rolling stone, sir. I've lived all over the place in me time. In the last fifty years I must have been in most of the countries in the world.'

Now he didn't look as though he was that old. I'd have put him somewhere in his mid to late fifties, I suppose. 'How old are you, if you don't mind me asking?' I ask him.

'I was born at the turn of the century. Bang on the dot of midnight on New Year's Eve. A chime child. Now you can't get much closer to being a child of the century than that.'

Bear in mind that this was 1967, so that made him nearly seventy years old, which was incredible. To look at him you would have sworn he was in his middle fifties – fifty-six or seven at the most.

'I tell you what,' I said. 'I just hope I look like you when I get to your age.' And he laughed.

So we drove on along the coast road, chatting away. I remember there was a brilliant sunset. It was one of those incredible Mediterranean evenings and there I was in a chauffeur-driven car being taken to some castle somewhere where a Spanish contessa was going to be using me as her plaything for the next couple of nights. My lucky star was certainly shining on me

'What's the contessa like?' I asked him.

'A real lady,' he says to me, 'a real lady through and through.' And then he shuts up and I realise I'm not going to get any more out of him on that subject, so I ask him how he's ended up living in Spain.

'It's a long, long story but I'll tell you a bit of it. I've been a wanderer since I was a child. It's partly the fact that the Irish have been forced to leave home in search of employment as far back as anybody can remember, and partly the fact that I was born a wanderer. When I was a baby, me mother used to have to tie me to the leg of the kitchen table or I'd have been off down the lane and across the fields and away over the mountain. Me sisters were forever fetching me back from somebody else's house or yard.

'I suppose ever since I was small I've always wanted to see what was over the wall, what was over the hill, if you like,' (and he waved with his hand as though he was blessing the mountains off to our left) 'what fine famed foreign country lay beneath those far off-clouds.'

He laughed. 'Well, I left Ireland in the twenties and went to America first of all. I travelled all over that godforsaken whore of a country working on the railroads and the buildings, and as luck had it I found meself there during the worst depression the world has ever known.

'God help us, that was a rough old time right enough. There was soup kitchens and starvation in the richest country on earth and millions walking the streets looking for work. I tramped all over the place sleeping rough and scratching the odd job here and there. I was young like yourself, so I didn't mind a bit of hardship. But it was terrible to see the way some of the people were living, and I'd left Ireland to get away from poverty. I'm telling you, what I saw in America was worse than anything I ever saw in Ireland.

'So, like thousands of others, I found meself riding the rods looking for work. I must have travelled hundreds and hundreds of miles jumping on and off freight trains over the years, dodging the yard bulls – the railway police, that is. I was lucky in the end, though.

'I jumped a box car out of New York and found a couple of old bums who'd been travelling hard for years already sleeping there. We rode together on that southern line all the way down to the Crescent City, old New Orleans herself. The two old bums went off looking for another ride down to the oil-fields and I got a job working down on Bourbon Street in one of the bars.

'I've always got on with people and it wasn't long before I had meself a good position. The owner liked me, he was half Irish himself. The rest of him was Seminole Indian, Creole and Chinese, mixed. He was a queer fellow to look at I can tell you, with red hair, yellow skin and blue eyes. He was about four foot ten high and four foot ten across, and nobody argued with him.'

'Was he a good fighter?' I asked.

'No, not particularly. He kept a Thompson sub-machine-gun under the bar, and if anybody got too out of hand he'd let rip at the ceiling with it as a warning. Still, you were asking how I came to end up here.

'One of the customers was the barber from next door but one, and he did hairdressing as well. The creole girls used to come to him especially, because he was great at styling strong kinked hair. He had a couple of guys working for him in the barber shop, and he used to do the special stuff himself. I'd always fancied meself as a bit of a hairdresser – I suppose it appealed to me as the sort of job where you met better clients. A better sort of person. I'm not talking just about the barbering, now, I'm talking about the hairdressing – you know, the *coiffure*.' And he said it as though it was a rich brandy.

'Well, I asked this guy one night if he'd teach me how to cut hair. He liked his liquor. A bit too much, some said, though he never got out of hand in our place. He got a bit maudlin and cried into his rye once or twice, but nothing to get the Chicago piano out for. So I said I'd flirt him a few free noggins if he gave me the grounding in the trade; and he said if I'd go in on me mornings off he'd show me, and he did. He was one of the best ever. François Arnaud he was called. His people came from one of the oldest families in New Orleans, but they'd all fallen down on their luck through gambling or women or both. I can't remember which; there was a lot of all that sort of stuff going on in New Orleans.

'But what a city – the music and the women and the night life! They were the best years of me life. I had a place in the French quarter in a house run by an old woman with one leg. The downstairs was a brothel, the upstairs was divided into two apartments. I had one and a voodoo queen called Marie Lebon had the other.'

'Voodoo queen!' I asked, 'What the hell's a voodoo queen?'

'She was a beautiful black woman, tall and straight with the biggest eyes I've ever seen in me life. She did spells and sold charms, mojos and hexes and such like. I was brought up a Catholic and taught not to have anything to do with things like that. I used to think it was a load of old malarkey, but I tell you I saw things with me own eyes that were incredible. Absolutely incredible.' He was silent for a moment.

'Anyway, I stuck it with old François for a couple of years, learning all I could about hairdressing and barbering on me days off. And one day I'm in the shop when an officer comes in from a big German ship that's just docked – New Orleans was a big seaport in those days. I'm cutting this officer's hair and he says to François, "Do you know any barbers who would like to work on a big boat?"

'So François asks why, and yer man says that the ship's barber has just collapsed with appendicitis and is stuck there in hospital. The ship was leaving in a few days' time and they had a ladies' hairdresser but they really needed a top-class hairdresser for the men passengers and the crew. François looked at me and said, "This is yer very man, here. The second-best gentlemen's hairdresser in New Orleans." He was as full of the blather as meself, was old François.

'At the time I was living with a woman who was giving me a lot of problems. She drank a lot and she wasn't clean in her habits. I can't stand that in a woman, I'm a bit finicky that way. She used to leave her stockings and her drawers all over the house, soiled and everything, and she used not to bath for days on end and cover up the smell with perfume. She stole money out of me pockets, too, and then she'd go off on the tear for days at a time. Then the police would come round and tell me to come and pick her up from the jail or some other place she was in wrecking. She was a beautiful-looking woman. But I'll tell you, son, looks aren't everything when it comes to a woman. A sweet temper is better than sweet looks any day. A sweet temper and a familiarity with soap are two great things. Anyhow, things being as they were, as you might imagine when I got the offer of a way out I jumped at the chance.

' "I wouldn't mind a couple of trips," I said. "But I've never been to sea before. I've no seaman's ticket, or anything."

' "Leave all that to me," says yer man, and a couple of days later I've packed up, collected all me wages, had a big leaving do, crept out when the quare one was asleep, and there I am on board this big German ship setting off down the coast of South America to Brazil. It was gas, I can tell you!

'Well, the other hairdresser on board was a big German girl called Helga. We ended up hitting it off famous. She was blonde and neat with big blue eyes the colour of the sea and a fine figure I can tell you. And clean! You could eat your breakfast, dinner and tea off the floor of her room and you wouldn't find any potatoes in her ears. Things went from good to better, and she taught me German and I helped her to improve her English, and one thing led to several others and after a couple of months we decided that we couldn't live without each other and we got the captain to marry us there and then at sea. It was wonderfully romantic, the moon shone on the waters and we could see the trees of the coastline and hear the surf and the birds and everything. It was like a film.

'Anyway, when we finished that trip we signed up on another one, and then another and another. They were great days and we saw most of the world together but we decided in the end that we needed a base. The wandering was all right but we wanted somewhere of our own. Somewhere to throw your hat, you know.'

He stopped the car to let a flock of goats stream across the road and into the olive groves on the opposite side. The car purred off again into the evening and he carried on with his story.

'Anyway, after a couple of years at sea we managed to save a bit of money between us, having no children and with all the tips you'd get and that. Then her mother, who was living in Berlin, died and left her a bit of money and a little tobacconist's shop right in the heart of the city. So we went back there to take it over. There was a shop next door that had come empty and we managed to buy that with the bit of money Helga's mother had left her. We knocked the two shops together and turned the new half into a hairdressing salon for women.

'I ran the tobacconist's and Helga did the ladies' hairdressing. I didn't bother much with the barbering because there were enough barbers in Berlin in those days, and in any case it was getting a bit rough for foreigners. The Nazis were just starting to come to power. I was Irish, so I was all right what with Ireland staying neutral all through the War, but the accent was enough to make people look at you queer at times. It was a terrible time. People were starting to get frightened of their own shadows. There was great fun too, though, there was a lot of heavy drinking and mad things going on. Berlin was raving during those years all right. Clubs and bars and bierkellers. It was wild I can tell you.'

'Did you meet any famous people?' I asked him that because I found it all really interesting. We'd done the Weimar years for A-Level history and it was amazing meeting this guy who'd been there during that time.

'The funny thing is, you see, you didn't know they were famous at the time. They were just people you saw in the bars or that came in the shop. Let me think, now. Did you ever hear of Otto Dix? He was in Berlin for a couple of years. I liked him. Yer man what's his name, the writer, Isherwood – he was stopping a couple of streets away. He came in a lot for cigarettes, smoked like a bloody chimney. There was all sorts of artists. George Grosz I knew from the shop, and from a bar we both used to drink in. Fritz Laing used to come in and Freda Herzog, one of the actresses in the Berliner Ensemble, used to have her hair done next door. I met Bertolt Brecht just the once. He cleared off when things got too hot for him in Berlin. Joyce used to come in too.

'James Joyce?' I asked.

'No, the other Joyce. "Lord Haw-Haw", as they used to call him. He broadcast to England for the Germans all through the War, propaganda stuff it was, and when they caught him after they hung him. He was Irish, his mother and father lived in Manchester they say. But by the early thirties a lot of the intellectuals were piling out of Berlin as fast as they could, the Socialists and Communists and that – it wasn't safe to be either in those days. And after the Reichstag fire in thirty-three it was the end of the road for all the fun and games. I was all right, though. I kept me head down and just got on with me job. The Irish are great survivors. We've had to be.'

'Did you ever see Hitler?' I asked. I was totally fascinated by now.

He was quiet at that, quiet for longer than you would be if somebody had asked you a question you didn't mind answering. Then he said:

'I'll tell you a story now and you can believe it or not, I don't really care. And it's a story I've only told to a couple of other people in the last thirty-odd years. But it was just after this happened that me and the wife came here to Spain, Spain was neutral too during the War and we came here and settled down in a little business. She died five years ago and it was then I went to work for the count. The wife used to do his first wife's hair so he offered me a job when Helga died. That's how I came to be here, but let me finish the story.

'You asked me about old Adolf. Well, in the April of 1937 a woman came into our hairdresser's, it was early on and I was just bringing coffee in to the girls. The tobacconist's was quiet after the morning rush. A blonde woman came in and asked could she have her hair done right away. She'd heard about how good Helga was, all her friends had their hair done by Helga and she wanted hers doing too. You see my wife *was* very, very good. She was one of the best and she'd built up the business until we were doing great. So she says, "Yes, sit down, madam, and I'll do you now."

'I spoke pretty good German by then, and I heard the girls whispering in the store-room. A bit later one of them comes into the shop for a smoke. They weren't allowed to smoke in front of the customers.

' "Do you know who that woman is who just came in?'" asks the girl.

' "Not at all," says I and begod I hadn't a clue .

' "That's Eva Braun," she says, "the Chancellor's girlfriend."

'Of course that was yer man Hitler. She comes back the next week, and the next, and soon she's one of our regular customers. Every time she comes she's dropped in a big staff car with the Reich stuff all over it, and then it comes back again and picks her up afterwards and whisks her away. There was a powerful lot of security about. There'd been a few attempts to kill yer man Hitler, and he wasn't taking any more chances. And then a couple of times himself comes in.'

'Hitler?'

'The very man. A little short-arse he was, not much bigger than meself. He seemed smaller, too, because he wasn't standing shouting on a bloody stage like he normally was. People look bigger when you see them on the stage or on a newsreel.'

'Did he talk to you?' I asked. I was absolutely enthralled. I'd never met anyone who'd met Hitler before!

'Not much. He just walked round, waiting for her to finish. Sometimes he'd tease the girls a bit. He gave off this amazing atmosphere of power, though, I've never seen anything like it. I suppose you'd call it animal magnetism or something. He had the women nearly wetting themselves at him – and it wasn't fear either.

'Then one day in October, just after war was declared by England, the time of what they called the "phoney war", he comes in and it's obvious he's annoyed about something. There's a sort of atmosphere you could have cut with a bloody knife and Eva Braun looked as though she could have murdered him. Anyway they came in, and Eva whispers something to Helga in the corner. Then there's a few smiles and Helga nods to one of the girls to come and fetch me out of the tobacconist's. I leave the girl serving cigarettes to someone and go through. It turns out there's been a row between old Adolf and Eva because he has an important newsreel film to make that afternoon and wanted to get all spruced up for it. His own personal man was sick or something, and Eva had this appointment. Anyway, the upshot is that he wants a trim and a tidy-up; and Helga goes and tells him, I'm yer man.'

'You cut Hitler's hair?' I asked. You can imagine how gob-smacked I was. Here I was, being driven along the coast of Spain to a rendezvous with a Spanish contessa by a bloke who'd cut Hitler's hair!

'Cut his hair?' he said. 'By Christ! I did better than that! I shaved his bloody throat. I had a cut-throat razor a midge's dick from his feckin' windpipe. I'll never forget till me dying bloody day how me bloody hands was shaking. *By Christ!*, I thought, *if I slip now I'm up shit creek in a barbed-wire canoe with no bloody paddle right enough. They'll never believe it was me bloody nerves.*'

'Did you not think of how you could have killed him? You might have stopped the Second World War?' I asked. It's obvious when you think of it. If he'd killed Hitler there and then, cut his throat and run, can you imagine what might have happened?

'Just think,' I said, 'there would have been no six million dead Jews, no three million dead Gypsies, no twenty-five million dead Russians. God knows how many dead English, French and American you could have saved. When you add it up, it probably comes to fifty-odd million people!'

'Well, anyhow, I didn't,' he says and he looked sideways at me, his face all shiny and red, and not from the sun either.

But I wouldn't leave it alone. 'Why not?' I asked.

'Because,' he says loudly, 'I was a bloody coward. It was his life against mine. And I wasn't chucking mine away just to take his. In any case we weren't sure then how things was going to turn out. No one was. It's easy in hindsight. We can all be bloody clever after the event. But I'll admit I've often thought about it since, and wondered would I have maybe stopped the whole bloody shooting match? And maybes I would, and maybes I wouldn't. But then again here I am, aren't I, living the good life in Spain and where's yer man Hitler now? Dead and gone, that's where.'

And he swung the wheel to take us round a bend in the road and the sun hit us full on, low down and sinking.

'There's the castle ahead,' he said and for the rest of the journey he said nothing, just drove on. He sat there with his little uniform cap on, his cap badge shining and his face and his hands on the wheel all blood-red as he drove straight on towards the sun setting behind the castle ahead of us.

I've often thought since it would make a good story for a film. If I could only write I'd put the idea down and sell it to somebody. I might get round to it one of these days. I can just see Milo O'Shea as the little Irishman. You can get people to write stuff for you, though, can't you, if you're no good yourself? Ghost writers?

Egg and Chips and Rock and Roll

Don Wilson married the first girl who ever gave it to him regular. Well, he had to. He ended up putting her in the pudding club, and in those days there was only two things you did if you got a girl into trouble. You either married her, or you joined the Army – and Don would have been as much use in the Army as a chocolate teapot. He was five foot two, with turn-ups on his underpants, and more meat on a butcher's biro; and he was so short-sighted he needed a pair of glasses to see to the end of his nose. Plus he had spots – or should I say the spots had him? He looked like he'd been hit with a colander, and some of the lads had taken to calling him 'Dot to Dot'. Which I thought was a bit cruel – but still funny.

He worked as a warehouseman, getting 'A1B 69 washers fibre' for this and 'grease nipples, half-inch BSA thread' for that. I saw him once at work and I'm telling you, in his long brown warehouseman's coat with thin black drainpipe trousers poking out the bottom, luminous dayglo socks and crêpe-soled brothel-creepers, his bootlace tie, his Tony Curtis haircut with a duck's arse at the back, sideburns down to his collar and a face like a scale model of a volcanic region, he hardly looked the stuff of romance. But one thing you had to say about him, he was a damn good drummer, Don.

His idols were Gene Krupa, Sandy Nelson and Louis Belson and he had every single one of their records. Skins Wilson, he liked to call himself. He even had it put on his drum: 'Skins Wilson' it said, in big letters that the bloke who did Passagno's ice-cream van painted on for him. But the bloke had used the same sort of letters, all florid and gold and red and white, so that it looked a bit like the side of an Italian hokey-pokey cart. Very odd.

The other side, where his foot-pedal hit, had a Red Indian chief's head painted on it because it had once belonged to the drummer from Morris King and the Mohawks dance band. Morris's real name was Levenstein, but he thought King was more showbiz. His band used to play regular at the Ritz, but they folded when rock and roll hit the streets. The old blokes in Morris's band couldn't groove to the modern stuff, so they jacked it in. Like Don said, 'You've either got it or you haven't, man.'

He spoke like that a lot, did Don. Down the Whisky-a-Gogo one night, with a cream moustache on his lip from his frothy coffee, he said, 'Dance bands is dead, man – too square. Know what I mean? Rock and roll is for youth. It's like history, man, yer Ruby Murray and that other one, Eve Boswell. *Come to the barbecue and sit by my side...Pickin' a chicken with you!* Bloody stroll on. What a load of crap!'

I knew what he meant. So did Morris King. He sacked the band, went back to his original job of cutting gents' hair, selling Durex and taking bets in his dad's barber shop, and at nights and weekends ran a trio that did weddings, socials and barmitzvahs. Don bought the drums.

Drumming with the Rebels was how he met Doreen. She was in the Exile of Erin one Sunday night, drinking Cherry Bs and sitting close enough to the piano to get a good look into the corner where Don was, with his drums. The piano wasn't used much now, except for the group to stand their amps on to give them a bit more room. A poster in one of the windows still said *Fri Sat Sun – Free and Easy With Fred on the Piano!!!* but that had been ages ago and Fred had gone to play somewhere else when Mrs Crowley hired the rock and roll group to play *Fri Sat Sun.*

'Who's *Fri Sat Sun?*' asked Tommy, the Rebels' lead singer. 'Sounds like one of them Japanese generals. *Ah so, Emperor Hirohito, General Flisatsun has destloyed John Wayne and Amelican fleet.*'

The Rebels' line-up was the standard one: lead, rhythm and bass guitars, drums and standard shaky-leg vocalist. They were good, one of the best bands around at that time. They did stuff like 'Boney Moroni', 'Blue Suede Shoes', 'Summertime Blues' and 'Whole Lotta Shakin''. They used to tear the place apart, specially when the punters had had a few. Tommy the vocalist used to pretend he had a bad leg like Gene Vincent. The trouble was, he'd walked with a pretend limp for so long that he'd caused some sort of extra wear on the other leg and was really starting to limp for serious. He couldn't half pull the birds, though.

All the lads had loads of girls, except Don. Don said the reason he couldn't cop was because he was stuck at the back, and the birds couldn't see him – and no one had the heart to contradict him. But Doreen saw him right enough that night, and knew he wasn't fixed up too. She'd asked one of the other girls where his girlfriend was, and she'd told her he hadn't got one.

'You'd better watch out, Don, she fancies you,' I said to him when I fetched him his staff pint. Waiting on, you get to know when things are happening before they happen – if you know what I mean. You develop extra eyes. Feelers, like. You can tell when a fight's going to go off ages before. The air starts to get kind of heavy, sort of sparky and electric, and you just know sure as eggs that in a few minutes pint-pots and tables will be flying and somebody will be giving somebody else a bit of knuckle butty and a face full of dandruff.

It's the same with sex, or romance if you want to call it that, you can always tell when they're hunting. Two lads out on their own, drainpipe trousers, drape jackets, hair slicked and flicked, Billy Fury look-alikes – the business. They stand at the bar, get a drink, then turn around clocking the room, rubbernecking like submarine periscopes. And the girls sit at the tables pretending they don't know they're being fancied and, what's more important, pretending they haven't already decided whether or not, and who's going with who, and how far they're going to go. That's what the ladies' toilets is for, sorting out the odds. And men think they make the running – the barmpots.

That's how it was with Don. He thought he was pulling Doreen, when in reality she'd made her mind up she was having him. She'd be about five years older than Don, twenty-seven or so I'd guess, dark-haired and Italian-looking. Big up top, nice bum, good teeth, nose a bit big though, spoilt her really. Of course Don was as pleased as a dog with two dicks when I told him she was looking him over.

He'd had girls before, of course, but mousy-looking things, whatever was left after the rest of the group had their pick. Pecking order: singer, lead guitar, rhythm guitar and bass. What was left went to the drummer. Mostly Don ended up with things that looked as though they needed a good feed and a wash, nothing so obviously sexy or classy as Doreen. I mean I could have fancied her myself if I hadn't been courting with Mrs Crowley's Deirdre – and you didn't mess around with Mrs Crowley or any belonging to her. I'd even started back going to mass at Saint Malachy's on account of Deirdre, and I hadn't got inside her circle-stitched bra yet.

That night, Doreen came up after the gig and pretended to be really interested in drumming, asking was it hard and saying what a good sense of rhythm Don had. It was painful, really, and me and the rest of the lads just looked at each other and rolled our eyes. But Don was like a sponge and five minutes later he's covered his drums with a bit of old curtain and locked his sticks and snare in the cleaning cupboard and they're walking towards the door together.

'Just walking Doreen home, lads,' he says. 'See you next Friday.' The lads gave him a bit of a ribbing as he went out but he just combed his hair, shrugged his drape jacket up on his shoulders, hitched up his drains and went off into the night like a myopic James Dean, his head on a level with her armpit.

'Hope she's using Mum Roll-On,' says Tommy.

So the next time we see them they're a couple, fixed-up like, and from then on she's sitting in the same place every night, checking out that nobody else is looking at him. She brings a friend along with her to keep her company after a while, a real boiler called Brenda. She looked as though she'd gone ten rounds with Rocky Marciano and lost. She'd a face like a box of frogs and a figure like a hundredweight of badly-wrapped mince. Every night after the gig Don has to walk them both home, dropping Brenda off and then going for a bit of a snog and a whatever down on the brick croft.

In those days there weren't many places you could go to do your courting, and the brick croft overlooking the canal was the only spot for miles around. Most weekend nights it was full of couples lying down on raincoats in the long grass.

Once when I was a kid we went there on Bonfire Night. They used to have a huge bonfire there for all the kids in the area. Well, a load of couples sloped off into the long grass just on the edge of the darkness. We waited till they got well settled down, and then me and my mates threw a dozen rip-raps into the grass. You know, those jumping-cracker things that leap all over the place. Laugh! I nearly passed me fags round! There was bums and legs and tits on show, with half a dozen couples trying to get dressed and jumping all over the shop, all spot-lit by the bonfire. There wasn't half some girls got clouted by their mams that night I can tell you!

So Don and Doreen are off every dry night, down on to the croft. Then her mam goes away for the week to Blackpool with her aunty to stay in a caravan they have – Doreen had no dad, he was dead in the War, or something. Anyway, when her mam's away Doreen has a party in their house and we all steam in, dancing and drinking. Elvis on the Dansette, Double Diamonds and Cherry Bs all round, plates full of crisps and little sausages on sticks and everything, sound as a pound!

I don't know if it's the drink, or whether it was the first time he'd done it in a feather bed, but Don told me long after, that that must

have been the night when he dropped one. She wouldn't ever let
him use a johnny because she was a Catholic, so he'd been getting
off at Bury instead of staying on to Bolton – if you know what I
mean. Anyway, not long after that weekend and not knowing she's
up the spout, he decides to finish with her.

'What you on about?' asks Joe, the bass player, when he told us.
'You've only been goin' out with her a few months.'

'Yeah,' says Don. 'But she keeps talking about gettin' married
and draggin' me to look in furniture shop windows at three-piece
suites. Jesus, on my money we couldn't afford a one-piece suite.'

'You can gerrit on the drip,' said Tommy. 'Two quid down, and
ten and six a week for two years.'

'Do me a favour,' says Don. 'I'm too young to get married.
Besides, she's wearing me out. She's after it all the time. Three or
four times, one after the other.'

'What you complainin' about?' I says. 'I haven't even been past
the tops of Deirdre's stockings yet.'

Anyway, that night he does finish with her. But the head-the-
ball tells her at the beginning of the night instead of the end. So
the band spend all night playing away, looking at her sat on one
of the front tables with eyes like a dog's bollocks after it's jumped
a barbed-wire fence, and a mascara beard half-way down her chin.
And Brenda the Boiler has her arm round her, glaring at the whole
band as though they'd all got something to do with it.

Then Tommy, like a dick-head, starts singing that Skeeter
Davis number about *Why does the sun keep on shining and the sea meet
the shore when you don't love me any more?* She starts crying out loud,
and some women have to help her out, and Don just keeps
drumming with his nose an inch from the skins and the women are
shouting 'You heartless bastard!' at him as they help Doreen out.

Nobody sees Doreen after that for a while. Don starts going out
with a little peroxide blonde called Lindsey from the firelighter
factory. She's smaller than Don, and even more short-sighted than

he is, but she doesn't wear her glasses because they spoil her looks so we reckon she hasn't clocked on yet that Don isn't Rock Hudson. They've been going out about three months, and he's really stuck on her, and there's even a rumour of them getting engaged.

Then one Friday night the band are in the middle of their second set when Doreen comes in with an older woman – and you don't need to be Charley Chan to know that it's her mother. She's like Doreen, only with a three-day moustache and a selection of chins. They come in, get their drinks from the bar and sit in Doreen's old corner. Halfway through 'Cut Across Shorty', Hammy the guitarist catches Don's eye, and nods towards the corner. Don goes very yellow-looking and mutters something painful under his breath, and looks as though he wishes there were a window open somewhere.

You've never heard so many dropped notes in your life. Don is playing the drums like he's only just been given them for Christmas. His rhythm's all over the place, and the guitarists are dropping bollocks left, right and centre, trying to keep their faces straight, while Tommy keeps forgetting which leg he's twitching and starts coughing and choking on his words until every song he sings sounds like a rock and roll version of the Laughing Policeman.

At the end of the night the lads scarper down the cellar for an 'after-hours' from Mrs Crowley, and Don's about to do a runner with Lindsey the blonde when Mrs Cassarotti bawls out, 'Come here Don, our Doreen wants a word with you.'

I'm stood behind the bar washing the glasses, but I hear most of what's going on, and there isn't no point in spelling it all out because it's the old, old story and it finishes with: 'So are you going to do right by her, or what?' from Mrs Cassarotti and Lindsey kicks him in the knackers and flounces out in tears leaving Doreen and her mam 'flushed but triumphant', as I read somewhere once.

The wedding was a quiet side-altar do in one of the big Italian churches down the ice-cream area. Me and the band enjoyed it –

well, most of them. Don had a sort of troubled look about him as though he'd rather have been somewhere else, like fishing, or Greenland, or both. But, seeing that her brothers and her uncles were all dressed in black, and looked as though they'd been drummed out of the Mafia for cruelty; and since he didn't want to have to learn to walk on the bottom of the canal in a new pair of concrete wellies, Don said 'I most certainly do' at all the right moments and even managed to smile for the camera. If he hadn't, I think Mrs Cassarotti would have ripped his head off with her teeth.

There was no honeymoon. They were too busy decorating a little two-up-and-down they'd got round the corner from the Exile. It wasn't a bad little place, and once she'd got over the initial shock of being a rush job granny Mrs C. buckled to and helped with the cleaning and whatever.

It seemed to suit Don, too, for a month or so. He even started to fill out a bit.

'Must be that Italian cooking,' says Hammy. 'All that pasta and garlic.'

'You must be bleedin' joking, man!' says Don. 'You know that Doreen of mine must be the only Italian who can't cook. That's like an Irishman who can't sing. They don't exist, man. But she does.'

'What does she give you, then?' I ask.

'Egg and chips.'

'What's wrong with that?' asks Tommy. 'I like egg and chips.'

'All right. Dig this, man. Egg and chips for breakfast, egg and chips for dinner and egg and chips for me tea. Some nights she'll say, "I'm a bit peckish. Let's have some supper, love," and do we get cocoa and a biscuit like ordinary people? No, do we bleedin' hell as like! We get a plate of egg and chips – between us. Sunday dinner: egg and chips. My birthday: egg and chips. Christmas bleedin' dinner: egg and chips with holly on, I'm not kidding! It's all she can bleedin' well cook, man!'

There's a weird, Peter Cushing look in his eyes by now.

'I could be married to her for fifty years. That's fifty bleedin' years of egg and chips, man! I worked it out last night. Do you know how many eggs that is? It's fifty times three, times seven, times fifty-two, that's fifty-four thousand six hundred bleedin' eggs. Plus two pounds of bleedin' potatoes for chips – she doesn't scrimp on the chips! Oh my God, no! They're rolling off the plate on to the table and off the table on to the floor.'

He took a breath, and some of the puce left his face. 'That's six pounds of spuds a day, that's forty-two pounds a week, that's two thousand one hundred and eighty-four pounds per year, times fifty, divided by one hundred and twelve, divided by twenty, that's forty-eight and three-quarter bleedin' tons of potatoes. And when it comes to lard...'

'Come on, leave it out!' I say, feeling sick. 'Buy her a cookbook, or get one from the library.' I knew how tight Don was.

'And d'you know what really gets my tits?' He was looking really wild now.

'You're egg-bound?' I suggest, but he ignores this.

'It's the way she says grace. *Bless us, O Lord, and these thy gifts which we are about to receive from Thy bounty through Jesus Christ, Our Lord, amen, help yourself to salt and vinegar* – Just like that, every bloody meal! – *Bless us, O Lord, etcetera, etcetera, help yourself to salt and vinegar – help yourself to salt and vinegar.* It's driving me round the bloody twist.'

It went on like that for three years. She had the baby, a little girl called Carmel – very sweet she was, with brown eyes and lots of black hair. Then she had another one, called Tony. Don thought the world of them.

The egg and chips didn't change, though, and after three years we stopped remarking on it. You get used to anything after a while. Don just got fatter and fatter.

Tommy got married in a rush that third year, though surprisingly he didn't have to. She was a little darling, half-Chinese, and worked in the local college as a cook. He buys a house two streets away from Don and a couple of weeks after they were married she invites us all round for a meal after the gig on Sunday. Well, it's Chinese and Indonesian stuff and none of us have had any of this type of tackle before, but after the first taste we're digging in like we haven't been fed since the old Queen died. Don was there with Doreen, and she was the only one who didn't like it.

'I'm sorry,' she says, with a face like a yard of cracked lino. 'I can't eat anything with garlic or onions in. I'm sorry.'

So Mary, Tommy's new wife, asks her can she do her anything else.

'Oh no thanks, don't bother,' she says, but there's a bit of a huff in her voice.

'She likes egg and chips,' says Joe, with a glum grin and Mary said that's no problem and goes off to cook her some. Don just stares at the carpet, his face all red, and carries on eating his chicken and ginger or whatever, but you can tell that his appetite's gone. When the egg and chips arrive he starts getting pissed in earnest, and Don wasn't much of a drinker at the best of times.

We couldn't hear properly what was being said, because we left a bit after them, but on our way home that night you could hear them ahead of us, streets away, over the rooftops, shouting at each other.

A few days later I'm washing the pumps through before we open, when in comes Wilf, one of the regulars. He's got a grin on his face that he's trying to hide, but it's so wide that one of his ears is in danger of falling in.

'I've just seen Don in the corner shop – he's bought five dozen eggs. And Marge at the greengrocer's says he's just bought forty-odd pound of potatoes.'

On my way home that night I walked by Don's. The lights were all on downstairs, and I knocked, but no one answered. The curtains were drawn, but I peeped through a crack and I could just make out a figure in the back kitchen.

I knocked again but no one came and I was peeping through the windows again when some women came down the street, going carriage-cleaning at the yards, and I didn't want them thinking I was nosy so I coughed and pretended I had something in my eye and walked on.

He didn't come in the pub on Friday. When I got to work his drum kit was gone and, when I asked her where it was, Mrs Crowley told me he'd called in and picked it up that morning.

'He's packed in. He's told the lads he's jacking in, but he won't say why. He wouldn't see them; he just told Tommy over the phone. They've already got another feller from Eccles, starting tonight.'

As you can imagine, the band and the regulars spent all night wondering and debating what had happened. Some said he'd been seeing Lindsey and that he'd run off with her to Rhyl. Hammy reckoned he'd been made an offer by another group – but no one really knew. The night went off all right, because the drummer had played with the lads once before when Don had been ill with mumps, and they only played standards anyway, so there was no great hardship. And the next afternoon we found out exactly what had happened.

Don had left town – done a complete flyer. He'd gone to one of the music shops, flogged his drum kit and vanished, done a runner, El Bunkingtanos.

But that wasn't the all of it. Doreen had been in Blackpool at the caravan with her mum and the kids for the week. When she'd come home that dinner time she'd found the entire house covered in egg and chips. There wasn't a square inch of floor or chair, table or sideboard, that didn't have a patina of egg and chips cold and congealed on it.

She'd given out a scream louder than when the boiler blew at Small and Parkes, and half the women in the street had come running, thinking there had been a murder or somebody had cut his throat and his wife had found him. Like when Harold Riley nicked all the punters' money he was supposed to put on this horse for them 'cos he thought it hadn't got a chance, and it came in first at twenty to one.

Well, when the women saw what had happened some of them wet themselves laughing, some of them wet themselves crying, some put their arms round her and made her a cup of tea and others just got brushes and buckets and started a clean-up.

It was while they were cleaning up that they found the note under a pile of egg and chips on the radiogram. It just said:

Help yourself to salt and vinegar.
Don.
Gone.

Moonshot

The fan in the high, smoke-yellowed ceiling turned slowly above the heads of the three European men sitting at the small glass-topped table in the bar of the Hotel Liberty. The biggest of the three reached forward for his drink and the wicker chair creaked loudly beneath him.

'What a bloody craphouse of a place!' he grumbled. 'Look at the size of that bastard,' and, grabbing a fistful of nuts from the bowl on the table, he gestured towards a cockroach the size of a mouse, steadily making its way across the polished wood floor.

'A veritable khazi,' said Corrigan, the cameraman, pulling a pack of cigarettes from the breast pocket of his safari shirt. 'But remember, oh Jameson bwana, *tee aye ay*.' Jameson groaned. T I A, This Is Africa, was a phrase they had learned from other Europeans within days of arriving, and they had all used it so many times in the last month that it had become an almost atavistic chant. It could suddenly stir up in all of them feelings of frustration, anger, boredom, hatred and even at times a half-lonely fear. The double door into the street opened and the outside world with its heat and damp and smells blew a breath into the air-conditioned room.

'You get through all right, Tim?' Corrigan asked Bell, the assistant cameraman, as he let the door slam with a thud behind him and walked towards them holding one finger up to attract the boy's eye. When they connected across the big room, he silently mouthed, 'One beer.'

'Anybody else for one?' They shook their heads. 'Yes, eventually, after fighting half the forces of corruption and "couldn't give a bugger, bwana" in Africa. Cost me ten dollars to get the soldiers who guard the exchange to let me through, because what did I do?'

They intoned in perfect unison, 'You forgot your passport!'

'Correct.'

'Bloody craphouse of a place,' muttered Jameson as Bell threw himself into a chair, his shirt mottled with patches of sweat and the wet, sweet, cloying air of the midday street hanging about him in a cloud.

'Do you want the good news or the bad news first? Okay, the good news is that Charlie said that most of the last batch was terrific. The bad news is that there there are bad hairs in the gate on reels fifty-six and fifty-seven. I haven't checked the shot list yet, but I think they're the night shots up-country.'

'Oh for Christ's sake, no!' Martens, the director, thumped the arm-rest of his chair and grabbed his drink. He was in his early thirties, edging towards being plump, with wire-rimmed stylish spectacles and thinning fair hair which the tropical sun had bleached until it now matched perfectly the colour of the bamboo headrest of his chair. He was one of this year's batch of new, young, bright directors tipped for better things, and he hadn't as yet adopted the quiet workaday pessimism and cynicism of the older business end of the crew. He picked up the Filofax on the table before him.

'Fifty-six and fifty-seven have got the moonshots on them. Bollocks!' He threw the book back down, took a cigarette from Jameson and turned to Bell. 'Are they bad?'

'It's a really bad hair on both reels. Bits are usable, but generally it looks bad. I think it's that new stock. Charlie said it looks as though some of the emulsion has lifted in the heat, and it's stripped tiny bits off going through the gate. He says there's a few on other reels, but nothing too serious. Most of reels fifty-six and fifty-seven are out, though. Apart from that, he said the quality's really good. All the low-light stuff with the fast stock has come out exceptionally well. He said some of the interiors of the initiation ceremonies were stunning – that was his word – stunning. I've never heard him say that before. The highest accolade we've ever had from him before was "quite interesting", so we must be doing something right. The line was lousy, though. I've had better lines from Australia. And by the way it's been pissing down for a solid week in London, and United lost.'

'You might as well be in bloody Australia as in this bloody place!' crooned Jameson as he took another drink. A big-boned, heavily-fleshed man, with an overhanging gut and the merest tint of a now lost Scots accent, he was the hardest and most seriously dedicated drinker in a hard-drinking crew. 'It's nice of the Irish to name a drink after me,' he used to say, pointing to the whisky on the shelf. That was when he could get it. Here, on that line where bush meets jungle, fifty kilometres from the nearest town of any size, the only whisky to be had was what Jameson called a cheap 'industrial strength' blended malt. So he drank that, indexed his sound tapes and belly-ached about the country, the people, the local whores, the snakes, the insects, the food, the shoot and anything else his jaded eyes lit upon.

'Well, that's it. Looks like we're here for another few days at least.' Martens ruffled his patchy hair. 'I need that moonshot for the final credits. Without it the film will just fizzle out.'

'What about stock shots?' asked Bell. 'Somebody must have some good footage of a slo-mo moonrise.'

'I don't want stock shots. It'll look too obvious – the colour, the terrain, it will look all wrong. I want my shots...' he corrected himself '...our shots. If we get it right, it will be the icing on the cake. It will, as they say, gob-smack them.'

Jameson laughed. 'Watch out, Attenborough – we're talking BAFTA here!' He rang the bell on the table and the boy came and took their orders.

'Still,' said Martens, 'I suppose in a way those hairs could be a bit of a blessing in disguise. The moon'll be full in a few days' time. We'll miss Wednesday's plane, but it could mean that we get a better shot than last time. I'll get Sally to phone the airport and check the times of moonrise over the next few days.' He looked towards Jameson. 'We can shoot it mute if you like, Joe, so you can stay here and get totally arseholed, give the old mozzies another hangover.'

'Christ! Yes,' laughed Corrigan. 'Anything that drank his blood would end up paralytic.'

'As long as it didn't sing "My Way",' said Bell, referring to the song Jameson insisted on groaning out after a night on the booze.

Jameson grinned at this gentle ribbing. 'No way am I sitting here on my jacksie if you go off up-country. Point one, the waiters might eat me. Point two, if you're braving your all for art then I'm coming with you. I'll do some wild tracking. You never know, I might be the first sound engineer to record the mating call of the greater painted-toed, blonde-crested, large-chested, hotel-billed PA.'

They all laughed as Sally, their PA, came in at that moment. She heard what Jameson said and gave him a good-humoured slap on the back of his head.

'You having a go at us poor production assistants again, Mr MacTubby?' She sat on the arm of Marten's chair.

'Och no, me hen! Jings help ma boab!' Jameson protested in a mock Scots accent.

'We're here for another week, Sally. We've got bad hairs in the gate so we've got to re-shoot the moonshot,' Martens cut in, employing his professional voice, the one he used for getting things done, for 'cutting through the crap' as he liked to call it. 'So you had better phone Tim and tell him to let shipping know that we'll be at least a week later than scheduled. And – sorry to hassle you, darling – but can you phone the airport and see if the met people there can give you the times of moonrise over the next seven days?'

Sally nodded. 'I'll do it now. It'll probably take me hours to get through, and another couple of days before they understand me. The moon will have been and gone by the time I get it sorted.'

'I know, love, I'm sorry to lay it on you like this. I'll get you a drink while you're making the calls. What are you having?'

'I'll have an extra large G and T with lots of ice,' and she left, small, blonde and her very walk showing how conscious she was that at thirty-four she was still an attractive woman. Jameson's pouchy eyes followed her with puzzled interest but without hope for, though the rest of the crew were unaware of the affair, it was Corrigan whose bed she'd been sharing since Gatwick.

So the day developed into a long boozing session that stretched through the afternoon into an early dinner and beyond. The prospect of perhaps another week of 'this craphouse of a hotel' and a general feeling of depression at the loss of two key reels of film put them all into a hard-drinking mood. In the three weeks they'd already been in the town, they'd discovered that beyond the run-down and badly functioning hotel, where black-outs were a way of life and there was only enough hot water for three and a half people to have a small shower every day, nothing much happened; while within the hotel itself, nothing at all happened.

The town had a hundred or so mud-walled houses with banana-leaf roofs, a few more important buildings of concrete and corrugated iron, a palm-fringed square with a bronze statue of a soldier that commemorated the liberation of the country from invading neighbouring armies, a Catholic church, a Baptist mission, an orphanage run by some French nuns, a post office open for four hours three days a week and a small military garrison. Every day a market of ten or so stalls and a few ad hoc pavement groupings moved into the square at dawn and displayed a haggle of scraggy, moulting chickens, strips of high, fly-dotted meat, boxes of biros, cheap Chinese transistor radios, baskets of tiny eggs and lengths of bright cloth. The only things that seemed in reasonable supply were the vegetables. Raked up in piles on raffia mats before the feet of butterfly-coloured, chattering women, they were fresh, bright, healthy-looking and colourful. 'That's because they don't use any artificial manure,' Jameson told them as they were filming market one day. 'Nothing but good honest shit on them. Mountains of it.'

Two times a day a bus rolled in and two times a day a bus rolled out, every inch of it, inside and out, covered with people and bundles and baskets, like a dusty-red smoky scorpion puffing out thick black smoke as it groaned off slowly, carrying its children on its back along the bush road.

There was nothing for them here, they had decided almost from the start, but dust, boredom and the unspectacular rhythms of a day bounded by sunrise and sunset and chains of clean uniformed children going to school and back. Beyond that nothing much happened. There was only one blacktop road in the area. It led here from the capital and ended twenty kilometres from town. Every other road was dirt, red dirt. A month earlier the roads had been rivers of glutinous sucking mud, now they were ribbed and rutted, hard-baked switchbacks that put up a thirty-foot high fog of red dust. From time to time military convoys would roar out of town, heading into the bush on those terrible roads. The soldiers rolled and lunged along them in their trucks, looking bored and murderous. Weapons in their hands and bandoliers of bullets about their necks, they stared down over the tailgates of the wagons at the whites in their hired Landrover.

A few beggars wandered round the streets followed by small children and mangy-looking dogs, and from time to time lepers came into town to be picked up and moved down-country to the nearest leprosarium. Occasionally survey crews in four-wheel-drives on their way to the oil-fields in the north, or engineers making their way out to far-off copper mines, stopped at the hotel. It was their custom that kept the hotel and its bar open, theirs and that of the dozen or so whores the town possessed, who, as well as looking after the oil gangs, serviced the Army garrison and any passing travellers. Bright and smartly-dressed in Western fashion, the hookers – mostly amateurs, local girls with children and no men – hung around the bar waiting for custom; most of them were well-fleshed and liable to loud laughter, but there were a quiet, slim few already showing the signs of the disease that would kill them. On Saturday nights there was a dance with a local band playing 'Eight Until Late', and then the hotel was packed with people and the stairs were thronged all night with couples making for bedrooms.

The Hotel Liberty had been opened ten years before by the then Minister of Tourism. It was, he had declared, 'A sign of the rebirth of the nation.' On that day, there had been a band in the marble forecourt playing everything from five-year-old Western MOR to African pop. A group of local dancers and musicians were brought in to perform their folk dances for a handful of foreign travel-writers and a few local dignitaries, the boys in grass skirts and tee-shirts with the President's face printed on them, girls suitably Westernised in grass skirts and tartan brassieres. Most of the country's great and good were there that day; the VVIPs arrived by Army helicopter and the rest came down the road from the capital in black government Toyota Land Cruisers. The only important people absent were the contractor (who, after making crooked deals on this and several other major constructions, including a dam that would never be built, had fled the country with a suitcase of Kruger rands), and the contractor's brother (who'd been jailed for fraud in his brother's absence). On that day the fountains had worked, and the bar had sold a fair array of Western and African beers and liquors. Now the fountain was dry, a few of the state-owned tobacco company's cigarette packets curled where expensive Japanese goldfish once swam, and the bar sold only one type of local beer, the ubiquitous Coca-Cola and brands of local gin, rum and whisky.

Tonight, because everybody else of note had gone into the capital for a firework display in honour of the new military ruler's birthday, the crew had the place very much to themselves. The owner, a Portuguese black, had made a great deal of money during the revolution and ensuing civil war in a neighbouring country, when a smattering of newsmen and newswomen of some of the world's press had covered the event from the safety of his hotel bar.

Sadly, a CIA-backed counter-revolution in that same neighbouring country had replaced the despotic socialist Sandhurst-trained colonel with the son of the old tribal ruler, and the press and their money had left.

But now there was another film crew here, working on a series called 'The Rites of Man'. Financed by British, Australian, Arab and Japanese money, co-produced out of London and Sydney, it would be sold to every major and minor TV corporation in the world. The series had been devised by an anthropologist whose name, much to the scorn of his fellow academics, had become a household word and, under his direction, over a period of three years, crews had been sent out to film peoples, primitive and otherwise, in a world-wide survey of man and his rituals, ethics, codes, decorums and protocols. Country, race, culture and creed went under the scrutiny of the lens and the tape recorder to surface edited, cut and packaged to crows of wonder and incredulity in sitting-rooms across the planet. Families in Birmingham would marvel over the life of the Inuit of Greenland, while the Inuit of Angmagssalik, coming in on their skidoos across the frozen fjords under the northern lights, would stare at the bar-room TV, marvelling at Birmingham football hooligans in the streets of the global village of the video world.

This particular crew had already filmed a baseball game in Philadelphia, a wedding in Nepal, wrestling in Kyoto, aborigines at Ayer's Rock, New Fascists in Brixton, and a festival in honour of the Virgin on a Greek island in the Aegean when, on the day of her assumption into heaven, white snakes appeared out of the dusty, thorn-patched hills as though from nowhere and made their way round the church and down the valley to disappear as they had come. They had filmed a goat being crowned at a fair in the west of Ireland and the dances and rituals surrounding female circumcision in the Sudan; the Abbots Bromley Horn Dance and a young girl being blooded at her first ride to hounds. Now they were here, as the narrator's voice would later declaim, 'in this still backwater, cut off from the mainstream of Western civilisation, deep in the Heart of Africa's Darkness', to film the initiation ceremony of one of the local tribes. The boys, after a period of fasting and isolation in the jungle, would go through a painful ritual scarring to mark their passage from boyhood to manhood. After the ordeal the boys were the centre of a week of feasting and dancing. The shoot had been, they all felt, very successful and filming was all but completed. The moonshot, the closing image for that particular programme, would be filmed again three days later when, as Sally had discovered, the full moon would rise over a high jungle valley some thirty kilometres away, giving them the ideal shot they were looking for.

And so, on this night, the shoot extending beyond projection, they were involved in that particularly Western (or is it perhaps singularly British?) ritual of drinking, mutual mockery, leg-pulling, belly-aching and bitching.

'Another week in this place and I'll end up going bush,' Jameson whined. 'Nig-nogs, flies, snakes, vampire bloody bats, rotten meat and sod all to do!'

'And tell me, Mr Jameson, what else don't you like about Brixton?' Bell asked in a mock interviewer's tone, and they all laughed. Then Martens and Jameson talked bitchily for a while about somebody at 'BH' who had the knife into someone in Features; heads were going to roll, and somebody else was brown-nosing his way up through Drama while somebody else had screwed her way up from floor assistant to director in three years. With one ear on this, and under what little cover the table and the gathering darkness allowed them, Corrigan and Sally were stroking each other's knees and flashing covert lust between them with eyes and lips. Outside, the night was a rising crescendo of sound as the tree-frogs and insects heralded the blackness rolling down from the hills and the jungle to swamp the town.

Towards midnight, as the conversation grew ragged round the edges and gossip had been replaced by bawdy, and when even that had run aground on the shoals of repetition and Jameson had told them twice about the man who shat himself on a train; then, when heavylidded eyes had become varnished over with a dull patina of alcohol, the crew were surprised by the noise of a Landrover drawing up on the gravel outside.

'Another patrol back from shooting a few rebel gollies, I expect,' Jameson muttered into his glass.

But the door opened and, as though appearing by some conjuror's trick, a white priest walked into the room from the outside night through a cloud of shimmering moths and flies. He wore a dusky khaki suit, NATO boots and a baseball cap. Gold-rimmed glasses shone on a flat, broad nose that looked as though it had been broken at some time and below his thick trimmed red beard was a clerical collar and a crucifix. He looked in his mid-thirties, though he could have been older. As he entered the room an embarrassing silence preceded him like the bow wave of a ship. He took off his bush hat and looked at them through eyes the colour of the Virgin's cloak.

'It's no wonder the Church gets itself such a name as a killjoy if a poor priest wandering into a place in search of a drink can strike everyone in the room dumb.' There was still a strong hint of the Kerry hills in his voice, and his smile as he came towards them was such a smile as you'd meet on any of the backroads round Killorglin or his own home village of Rathmore.

'I'm sorry, Father,' said Bell. 'It's just that you're one of the few white faces we've seen in almost a month, and I think a white man and a priest was a bit too much for us all in one go.'

The priest laughed and Bell fetched him a chair to bring him into their circle, introducing everybody by first name, telling the priest about the film they were working on and explaining their respective jobs. The priest introduced himself as Mike Lynch and Martens waved the boy across for more drinks. When he arrived to take their order, the priest surprised them all by talking to him in the local language. They had a long conversation which left the boy going out for the drinks with a smile halving his face.

'You savvy parley good him fella,' said Jameson in what he imagined to be fair Pidgin.

'Oh me tok goodfella tok mista!' replied the priest. 'Me no bush Kanaka mista. En me no long long mista!'

Out-faced, Jameson laughed and lifted his drink in toast to him. 'Are you with the mission in town, Father?'

'No, I'm just passing through on my way back to Rome. Every so often my Order calls me back for a year to teach the languages, customs and dialects of this area to other priests bound for the missions. There are more than ten separate languages in this country alone, and within each language twice as many dialects.'

'Do you teach at the English College?' Jameson asked.

The priest looked at him for a second before answering. 'No, I am a Holy Ghost Father, we have our own place in Rome. To tell you the truth I don't like having to go back to Europe at all, I love it too much out here. But my superiors insist and as you probably know I am bound to them by the oath I took when I entered the Order. Whatever they say, I must do.' He raised his glass to them and toasted them in a wide sweep of his hand. 'Good health to all here. *Slainthé.*'

'Are you staying here tonight?' Sally asked.

'Lord save us! No! It's a cheap enough hotel for its type, I suppose, but even that would be too expensive for a poor missionary priest. We haven't television money,' he smiled. 'I have some things to sort out in town and up-country before I leave, so I'll be staying with the Sisters at the mission tonight, going up-country tomorrow for a few days, and then I'll be off to Rome for a whole twelve months.' He drained the last of the liquor from his glass, tapped a cigarette on the arm of his chair and lit it. 'But I'll miss the old place.'

'There you go, Joe,' Corrigan laughed, 'and you said you couldn't understand how anybody could like it here at all.'

'I still don't,' said Jameson.

'Ah, you've let Africa get to you in the worst kind of way. You've let it wind you up and stress you out. Relax. You're not going to change a continent overnight. It's been here a long time, and they had a civilisation here while we were still banging flint on stone to make fire. Africa's a very strange place. It takes a long, long time to get to know. People come here and suddenly they're instant experts; after six months they can pronounce on everything from politics to diet. I've been here nearly fifteen years and I've learned only one thing: that every day is different and nothing is sure. Nothing is ever quite as it seems. The taxi-driver with the crucifix hanging from his rearview mirror will still believe in ghosts in the bush, will still tie a red string around his little finger so he can't be bewitched or taken by zombies. I've spent most of my last fifteen years here, eleven months of every year, and I don't claim to understand even a tenth of it. It's a wiser and deeper continent than you or I could even imagine.'

'I dare say,' Jameson came back. 'It's just that I'm fed up with being ripped off by little brown men. Hands out everywhere, dollars for everything, and worst of all is the way they smile at you to your face and screw you behind your back. Everybody rips you off, our driver, the boys here, even the fixer here, Collee, who sorted out all the arrangements – we find out now that he's into twenty-five per cent of all the bills.'

'It's a small price to pay for the way that the West has destroyed this place. Don't forget the rape and the enslavement of a whole continent in the name of God and Trade that took place under Victoria and the Kaiser. They sliced a whole world up between them. You know when they drew the borders up between Kenya and Tanganyika, Victoria said, "Poor Willie, you've got no mountains and we've got three." And they re-drew the border so that the Kaiser got his mountain. That's why Kilimanjaro is in Tanzania today. White men slicing up the world.'

'Politics apart,' Sally, who was a knee-jerk Tory, interrupted, 'it's just so corrupt. We were talking to one of the Baptist missionaries a few days ago. He's been setting up a workshop with mission money, some kind of local small industry they're trying to set up. He told us that as soon as he leaves, all the machinery that they put in will be ripped out and sold. What can you do with people who won't even let you help them?'

'You're here as outsiders,' said Father Mike. 'You've come here to observe, to peer at the people and the country through your cameras, your magic crystal balls, your lenses and your microphones. You spend such a short time here, you see so little. Your job is to move quick, hit and run, get in, make your film and get out again. How long is your programme? An hour?'

'Twenty-six minutes with credits and the commercial break,' Bell answered.

'You see,' said the priest, 'we live in the age of the sound-bite, the quick-fix approach, summarising everything.'

'But that's the name of the game.' Martens was a little exasperated at what he thought was a slur on his profession. 'We're professional enough to do our research and track down what we want fairly quickly. It's a matter of selection.'

'Sure,' said the priest, nodding. 'I'm not condemning you for that. You take the noises that a country makes and the movements it makes and fix them, like you'd fix something in formaldehyde to preserve it in a jar in a museum. But in truth at the end of the day you see very little, and of that you see only two dimensions. It's not your fault, it's the fault of the medium. It's a question not just of journalism or of technology but of metaphysics.' Some of the crew were starting to look confused. 'Look at it this way. Even a hologram is only an electronic image, it bears less resemblance to the reality that created it than a fossil does to the living waters of the Pleistocene seas. You preserve it all right, but once you've done it, once you've taken the picture, once you've recorded the sound, it's dead. No amount of replay will bring it back to life again. You see films for example, newsreels say of the Yalta conference. Look at the screen and there they are, Stalin, Roosevelt and Churchill, carving up the world, the most momentous decisions three men have ever made in the history of the universe. They moved air and reflected light and those impressions they made were kept on tape and on celluloid – but the men who made them are dead, they're gone. Their accidence is there, but nothing of the essence, nothing at all.'

123

Jameson looked up from his drink. 'But you could say in a way that the film was a relic of these people, a trace of their existence.'

'The fact that they made an image on an emulsion of silver halide crystals or that their voices affected particles of magnetic iron oxide on a vinyl tape may give you evidence that at one time they existed,' said the priest, 'in the same way that the shape of an ammonite fossil in limestone tells you that it was there once – the animal's no longer there, only the shape its form made in the thickening ocean bed. But, in that it is a physical mirror of the substantive shape, the fossil tells you more about the real ammonite than a film tells you about the reality, the life-blood, the soul if you like of Stalin, Churchill, Roosevelt or even this place.' And he waved his hand towards the door. 'The world out there has a soul you can never see through a lens or with a pair of earphones. The real soul of the place flows under and through and around it all.'

'What do you mean by the soul of a place? I thought only human beings had souls?' asked Sally.

'How many days have you got?' laughed Mike. 'I suppose I mean the essential, the "thingness" of Plato.' He took another drink. Bell was almost asleep, Martens had decided that the priest was jabbering on because he saw Western faces so infrequently, and Corrigan and Jameson had both decided they were too pissed to take in much of what he was saying. 'There are some single-celled organisms, protozoa or a kind of amoeba, I forget what they are called. They're very basic life forms, as simple as you can get. They normally live in puddles, the sort of things you get in ruts, in cart tracks. When the puddle starts to dry out, the cells, these individual cells, clump together and form a communal animal that rolls along the ground rather like a tank's track until it finds another puddle. When that happens the "animal" breaks up and becomes a lot of single-celled organisms again. Now where does that knowledge come from? DNA, electricity, genetic patterns? If so, do we have the knowledge of all our forebears within us, the history of our race stamped into every one of our cells? They've now got a micro-chip the size of a matchhead that can do the same job it took a room full of computers to do twenty years ago. Our cell structures, our brains, the chemical composition of our bodies, are infinitely more complex than any computer.

'If you find it hard to believe, remember that as far as the scientists are concerned we all have a massive area of our brain that we seem not to use. Is it not perhaps there that we keep our prehistory through which and over which the individual soul wanders? We are all individual souls who are part of that continuum and our sole function (no pun intended) is to pass Life on.

'Now Time, in which all this happens, is another thing entirely. Time as a sequence of events we're all aware of, but God's Time, the time of the infinite, Absolute Time, like Absolute Truth, is outside the bubble. Our linear time runs on a straight track, infinity marches to a different drum, it is cyclical, its end is its beginning. Our Time has no link with infinity, it exists outside Infinity. It is no more part of it than a chord played on a piano is a cathedral. So what I mean by the soul of a place is that essence that runs through it, the race memory of its individual people forming one great memory, the vibrations of its physical history, its volcanoes and rivers and trees, all running through time.'

'Wow! I think it's a bit late for me to take all this in – or else this gorilla pee is stronger than it says on the bottle,' said Corrigan. 'Can we talk about something I know about, like football?'

'You can talk about what you like, I'm knackered. I'm for my bed,' and Bell moved in a wavering walk towards the stairs.

They all laughed and when Bell had gone, they did talk about football for a while, for the priest had been a keen Manchester United fan when he was at the seminary in England in the days of Best, Styles and Charlton and had carried on taking an interest in the team since. So the talk ranged from football to England, to politics, to the political problems of Northern Ireland, to the breakdown that seemed to be taking place all over Western society and, just before the night drew to an end, came round again to the nature of the world outside and Father Mike's part in it.

'It's a long way from Kerry to the Hotel Liberty,' Sally said. 'Don't you ever miss home?'

'Sure, but I have a job to do. I'm here because of Sin,' he smiled. 'Sin is sin, you know, whether it's here or in London or New York or Kerry.'

Sally felt the rising of a sudden fire sunk far within her that spread as though in a mess of tinder until it shone out of her face. She wondered if anybody else had noticed, but the others were too busy in the rummage rooms of their own consciences to see her reaction.

'My faith tells me that there are legions of souls here in a state of ignorance, and my vocation is to take the teachings of Christ to those souls.'

'I think it's a bit arrogant to believe that these people are damned if you don't convert them to Christianity,' said Martens.

'Ah no, it's not quite like it used to be. The Church no longer believes in aggressive missionary work like in the old days. We're much calmer now, and much more prepared to accept that the cultures of the people we work among are valuable and not to be destroyed. We no longer have a place called Limbo where the poor souls who die in Original Sin are banished for eternity, and most of us younger priests now believe that the kingdom of heaven is not a club reserved for Catholics alone.'

'That's a relief,' said Corrigan, half-trying to make a joke.

'No,' the priest laughed, 'men and women, Jews, Muslims, Hindus or atheists, can damn themselves every bit as much as Catholics. Although I think in fact that in an unclaimed state the pagan soul can turn, and often does turn, to the Prince of Darkness, the Father of Lies, Old Nick, Satan, the devil, call him what you will. He's certainly out there. And if I hadn't seen it with my own eyes and heard it with my own ears, who knows, I too might have ended up working with a film crew staying in expensive palaces like this.' And he laughed loudly before ordering another round of drinks.

'Do you mean to say you've seen the devil?' Sally asked, a shock wave building inside her and electric pulses just within her temples pressing in, ticking.

'Not face to face as such, but I have seen him in possession of souls. I've seen him in complete possession of natives in some of the up-country tribes.'

'How?' asked Martens. 'What did they look like?'

'Like their brothers and sisters, no different. Our old enemy is too clever for that. He'll hide within children, women, the old and the young, whatever suits his purpose.'

'And how do you know he's there?' Bell asked

'In many ways. Sometimes the possessed person will howl like a dog when I go near, or if he or she sees the crucifix around my neck. I've seen him have people foaming at the mouth and twisting, thrashing and writhing in agony on the floor when I've approached them with the Blessed Sacrament. I've even had him speak to me through them.'

'You've heard him speak?' Sally could feel the pulse in her temples again, like a tiny drum.

'Over the last fifteen years it has happened three times. Way up in the bush, where there are tribes that have never seen a white face, I saw two possessed people. One spoke to me in English and one in Irish. These were totally uneducated natives who had no conceivable way of knowing those languages.'

'That's incredible,' said Martens. 'Are you sure the voices weren't just in your own mind?'

'There were other people there with me at the time. They heard the voices, too. There was a witchdoctor way back up-country the year before last, and the same thing happened with him. By the way, not all witchdoctors are possessed or evil, not by a long chalk; some are just fakes, some are simply herbalists. Quite effective some are, too. But anyway, as I was saying, I was working way out in the bush and one day I drove, with a boy who was helping me, out towards the village of a tribe that spoke a very little-heard local dialect. We left the jeep at the road and walked for three days.

As soon as we arrived in the village, the witchdoctor ran out and began shaking at the first sight of me. He knew we were coming. He came across to us, the whole village was watching, he bared his teeth like an animal and screamed like a hyena. Then he spat at my feet and in a voice that was the voice of my old Latin teacher in the seminary, the exact same voice screamed, in Latin, "Go, or I will kill you!"'

'For God's sake,' said Martens, who didn't quite know how to take the story, 'it sounds like there could be a film there. It would make a marvellous documentary.'

The others, likewise captured by the tale, said nothing; except for Sally, who asked, 'What did you do?'

'I sat it out. I stayed and forced him out of the village. The people saw that it was a battle of wills between myself and him. I prayed, baptised people and made sure that the boy stood watch while I slept and I stood watch while he slept; and to make sure he didn't poison us we cooked and ate our own food. Finally, after a month, he disappeared into the bush, screaming vengeance. And, so far as I can discover, he hasn't come back.'

'That's incredible! Just incredible. There's got to be a film in that somewhere.' Martens took one of Corrigan's cigarettes.

'So here I am and after a year in Europe I'll be back, God willing,' said the priest. 'This is my place. These are my people. It's the only place outside Kerry' – he smiled – 'that I truly feel I belong.'

After that, one by one, the crew made their way to their beds, leaving Jameson and the priest down in the bar, still drinking. A little while later, in Corrigan's arms, Sally asked, 'Do you believe what he said. About the devil, I mean?'

'Bullshit. Total and absolute bullshit larded with a bogman's love of fairy stories. What a windbag. I thought he'd never stop talking. You've heard of the Blarney Stone? Well, he didn't kiss it – he swallowed the bugger. He sounds like my old man after a night at the Irish Club. This place has gone to his head – it's scrambled his brains. I've seen it before. "Jungle-happy", they call it, "going bush".'

Downstairs, under the slowly spinning fan, Jameson leaned forward in his chair. 'Were those stories for real, Father?'

'Every word,' he smiled. 'Are you doubting the word of a priest? As a Catholic you should know better.'

'How did you know I was a Catholic?'

'Only a Catholic would know about the English College in Rome.'

'I'm afraid I'm not a Catholic now, Father. I lost my faith some time back. I'm afraid you're talking to a lost cause.'

'There's no such thing as a lost cause! Even if there was, sure couldn't I pray to St Jude, the patron saint of lost causes, for you?'

They both laughed at that, then after a few more drinks they said goodnight. Jameson, as he stood at the foot of the stairs, turned and saw the priest vanish into the night, haloed by constellations of fluttering silver moths.

The last light of the falling sun was mirrored off the underbellies of a few clouds and was fringing the leaves of the far trees at the head of the valley as the long-wheel-base Landrover climbed the dirt track leading from the bush of acacia and bao-bao up into the higher ground where the jungle proper began. The vehicle groaned along the track under the moss-draped limbs of tall trees as the high green walls of the jungle moved in to surround them. There was a clearing where some surveyors had dynamited trees to make a camp. They stopped there and looked down at the jungle valley below them. They were on a mountain ridge below a pass that led through the jungle to the next valley. Bell hurriedly set up the tripod and mounted the Ariflex camera on its ball and socket. Corrigan moved about the clearing, taking readings with a light meter. The night of Africa, that sudden duskless night, washed over the world, a dark hot blanket filled with noise.

'There's a fair bit of residual light, you know,' he said to Martens. 'There's just enough to give us a bit of foreground detail. If it drops any more we can put up a light and wash it in a bit.'

'Wonderful!' said Martens, in a flat voice. It was one of his expressions and could mean anything from 'wonderful' to 'so what'. This time it was somewhere between the two. 'Start tight on that spot just to the left there, where she should rise, slowly zoom in as she clears the trees, going in from the vee of the valley, keeping it fairly tight, right on the end of the bottle, so that she looks big and fat sitting in the fork of the vee. It should take about five minutes. The credits will last forty seconds, so a time lapse of seven and a half to one should give us enough to go at.'

They rehearsed the shot a few times. Jameson slung his tape recorder round his shoulder, pulled his earphones on and turned away from the camera, the microphone held in his hand like a fat-barrelled pistol in its windshield. He moved away from the noise of conversation to record the sounds of the darkness, turning off the rough track to follow a path into the bush that had been carved out by hundreds of years of travelling feet.

'He's pissed, isn't he?' said Bell.

'Absolutely out of his tree,' Sally answered. 'Have you seen the way he's been drinking for the last three days? It's been non-stop!'

Corrigan nodded. 'He's been at it today, all day. Started in his room after breakfast, carried on in the bar through lunch, missed his meal completely, and drank all the way through the afternoon. He's just about as pissed as I've ever seen him.'

Jameson walked softly through the bush, his mind awash with drink, stopping every few moments to listen to the galaxy of sound that was coming off tape and through his earphones milliseconds after it had been created. He was recording and listening when, above the thick carpet of calls of birds and insects and frogs, he heard what sounded like a scream – possibly human, but perhaps animal. It was hard to tell. In the thick, growing dark, he turned up the playback volume and pointed the microphone towards the blackness ahead of him and the source of the sound. And he heard it again, louder this time, and what he heard made his skin walk, for further down the jungle path, in among the cheepings and whirrings, and the screeches and cries of things on the edge of night, some merely bedding down to wait for dawn, others killing or being killed, in among all that great broth of noise, somebody was calling his name.

'Joseph, Joseph, pray to God for mercy!' the voice ululated a dozen or so times, in what was sometimes a call, sometimes a cry, at others a sob.

He moved towards the source of the sound, the volume control full up, the tape and the jungle hissing in his ears. His torch cast its weak light a short way ahead of him through the bush, the rising moon helping him a little, fringing the stark branches and the creepers as he moved through them. With the jungle screaming in his earphones, and the siren calling 'Joseph' luring him on, he pushed forward, brushing the trees, creepers and flying things drunkenly away, his mind a cauldron of fear and curiosity. He crashed out of the bush into a clearing. There, on a fallen creeper-covered log milky with moonlight, sat an old black man, dusted with moonglow and naked but for a pair of tattered shorts.

'Joseph, Joseph,' called the old man, rocking backwards and forwards. Jameson walked slowly towards him, terror screaming louder than the jungle in his mind.

The old man's lips moved, then a millisecond later his voice came off the tape. 'Joseph, Joseph,' said the old man. He looked at Jameson. His cataract-skinned eyes were milky pearls in their sockets. Opening his mouth again he said in a voice that came from deep inside him, a voice with a rich Kerry burr, the voice of Father Mike Lynch:

'*Now Israel loved Joseph more than all his children because he was the son of his old age: and he made him a coat of many colours. And when his brethren saw that their father loved him more than all his brethren they hated him and could not speak peacefully unto him. And they took him and cast him into a pit and the pit was empty, there was no water there.*'

Jameson remembered nothing after that. He came to lying on the earth by the Landrover, his head booming. He'd been sick down himself and had cuts and deep scratches on his face and hands, caused, he thought later, by his flight through the bush. The others fussed around him, Sally was trying to clean him up.

'I'll be okay,' he said and sat up. 'Just threw a wobbler, that's all. Too much to drink, I suppose, and too much sun. I was drinking out on the terrace this afternoon, didn't have my head covered, fell asleep in it. The bloody heat must have done it. Bloody arsehole of a country.' He was on the edge of crying.

All the way back to town he sat frozen and wordless in the back of the Landrover, his heart drumming in its bone cage. He didn't mention the old man in the clearing and it wasn't until he returned to his room that he played back the tape and heard what he had heard in the jungle coming back at him from the spinning reels on the bed. He ran faster then than he'd run for years, out of the hotel and across the dark and moonlit square to the door of the mission. A black caretaker opened the plain wooden door to his banging. He peered at Jameson.

'Go 'way,' he said.

'Is Father Mike in? I must see him.' Jameson was frightened at the urgency in his own voice.

'Who is it, Patrick?' a voice called from within.

'Him white fella no belong dis place, Fada,' the man called, looking over his shoulder.

A white face appeared alongside the black one. 'What do you want?' It was not Father Mike, but the voice was not unfriendly.

'I'm looking for Father Mike.'

'He's up-country tonight. I'm afraid he won't be back now for two days. Can I help?'

Jameson thought for a moment. 'Will you hear my confession, Father?'

'Are you in a state of mortal sin, my son?'

'I am, Father, God help me.'

'Come inside, then,' the old priest said tiredly, 'and I'll confess you.'

And in a cool room, smelling of bees' wax and disinfectant, the same smell that he remembered from the chapel of his school when hands innocent of sin had clutched the wooden pew rail, Jameson unburdened himself of the sewage of his heart before the tubby little priest with the shaking hands.

Two days later he and the rest of the film crew drove to the airport and flew out. Jameson, sober and quiet now, was attracting worry and concern from the others.

'I'm all right,' he had insisted, grinning, embarrassed in the airport bar. 'There's nothing wrong with me. I've just given up the booze, that's all, for good. Before it gave me up.'

'He's had the gypsy's warning,' Corrigan said, laughing.

'You might say that,' Jameson replied, sipping his lime juice and soda.

Father Mike arrived at the mission later than he'd expected. He'd arranged confirmation classes for a lot of the outlying missions and it had taken longer collecting names and information for the Bishop than he had wished. The fat little priest opened the door to him when he heard the Landrover come into the mission yard.

'And has there been much change in the world since I went away, Father Nolan?' asked Father Mike.

'We found a family of snakes in the well, somebody's stolen one of Sister Carmel's goats, Patrick fell and broke a tooth and I had a soul come back to God.'

'You did?'

'I did indeed. The poor fellow was banging on the door at half-past midnight, begging me to confess him. An English fellow, one of those you had a drink with in the hotel. I confessed him, of course. You'd have thought he was a murderer the way he was hammering at the door. He asked for you at first.'

'Me?'

'I told him you were away. The poor man was frantic to cough it all out, and truth to tell it was nothing much. It was the old sad story, mad times with the roaring boys, sins of the flesh and the passion. Not a murder in it.' He laughed and pointed a thumb over his shoulder. 'And there is a bit more news. There's an old friend in the garden, come to say good-bye to you.'

They walked together through a door and out into a walled garden where a group of nuns were playing with some small children. On a bench in the shade of the cloistered trees an old man sat rocking to and fro, staring blindly ahead with eyes that were pearls.

Father Mike leaned over him and with deep affection said, 'Well here's me come a surprise, me fella. Long time me luk you see,' and he took the old man's hand. 'You savvy. Me fella go Inglan by an by,' and the old man nodded sadly.

'You by an by tok-tok Inglis for me fella?' Father Mike asked. And the old man smiled and intoned parrot-fashion in a deep bass voice that came from far inside him, halting and over-pronounced:

Now Israel loved Joseph more than all his children because he was the son of his old age: and he made him a coat of many colours. And when his brethren saw that their father loved him more than all his brethren they hated him and could not speak peacefully unto him. And they took him and cast him into a pit and the pit was empty, there was no water there.'

'Joseph, you remembered!' said Father Mike, smiling, and he touched the old man's face.

When the Birds Came Back
to Belsen

I was there that incredible spring when the birds came back to Belsen. I have lived a very ordinary unremarkable life and mine is, in the main, the story of countless millions of others, ordinary people who lived and loved and had children and died. But among it all there is this one event in my little uninteresting life, when the birds came back for the first time in years to Belsen; this one event that has come back to me again and again over the years, and has eaten into the edges of memory getting bigger, little by little, until now I have decided to write it down. Or perhaps the story itself, like all great and true stories, is shouting out, wanting to be told, knows itself that now is the time.

For it is a true story and when I die it will end and die with me unless I set it down and let its ghost live on in these words you read, these little black marks stamped on the page in your hand. Look closely at the words, it is not my voice you hear; it is your voice inside your head. Our common humanity links those two voices, my thoughts come crackling down the wires of time to become little black lines and circles that stare at you from the page. Confused and approximate, they struggle none the less, choking on their own passion, hungry to be heard. Look very closely and all you will see will be the inky symbols that approximate to what I am trying to say. Marks on the page, marks made by a stick in the sand on the beach that the tide will obliterate, the writing of a Jew in candlesmoke on a cellar wall – all of them marks and smudges, ghosts of ghosts of stories.

There is a poem by a little-known Irish poet, Christopher O'Neil, called 'Alphabet'. Do you know it?

> Twenty-six flowers.
> Oh what a web of tales they spin!
> What worlds, what gold imaginings
> What night-dark bowers.
>
> Twenty-six flying birds in your hand
> All colours, flock and swarm, take to the sky
> Who knows how they fly
> Or where they land?
>
> Twenty six tongue-stones,
> What pathways they build
> What stairs, what walls
> What palaces, what cells, what dungeons!

I'm afraid that you will find my little narrative, or at least my way of telling it, very dull because I am going to set it down as barely and as plainly as possible, since I think that it's important that I try and tell the story as accurately as I can.

I am not a writer, you see. I am an engineer used to working with the certainties of measurable dimensions and forces, not with the shifting vagaries of words. I am not even an Englishman, so you may find my way of expressing myself clumsy and stark. I was born in Hungary and came here as a youth, as a refugee with my parents after the uprising. So in a way it is presumptuous of me to try and write this down in English at all. But now my parents are dead I hardly ever speak Hungarian, and English is the language I have adopted though I still find myself thinking in Hungarian.

So that is it, and you must forgive my plainness of style and mistakes. But I know in myself that it is important that I write down what happened as closely as I remember it happening as is possible, so that what you read is as near to the truth as I can get it.

Truth? If there is an Absolute Being then he alone will know the Absolute Truth of what happened in those days when the world went mad. For the rest of us it is all a shadowy play in a darkening room where the actors change shape and position in the winking of an eye. I have told this story to no one before lest it should be changed in any detail by the telling, as is the way with stories. I have tried to set it down exactly as I remember it happening. After I tell it here, on this paper, I will tell it no more.

In April 1971 I was travelling through Germany, working for the British Army on the Rhine. What I was doing doesn't matter, since it isn't important to the story, but I found myself after a long drive down the autobahn arriving in the evening of a sunny April day in the garrison of Hohne near Hanover that is also known as Bergen-Belsen. Spring had returned to that cold German plain and the brown earth was covered with the new green. Somebody in the garrison told me that Bergen had once been the training-camp for young SS officers. The Round House, where we were working, was a Bauhaus structure with linear, plain, metal lamp-holders strutting from the bare stone walls of the vast meeting hall. It was the place where Hitler had addressed the young SS elite, his Aryan angels, from a reviewing station high up in the walls. There was something very depressing about the whole place and I remember thinking almost as soon as I arrived that I wanted to be gone from it as quickly as possible, even before I knew of the camp's past history. I felt there was a chill, a greyness, a sense of darkness about the place.

I wasn't surprised to discover later that three kilometres from the Round House was the site of the Belsen concentration camp. It had been levelled to the ground after the war and its vast acreage stood empty and grassed over now, left as a monument to man's amazing ability to wreak Hell upon his fellow men. It stretched, acre after acre of grass with no features as far as the eye could see.

'You know here are no birds in Belsen?' a young officer said to me one night in the mess.

'What do you mean, there are no birds?' I asked.

'Apparently, since the trucks came in with all the quicklime and filled in all the pits and the bulldozers levelled the place, not one single bird has been seen out there. All those acres of flat grass and not one bird, not for years. What do you make of that? You're an engineer, a practical man, so maybe you can explain it. The electronics guys in Signals reckon there is some strange magnetic variation there, too; they reckon that a compass out there starts to do all sorts of crazy things, almost as though the evil that went on there left some sort of kink in the magnetic web. Extraordinary, isn't it?'

I made some inane reply and muttered something about spiritual vibrations, then the conversation, as it will, wandered off on its own round the Russian experiments with parapsychology, UFOs, spontaneous combustion, leylines, crop circles, stones that move on their own, the earth markings at Cutzco, the stone circles of Carnac and Stonehenge and such. But later that night, as I was getting undressed in my billet, a sensation came over me which I had experienced only once before in Australia. I had been out there working on a big project and one night my journey took me to the middle of the Simpson Desert. I was with another engineer, making a survey for a mineral exploration group.

We stopped the Landrover to make camp for the night and got out into the darkness. The engine took a long time to cool down and it was ticking and creaking as it did so, but after it had stopped a silence thicker than any I had ever heard stretched as unbroken as the landscape all around us. There was not a breath of air moving. Above us the bowl of the southern sky with all its different stars stretched from horizon to horizon. We stood looking and listening.

'Quiet, isn't it?' the engineer said.

'Beautiful, just beautiful,' I replied.

Then it seemed that I could hear something, something that was almost a low murmuring, like a chant, or a rumble of voices, a humming perhaps. It flickered about, at times becoming hardly audible. It was extremely low in pitch – somewhere round sixty cycles, perhaps – but it was always there, almost like a low groan of pain. I wondered if perhaps there were aboriginals in the area.

'Can you hear a noise, something low, rumbling?'

'Yes,' he said, 'I can hear it. But only just.'

'I wonder what it is? Do you think it's aborigines chanting?'

'No way. There aren't any abos for miles.'

There was a pause as we listened once more, then in a low serious voice he said, 'I've heard it before, just once, on a night like this. It's the sound of the world turning.'

It was then I experienced the same sensation that came to me all those years later in Belsen; a mixture of helplessness, of fear, of timelessness. It is very difficult to describe; words are perhaps not the tools to use here. Perhaps music or a painting could tell the story better. It was a terrible sense of the vastness and mystery of all of Life, of dimensions that I hadn't even suspected existed before, of something eternal and immense moving about the universe, and it hit me like a slap the way, when swimming in a warm sea, a cold current can suddenly squeeze the breath from your lungs.

The same thing happened in Belsen-Bergen only it was much worse, much more frightening. A dizzy nauseous feeling came with it this time and as well as the feelings of awe and emptiness and insignificance, was the sure and certain knowledge that what had happened in here could have happened to me, too. I had been a refugee and knew what it was like to be displaced, to be driven across Europe leaving everything we knew behind.

But it was not that that struck me now, it was the thought that if I could have been one of the victims here, I could also have been one of the gaolers. And how would I have been then? I with my liberal ideas, my acquired English sense of 'fair-play'? Would I have had the courage to disobey orders, to get down in the pit with the naked and the dead? Or would I have been swept along by the tide of passion? Would I have become a Jew-hater too? Would I have loved my job?

It is easy for us to imagine in our little houses with our little cars and our little jobs so far removed from that madness, that no evil lurks within our small suburban souls. But it must be there as surely as the goodness and the love is there. If it is in me to hate what they did, it is also in me to love it.

Make no mistake, you and I could have herded the shivering, naked wretches towards the cyanide and the ovens. We too could have been the man or woman in boots and field grey or SS black ushering the chosen people to the charnel-house. If it is in them, then in my humanity it is in me too. None of us is innocent, our common nature taints us all, and we should all be on our knees giving thanks that we were not there, that we were not touched by the madness, the evil darkness of those days; that we were not forced to make choices.

All of this came to me during that night and I woke six or seven times sweating and shaking, shaking so hard the bed actually rattled.

All the next day I wandered round in a half-stupor that stayed with me until the evening when, after dinner, I wandered into the sergeants' mess and got involved in a game of darts with a tall, grey-haired sergeant, about fifty or so years of age. He was neatly dressed, quite handsome and quietly spoken, but confident without being pushy. After the game, which I remember now I won, we sat down; he as the loser bought the drinks and in a quiet corner we started to talk.

I couldn't place his accent at first. Having travelled all over Britain in my job, I'm used to the variety of dialects and accents that can be found spread across that land. At first I thought he was Welsh, then perhaps Cornish, but there was a strange burr to some of his 'r's, and his 's's were very pronounced, sounding almost like zeds.

I suddenly placed it.

'You're Polish, aren't you?'

'How did you know?' he asked, smiling.

'I have a Polish friend and his English, like yours, is excellent. But he has just a tinge of an accent, like you have. I have been trying to place it for the last ten minutes. I had you down as Welsh for a while.'

He laughed. 'I was stationed in Wales just after the war. They thought I was Scots.'

We talked about England and places he had been for a while and I was just about to ask him how he, a Pole, came to be a sergeant in the British Army, when somebody called him away. I finished my drink and walked across the camp to my billet and bed. That night, knowing I would be leaving in a couple of days, I slept well.

The next day, as I was working in the Round House, word went round among the swaddies on the job that the birds had come back to Belsen.

'Saw them this morning on the way here, he said, shitloads of them. Says they were nesting. Thrushes and all sorts. He knows about birds, that Jürgen. Says he saw some there last week, too. Been coming back for weeks he says.'

'He the one that works in the kitchens?' asked a signaller.

'Yer.'

'They must be payin' 'im well. 'E turned up in a bran' new BMW yesterday. Must be workin' a fiddle or somethin'. You don't get bran' new motors like that on what the Naafi pays.'

So the conversation left the birds and wandered on to cars, money, fiddles, tax dodges, the things that money can buy, and then on to the usual things bored men talk about when working on something that only needs the mental application of a goldfish: sex, women, sex and women again. That evening in the sergeants' mess, still curious, and feeling I had more than a little in common with him, I sought out the Polish sergeant and asked him as we sat with our drinks how he had ended up as a sergeant in the British Army.

'Not a sergeant,' he said, smiling. 'I was a band-master sergeant once. Until I got busted.'

'What happened?' I asked.

And over many more drinks, as the evening moved through to night, he told me his story. And as closely and truthfully as the years between will admit this is how I remember it.

I was born, he said, in 1929 near Lodz. My father was a goldsmith. I had two brothers and a sister, Eva. She was the baby of the family. She was so beautiful with black, thick, curly hair, and big brown eyes. We were Jews and even then, before the war and the Nazi invasion, there was a lot of anti-semitism in Poland. Polish thugs attacked Jews in the street simply for being Jews, there was a political coalition of anti-semitic groups and people's homes and businesses were confiscated. The Poles don't like you to know this but it is the truth. All over Poland you will find monuments to the murdered of their cities and towns, but all of them are to the Gentile dead. Not one candle burns for four million Jews.

But when the Germans came, the real persecution started. In 1939, as you know, the Germans invaded Poland and in 1940 Lodz was turned into a factory to feed the German war machine. Nearly two hundred thousand Jews were herded into the ghetto and forced to work in the textile workshops making German uniforms. My father, my mother, my brothers, cousins, grandfather and grandmother – we all had to work for the Germans war machine too. I wanted to be a musician. I had taken violin lessons under a great teacher, Mendel Grossman; he died on one of the death marches. But I had to give up the violin and work as a carpenter instead, there was no time or money for lessons and the violin had to be sold.

The leader of the Jewish community, Chaim Rumkowski, collaborated with the Germans all along. He was not a bad man, he was trying to make the best of an impossible job, trying to 'normalise the situation' I think you would say. He collaborated in the formation of the ghetto in the hope that that would placate the Nazis. It didn't. Nothing would have placated them by then; they had turned from being human beings into becoming mere cells that were part of a larger killing animal dedicated to the extermination of the Jews as a race. Make no mistake about it, if they had taken Britain then the Jews there would have gone the same way. There would have been forced labour camps outside Coventry and Newcastle and extermination camps on the moors; and there would have been plenty of English men and women only too glad to staff those camps.

Anyway, in 1941 the Germans decided that the Lodz ghetto was a good place to dump all the old and the sick, all the other unwanted Jews from the cities of western Europe. We were already overcrowded and underfed, people were sickly and weak. The Germans just allowed us enough to stay alive and work for them – no more than that – everything else was for the Reich. But you know it was amazing what they did!

Their war machine was so good. Suddenly they had railway timetables and trains and more than twenty thousand Jews were shipped to Lodz from Berlin and Prague and Luxembourg, from Frankfurt and Vienna.

The winter that year was terrible. Five thousand people died that winter. I saw people die of starvation. I saw people die leaning against a wall and they froze there, standing up, the snow and ice came and they were there like statues frozen to the wall.

Then in the summer of 1942 the Nazis began to move us out to the death camps. Eighty thousand people were deported, my grandparents and cousins, my aunt and uncle among them. Forty-four thousand went to the extermination camp at Chelmo. Nobody knows what happened to the rest of them.

He stopped and ordered another two pints of beer, lit a small cigar and looking down at the table, as he had done since his story began, he carried on speaking in a slow sure voice. He never hesitated once. It was as though his story had been rehearsed in his mind a thousand times or more, and now it had found an audience.

They left us until the last. My father was a valuable man to the Germans. He could do amazing things with gold and they forced him to help the officers smuggle gold out of the ghetto, gold that should have been handed over to the Reich. He made fountain pens, badges, lighters, all of them dummies and all made in solid gold. He even made a solid gold Lüger pistol for one of the officers. And painted it so that it looked like the real thing. Thousands and thousands of pounds' worth in today's money.

And so we clung on from day to day, my father working in his little workshop, I working as a carpenter, the rest of the family working ten hours a day in the factory making German uniforms. We got two hundred and fifty grams of bread a day and half a litre of turnip soup. God, I think back on it now and remember how we longed for that soup! We looked forward to that bowl of lukewarm dishwater all morning, and when it had gone we looked forward to the next day when we could look forward to it again. You kept yourself alive by hopes like that.

We knew about the camps. Rumours came back; the watches from some of the earliest to go found their way back to Lodz, and my father saw them, read the names he himself had inscribed on the back. But we thought it wouldn't happen to us, we lied to ourselves, thought that somehow we were different, we refused to see the truth. Perhaps that is the fate of all mankind, to refuse to see the truth until it is too late. By June 1944 we were still there, my mother and father and brothers and sister. There were seventy-six thousand seven hundred and one Jews registered in the ghetto, all that was left of more than the hundred and sixty-four thousand Jews of that city and the twenty thousand that were deported there.

Then the time came for us to go, too. The Allies were eight hundred miles away to the west and the Russians were pushing their way forwards from the east. The Germans decided to destroy the ghetto. They made an announcement. I'll never forget that it was called Announcement Number Four Hundred and Eighteen and that it was headed *The Transhipment of Jews from the Ghetto* . That was on the fourth of August. On the seventh of August came Announcement Number Four Hundred and Twenty-Two. We were ordered to prepare ourselves immediately for departure, taking only what we could carry. We knew that the Allies were making their way towards us and that if we could hold out then they would eventually reach us and release us. So we went on strike, and refused to move. The authorities insisted that we leave and still we refused.

We were told to gather to be addressed by the Chief of the Ghetto Administration. His name was Hans Biebow and he was a graduate of a German school of business administration. He told us that Allied bombers would destroy Lodz and the Jews with it, and that our only hope of survival was to move west. All the Jews were needed for the factories in Germany since many of the workers had gone to fight at the front. Food had already been loaded on to the trains and the journey would only take from ten to fifteen hours.

We reasoned that at least in the west there might be more food and that in any case we were only exchanging one workshop for another. So we gave in and packed our seventeen kilos of luggage and made our way to the railyard.

We did go west, but not to any factory or workshop. We went to Auschwitz. Only one Jew had been spared deportation, Chaim Rumkowski, the elder of the ghetto; but when he heard what had happened to his people he walked out to the railway yards with his family and climbed on board the last transport to Auschwitz.

I don't know how many days we were in those trucks. We were crammed in more than sixty to a wagon. People died and fell to the floor and we stood on them. No water, no food, the shit and piss and menstrual blood ran down our legs as we stood. We held my baby sister Eva up so that she wouldn't get trampled. The train stopped, it started. It shunted into sidings. It waited. We died and we were stood upon. We rattled across Europe by night, the solid free earth passing beneath our feet.

And where was the eye that saw this? Where was the God that would put out his hand and put an end to it? Nowhere. When we reached Auschwitz they opened the doors and the light came in and we were blinded. And we swallowed the fresh air like wine, but it smelt sweet yet sickly. There was something in it that I didn't recognise. It was the smell of roasting Jews. We got out and stood in line by the tracks. I thought I was in some kind of lunatic asylum, and in a way I was. There was an orchestra playing, a group of men and women dressed in striped uniforms were playing Strauss waltzes, and there were flowers growing all around the bandstand.

The SS were there of course, marching up and down, sorting out the living from the dead, but everywhere there were people in striped uniform with crazy-looking caps on their heads, muttering in Yiddish. One of them saved my life. Most of the others ignored him, perhaps thinking he was mad, but I listened to what he was gibbering over and over again: 'You're eighteen, you have a trade, you're eighteen you have a trade,' so that when they grouped us into line and made us walk to the selection platform I knew what to say.

'How old are you?'

'Eighteeen, sir.' I added two years to my life to save it.

'Do you have a trade?'

'Yes. I'm a carpenter.' So I was sent to the left at a nod from this man, and my father and my mother and my little sister and younger brother, who was eleven and had no trade, were all sent to the right. I soon learned what happened to those sent to the right. They were for the ovens. They were to go, as they used to say, 'up the chimney' and there were twelve chimneys at Auschwitz – that's a lot of Jews.

My sister was three years old and stood looking round her, terrified and exhausted. My father looked as though he was in a dream. I suppose in a way he was. My brother was shaking with fear – I think he knew what was going to happen to him. My mother was still and very, very pale, hardly breathing. She wouldn't cry because she knew that would have made it worse for me, for all of us. There was an order and those who had gone to the right were marched away.

I had never known that such simple words as *right* and *left* could also mean *life* or *death*. Words are powerful things, my friend, such powerful things. One word, 'right' – you die; another word, 'left' – you live. And that was the last I ever saw of my family. Is there any way you can imagine that? To watch all your family, the only people you have and love in this world, walk away from you to their deaths?

An SS man saw me looking after them. He came over and pointed toward the gates of the camp. 'Do you see that gate?' he asked me. I nodded. You never spoke to an SS officer unless he told you to speak. 'That, little Moses, is the way in and that –' and he pointed towards the big chimneys smoking above the crematorium ' – is the way out.'

My older brother, Avraham, was sent to the left with me. He was saved from the gas chambers and the furnaces not because he had a trade, but because he had a club foot. They didn't save him because of any mercy they felt for the lame, or anything like that. They saved him so that they could experiment on him. He was killed and dissected by Mengele, the famous Doctor Mengele who saw my lovely brother, my beautiful brother who was studying to be a rabbi, as an example of the degenerate nature of the Jewish race.

At the camp we were stripped, our heads were shaved and we entered the world of the mad. In the camp one of two things happened to you. You either fought them, inside yourself, and you survived; or you gave in and you went under. You told yourself you were going to survive, you woke up each morning and thought of something to look forward to that day. That gave you something, something to hold on to.

It was as though you were on a cliff-edge with your fingernails hooked on to a tiny ledge in the flat face of the cliff. You held on, gripped on to this mad reality, it was the only way. You were in another world, in the mad world of the camp, and you could only exist in that world by learning the rules, memorising the codes, understanding the system.

And there was a system, make no mistake about that, and eventually you knew the rules and the mad world of the camp became the norm – anybody who has been there will tell you that. And afterwards, when you look at the world outside, it is only the camp written in smaller letters, more subtle. What's the difference between the My Lai massacre and what went on in Belsen? What's the difference between napalming children in Vietnam and gassing them here? And we all ignore it. It is not our problem. The people who watched the smoking chimneys of Auschwitz, Ravensbrück and Dachau and pretended they didn't know what was going on are no worse than those who ignore the Palestinian camps today or the Colonels in Chile with their tortures and massacres. We know it goes on, but we choose not to admit it.

The camp was just a more refined academy of horror, the Bolshoi of terror, what you might call a centre of excellence. There the ballet of death and torture was brought to its finest state and there in this camp the rape and murder of the human spirit became a craft or art so practised that it became at times as subtle, as awe-inspiring almost as a brush-stroke by Picasso or a Beethoven sonata. We Jews have words for what happened to us then. We call it the '*churban*', the destruction, or the '*shoa*', the holocaust, the abyss, the cataclysm, the great darkness, the pit, the end of everything.

So there were two possibilities: you survived or you gave up. But you could always tell when people had given up. You knew then they were finished. Usually it started with them going very quiet, then one day you would see them crying. Once you saw them crying you knew that was the end, they couldn't take it any longer. But me, I became hard. So hard you would not believe. And I swore then to myself that for the sake of all my family, for what they had done to them, I would not let them beat me.

All around you would see madness: sick men stealing food from sick men; men trampling on the faces of the dying to reach the light; men fighting to the death over the corpse of a rat. We could all do it, you know. Humanity goes out of the window. And that is exactly what the Nazis were doing to us, they wanted to destroy our humanity. To justify them thinking of us as animals they tried to turn us into animals. It's hard to think of a skeleton crawling in his own shit as a human being.

But I swore with all my heart that I wouldn't let them do that to me. I gave people my bread, sometimes I gave my soup away just to prove that if the Nazis were monsters I didn't have to be a monster too. I could have been, we could all have been monsters, we could all have given up, but I didn't. The one thing they were not going to take from me was my humanity, my ability to say 'No'.

One day, it was an incredibly hot day in that late summer of forty-four, incredibly hot (it sticks in my mind like a picture, every detail), I was working with a party laying concrete for a hut base. It was hard work and it was even harder because of the heat, and we were hungry and tired and worked slowly. That made the guards angry and they were more angry also because of the heat. A man fell over and they told him to get up. I went to help him and they pushed me back. 'Get up!' they said and he didn't, he couldn't, he'd collapsed with the heat, with exhaustion and starvation. So they beat him to death in front of us with their boots and rifle-butts and whips. As he lay on the ground dying one bastard smashed his skull in with a rock and his brains came out on the floor in front of us. They made us bury him there and then in the wet concrete. We did as we were told and down he went, barely deep enough to cover him.

A rabbi who was working on the detail asked could he say a prayer over the dead man. I thought the rabbi would have been shot there and then. It's true! I thought the guards will kill this man too, but they just nodded and we said our prayers over the concrete. One hand stuck out as though it was grasping at the world above, and somebody got a stick and pushed it under as we

149

prayed. Then as we were praying a beautiful thing happened. A cloud of golden-red butterflies came, from god alone knows where, and fluttered about our heads and all around us. And I knew then that I would get out. The butterflies coming into the madness of that charnel-house had told me something in a way. It sounds crazy, I suppose, but at that moment I knew that I would survive, that I would get through. I the victim would be the witness.

It went on for months until we were all like you see in the newsreel pictures of the times, the living dead, zombies, walking skeletons. Then word came through the underground that the Russians were breaking through and that they were coming towards Auschwitz, that they were only a matter of days away. There was a buzz around the whole camp and on January the eighteenth 1945 we were ordered out of the camp, on foot, marched through those terrible gates with that terrible lying sign *Arbeit Macht Frei* above us and we went in column to the railheads to be shipped west, away from the Russians.

Those who were too weak to march were shot there and then, and any that fell by the wayside were shot and thrown into the ditches. We could hear them, the shooting went on behind us as we marched and we daren't look back. If you looked back you would have been shot too. We counted the shots as we marched, one day it was three hundred and twenty-one, another day it was five hundred and fifty-five. An exact number, that, and it stuck in my head because the first pack of cigarettes I was given when we were liberated had those numbers on the front: five five five. There was no food; a few people tried to escape and were shot. It went on for six days and then we reached a railway depot and they put us into cattle trucks and brought us here.

What? They brought you to Belsen, they brought you here?'

Yes, to Bergen-Belsen, to this very spot where we are now. We were ten days in those cattle trucks and of the thousand or more of us that climbed into those trucks less than two hundred reached

Belsen alive. Here, in the first week of February 1945, I marched through those same gates and stood in line for a piece of bread and I weighed just over four stones. Thousands were pouring in from the extermination camps all over the east, brought here to get them away from the invading armies. Five hundred died here every day. I thought Auschwitz was bad, but here was worse. Typhoid wiped out thousands. The camp commandant was a man called Kramer, who watched five hundred people a day die of typhoid and starvation in Belsen. When the British arrived, they discovered eight hundred tons of food here and a bakery that could produce sixty thousand loaves a week. They asked him why he hadn't fed the dying people in the camp, and he said it would have meant filling out special forms. A strange thing, the German mind.

So the Jews who had escaped Auschwitz and Dachau and Ravensbrück carried on dying. I was part of a burial detail, but we couldn't keep up, in the end everybody gave up. I saw them eating meat from the garbage bins that was so rotten it had turned to yellow slime; and I saw human beings drinking the water that the shitty underwear of the dead had been washed in. They were drinking raw typhus. There was cannibalism too. We found bodies with their lungs torn out, slices of meat cut from their thighs. Ann Frank died here. That beautiful little girl who never harmed anybody died here, while Irma Grese, twenty-one years old, the Bitch of Belsen, strutted round with her gold-blonde ringlets and blue eyes, turning her dogs onto the dying Jews and laughing as they devoured them. Starvation and typhoid. They died in their thousands.

By the time the Allies came in April there were ten thousand bodies rotting above ground, and the dying were gnawing the flesh from the bones of the dead. Here, no more than five minutes from where we are sitting tonight.

Then, on the fifteenth of April, the British Army came into the camp. The Germans saluted and welcomed them in. Kramer stood in his Sunday best uniform and surrendered the camp to the

British officers. And the British soldiers couldn't believe what was before them, behind the façade of the saluting SS. I remember the first tanks squealing in through the gates. We younger ones walked towards them, we thought at first it was the Russians, then we saw the Union Jacks and a soldier jumped down and others got out of their tanks and stared at us. There were hundreds dying on the earth as the soldiers walked among us and though the gates were open, those of us not dying or too weak to walk had nowhere to go. We were free but we didn't know what to do. It seemed a dream that would turn back into another cruel reality.

And in any case we were like goldfish that have spent so long swimming round and round in their bowls that when they're let out into the big pond they still keep swimming round and round. We were burnt out. We had ceased to exist. We were the walking dead, ultimate proof of the darkness of man's heart. And do you know, it's ironic, but the first three soldiers into the camp were British Jews. One of them, a rabbi, a chaplain, spoke Yiddish and I'll never forget him weeping as he looked around him at what was left of his race.

They fed us and cleaned us up and buried the dead. You've seen the film of the squaddy smoking the Woodbine as he bulldozes the thousands of naked skeletal bodies into the lime-pits. Ten thousand dead and unburied when the British came through the gates. When they fed us a lot more died because of the richness of the food. The dried milk and the rations were too rich for some of the weakest, and they died eating their first meal in freedom.

Then, after they had filled the pits with bodies, they torched the camp to kill the typhus, burnt every stick to the ground. Only one bare tree was left. And they moved us down the road here to the SS training-camp, to this very building we're in now. I was seventeen years old, the only one left of my whole family.

There was a school for the children, and we studied. We studied like crazy because we had all lost our childhood and our education. I was old enough to be able to teach some of the children. There were Poles, Ukrainians, French, Hungarians and yet we all had one common language – Yiddish. And there is one thing that happened at that school that I'll never forget; until the day I die it will be printed on my brain.

The children never laughed, never smiled, their faces always had this same empty look, particularly the small ones, the four- and five-year-olds. And one British soldier had noticed this, a medic. So they decided to get a clown for the children. The clown is international, the clown is universal, the clown doesn't need a voice, the clown doesn't need language, because the clown always tells the truth. The clown cannot say 'right' or 'left.' The clown falls down, slips, pulls faces, the clown smiles, dances, makes little dogs from balloons and flowers from dust. The true clown turns the spark in the human soul to fire.

He came, he danced, he laughed, he smiled, he played a concertina. He also was a soldier. Before the war he had been a great circus clown, but circus clown is not a reserved occupation. For an hour he danced and sang and jumped and made magic, blew bubbles from his fist, hit his thumb with a rubber hammer, sat on a nail and rubbed his bottom, hooted his car-horn, magicked flowers from a small girl's ear and a golfball out of his mouth. He fell over, got up, poured water down the front of his baggy pants, and ate fire. He made a coloured rainbow stream right across the room from window to window and he made small chocolate flowers wrapped in glittering paper fall from the roof of this Round House like multi-coloured magic snow. And there was not one smile on those two hundred faces, not one spark of brightness in one single eye. And at the end of it all the clown stopped and got off his unicycle and stood looking at the children before him and he cried and cried and cried, the tears rained down his face and when he wiped them away the grease-paint smeared and it was as though his face had melted away before us. Then a soldier led him away and the children sat quietly cross-legged, staring at the space where the clown had been, doing nothing, and waited until a voice told us it was all over and we trudged off back to our beds.

I stayed in the camp for three years, there was a whole shtetl inside. We survivors began somehow to remake our lives. We became a symbol of survival. The Jews left in all the other camps came here. We had a hospital, schools, a seminary. We used the small theatre here and put on plays in Yiddish and we had an orchestra and I played in that orchestra.

For the first time in years I had a violin in my hands again and I could make the wood sing. And I made it sing the songs of my people, songs of the ashes and the burned stumps that were the Jews of Europe. Then on May the fifteenth 1948, we danced in the camp when the state of Israel was proclaimed. Many of the survivors went to Israel, many to America.

I went to England, became naturalised, and I joined the British Army. In the army, this crazy army, they discovered I was a musician. I told them I'd learned a little violin as a boy so, typical army, they taught me the trumpet. And I did well, over the years. I became a band-master. Then a band-master sergeant. Music became my whole life. I had always loved it, now it was everything to me. I never married. I had too much sadness within me I suppose. I was quiet, I got on with my job. I learned to speak almost perfect English and I was one of the best band-master sergeants in the whole of the British Army. My bands won competitions everywhere from Calgary in Canada to Famagusta in Cyprus.

I was in Cyprus for six years, Aden for four, Hong Kong for three, Gibraltar for two, then back to London as a band-master sergeant instructor. Then guess where they sent me? Here, four years ago. Hohne it said on my orders but I knew it was Belsen. I could not believe it. It was a posting I could have refused but I thought I could hack it. I thought I'd beaten them, I was too hard, too emotionally dead to let anything get to me. As the coach came into the camp I recognised the gates, the Round House, the road we had walked down to be murdered. But funnily enough, for a while I did cope. The hard man of Belsen came through again and I bit my lip and carried on.

Here in the charnel-house, in the slaughter yard, I carried on as though nothing had gone on here at all. I conducted the band, did the arrangements for all the visiting NATO brass, all the bullshit and the crap, I did it. I thought I had beaten them. I carried on, day to day, just like I had done in the camp before. I carried on. 'Don't let them get you,' I thought, 'don't let it get to you.'

Then one day, just over a year ago, a party of young New German Army officers came to Bergen on manoeuvres. Some NATO exercise was on, I can't really remember what. And one night in the mess they got a bit pissed. It was stupid really, they were very drunk. I should have gone home, stayed out of the way, but I didn't.

I had got a bit drunk myself, a lot drunk if I am honest, and they started to take the mickey out of us all in German. I'd learned the language well while I was in the camp, and had learned even more from living here, so I knew what they were saying. Then they started laughing and a couple of them, Bavarians they were, started saying that maybe Hitler wasn't all that bad and that if they had him today he'd be able to sort out 'these *gastarbeiters*, these bastard Turks' and they pointed up to that balcony over there where he used to stand to review his SS officers and started laughing.

I went berserk. I just went for them, piled into the middle of them and started laying about them. It took six red-hats to drag me off. Tables went over, there was blood everywhere. I hit them with everything I could, I don't need to tell you why. I put four of them in hospital. In the end I suppose you could say that I'd given in. I had forgotten for a brief moment the lessons of the camp, that they too were human. This place, if only for a second, had won. But it was for long enough. I had found myself saying 'right' and 'left'.

So I lost my stripes and here I am, no band, no master any more, looking after this hall, sweeping the floor, switching on the stage lights, checking that the curtains open, an embarrassment to the Army; like a caretaker, waiting for retirement and my pension.

I'll probably go back to England, I have a small house and a few friends there in Ipswich. I've no family anywhere else. I have my music, I still play a little. And so, my friend, that's my story.

I looked at the floor. There wasn't much I could say. I thought of the small boy in Lodz, of the Jews pressed into the chambers, of the young stupid German officers, of the thunderous sound of cattle trucks rattling through the dark nights of Europe, but most of all I thought of this old soldier and the terrible journey that had brought him here.

As a refugee myself I felt I knew some of his pain only too well and felt that I had to talk, to say something to break the awful silence, but what? In the end I said something that I now see was meaningless, perhaps even stupid, but it was something that came out of a need to respond to the terrible weight of the story just given to me, for every story is a burden which gives the listener the duty of carrying that story on. Like the Ancient Mariner, we are all doomed to pass on our tales. I sketched a meaningless circle in the small puddle of beer on the table.

'Do you know the birds have just come back to Belsen?'

He looked at his drink for a second, then said quietly, 'The birds, my friend, have nothing to forgive.'

Haul on the Bowline

Tommy and me were rotten drunk when it happened, steaming drunk, a danger to shipping. We were lucky to get away in one piece, now I think about it. I mean we're fairly hard, but there were ten times as many of them as there was of us and we were on another planet anyway. Somebody up there must be looking after us, is all I can say.

We'd just sailed back from Holland. We work on the ferries, merchant seamen by profession (if you want to call it that, but general dogsbodies would be a better term). Tommy loads the cars on and off and I serve greasy chips and deathburgers in one of what the brochure calls 'our many restaurants'. Even the ship's cat has ulcers.

We'd done ten days on, so we were desperate for a bit of a laugh. Tommy's missus had just left him after seven years and two kids. She'd run off with the bloke next door and gone to live in the Midlands. He was still a bit choked about that, particularly since it was the bloke next door's cat that had got into his loft last year and done seven of his best show birds in. Tommy reckons now he should have laid poison for the bloke next door as well as the cat. Maybe they'd have found him stretched out on the chip-shop step as well.

I still have to laugh, though, when I think of Mrs Binson seeing the cat on the doorstep next morning and knocking on the door to tell them they'd left their draught excluder out all night and it was wet.

His missus had left the kids behind when she did the runner, but Tommy's mam lives just around the corner and they spent more time with her anyway, so she looked after them while he was at sea. He worked hard and made sure the kids were really well looked after, but his job was an away job and that's all there is to it. As he always says, 'You can only do what you can do.'

I didn't have any missus to run away from home. I'd lived with a girl for a couple of years but it hadn't worked out. She didn't like my lifestyle she said, but when you're a sailor you're a sailor and that's all there is to it. I think it gets into the blood. I still get excited when I'm walking down the dock road and I can smell the salt sea on the wind. It always makes me think of foreign places, sandy beaches, strange ports.

I used to work out foreign a lot, but when I met this girl I packed it in and got the ferry job. And it still didn't work out. It's a sailor's life and that's all there is to it. Some day soon I'm going to try for a job on one of the bigger lines, get on the container ships and get out and see the world again.

Any road up, on this particular night what with his missus and the pigeon loft, Tommy needed a bit of cheering up. So we'd gone straight in the Lord Nelson after we'd docked and had several there, then we'd gone on to the Sailor's Return for a game of bar billiards, but we got thrown out of there when Tommy got too enthusiastic trying to pot the black, and one of the regulars ended up with a big turtle egg in his pint of mixed. Tommy told the landlord his pool table was greasy, and that didn't help.

He also told him he was going to stay and finish his pint, but the landlord whistled and a rottweiler stuck his head on the counter between the pickled eggs and the pile of pennies, so we went and had a vindaloo. It seemed funny to be eating curry at four o'clock in the afternoon but Tommy reckoned we needed a good lining on our stomach for the evening's session, plus the Light of Bengal had a licence. And so we had several more pints of lager with our dinner and made it last until opening time. We had a couple of brandies after dinner because we were too full for any more cold lager, and then we went to a pub called the Frog and Parrot which brews its own beer.

Even though it had only just opened, it was full of businessmen in suits, all drinking halves of Old Scrotum or something and going on about specific gravity. Tommy shouted something about 'Never mind the gravity, we have lift-off!' but they all looked at us as though we'd fallen off a star, so we only had one there and then went on to another pub, down near the docks, where we'd heard a bloke once got stabbed by the landlady for refusing to go to bed with her.

I don't remember much about the next couple of hours except us getting thrown out of Yates' Wine Lodge, which takes some doing since they normally throw people into there, but the annoying thing is that I can't remember what it was for. Anyway, round about eight o'clock we went down to an old boozer in the Land of Green Ginger that Tommy knew from when he'd had a shellfish round until he developed his allergy.

There was a sign on the door that said *Windlass Folk Club Every Friday*, and it was Friday as it happens. So we go in the pub and have a pint in the old saloon and from upstairs we can hear all this singing and music and we decide to go up. Seven and sixpence it was to get in. I'll never forget, we thought that was cheap.

'It's a singer's night,' said this girl on the door with round glasses, long hair and no make-up.

Tommy was even more steaming than me. 'What's that when it's at home?' he gargled.

'People get up from the floor and sing, anybody can do it.'

'Listen, bonny lass,' said Tommy, 'if I get on the floor I'll never get up again, never mind sing.'

We went to go in but she said that we had to wait until the singing had stopped, and when we heard the clapping she let us in. We had our beer with us, which was a good job because there was no bar in the room. There was just tables and chairs, and the

tables had candles on them – which was all the light there was,
except for a bit of a spotlight on a tiny stage at one end of the room.
There was a big pair of horns behind the stage and a scroll that said
something about The Royal Antediluvian Order of Buffaloes.

'That cow must have been going a hell of a lick when it hit that
wall,' Tommy says to this bloke beside him, being friendly like, but
I think the bloke had heard that one before because he just
grinned a bit and didn't say anything. We stood at the back and
looked around.

'Bugger me,' Tommy says to me. 'I'm not sure this is our scene,
bonny lad.'

Most of the people there had long hair, glasses and beards.
Some of the blokes did too. No, you know what I mean – they all
looked like hippies or art students, and if we tried to speak they
kept turning round and shushing us. There was a compere sort of
bloke, wearing sandals and socks and a fisherman's smock. He had
this long red beard and a pewter tankard, and he sang three songs
about the sea and everybody joined in with the choruses. One was
about going to sea no more and was quite jolly. We joined in with
that one, once we'd learned the words.

No more, no more, I will go to sea no more.
A man must be blind to make up his mind
To go to sea once more.

Me and Tommy liked it so much we sang it about seven more
times after everybody else had stopped singing and people had to
tell us to stop.

Then he sang a song about rounding the Horn and hauling on
the bowline. Tommy said when was he last at sea? There was no
bowline any more, just motor winches and a bloody big diesel
engine banging away. Another was about some bloke going to sea
in a slaving ship and that went on for hours and he pitched it too
high and his face went red and he squeaked and had to start again
and nobody laughed but me and Tommy. That song went on a bit

and didn't have a chorus and was all about throwing the slaves overboard and getting hung at Newgate – very jolly, I don't think. Then he did a funny song about a sailor coming down a street and finding a bit of string hanging out of a bedroom window and he pulls on it, and a woman comes down because this bit of string has been tied to her toe and she lets this bloke in and he gives her one. Not another bit of string, though – a bit of you-know-what. Me and Tommy thought that was quite a jolly song and remarked how we'd keep our eyes open for bits of string hanging out of windows in future. Then it turns out that the woman's husband finds out about this bit of string caper, and fastens a chamber-pot full of good-for-the-roses to the string instead of his wife's toe, so that this time the Jolly Jack Tar gets a right drenching and isn't very happy about the quality of the rain. So we changed our mind about the bit of string after that.

Then a girl got up with a guitar and she sang a song about some old man she was married to with 'no ding dorum' that was quite funny; though the girl herself seemed to take it all very serious. And then she sang another one about some queen going to confession, only the bloke she goes to confess to isn't a priest but the king her husband who hears all about her having it off with every Tom, Dick and Harry and especially Dick. I thought that was very good but Tommy nodded off leaning on the wall, and I had to wake him up.

Tommy went and got three more pints each to save us having to go up and down the stairs all night, and while he was gone this girl sang a song about a drowned sailor that I've got to admit had me going a bit. A few tears come out, I can tell you. She had a lovely voice.

Well, Tommy came back and we drank a couple more pints and now we're in no pain at all. A bloke with a fiddle played a few tunes and they were good – really good – but there was no room to dance. It seemed stupid to me that, playing dance music when you can't dance.

Any road up, then this compere bloke got up and said that if there were any more floor singers he'd like to hear from them, and that there was a free pint for every singer. And so this other bloke with glasses called Tony gets up, and he's got a beard and a pewter tankard as well, and he tells us he's going to sing a song about some shipwreck. And this is amazing because what he does is he tells us the whole story of the song before he sings it! And we think he's being funny, because it's all about these sailors that get shipwrecked and end up eating each other, but it obviously isn't supposed to be funny because nobody but me and Tommy laugh as he's telling us the story, because I say I wouldn't fancy eating any of our crew, unless it was Joyce from the purser's office, and we get told to shut up again – only this time they aren't smiling when they say it.

Anyway he sets off singing after he's told us the entire plot, who done what and everything, which seems a bit stupid to me. I mean if you already know the story what's the point of telling it all over again unless you tell it in a different way or make it better somehow? And the thing is, he's got a really crap voice! I mean I'm no Caruso, and I wouldn't have the bottle to get up in front of people and do a turn, but this bloke was all bottle and no talent. His voice was all out of tune and he made it wobble like a bleaty old ram being kicked to death on a barbed-wire fence, and the bloody song went on for bloody ages. There must have been a hundred verses! Well I got the giggles for a bit, then I just got bored, then I got angry and wanted to shout or knock something over, then I got the giggles again. Tommy just fell asleep standing up again and when the bloke finished and everybody clapped Tommy wakes up, sees we haven't any beer left and shouts out, 'I'll give you a song!'

'You daft bleeder,' I say, 'you can't sing.'

'Listen bonny lad,' he says, 'for a pint of ale I can be Bing Bloody Crosby,' and he wobbles to the front. He's half-Irish is Tommy, so he's got a bit of the Blarney in him, but I've never heard him sing no folk songs. Bits of Elvis now and then, maybe, and some Beatles stuff and he knows loads of Hank Williams songs. But no folk songs ever, I could swear to it.

Well, he gets up on this little stage and says: 'This is one I learned from my old grandad,' and he sings a song about a girl going to this wake that he says is a fair. People are enjoying it – you can tell from their faces – because he's pissed and he's putting a lot of actions into it. Then you can see their faces change when he sings a bit about this girl meeting a bloke called Roger the Lodger who introduces 'Old Fagin coming home from the wake', which is obviously not a person he's talking about but a certain part of his anatomy, i.e. the old pork dagger. In the next verse she has a baby and 'calls it Fagin's bastard coming home from the wake.' He finished that and there was a lot of clapping, most of it polite, though one or two people had enjoyed it. Some of the others had frozen faces, and you could see they thought Tommy had gone too far.

Then he launches straight into another one about some girl that he loves in her jumper and skirt and her trousers and her smock, but especially in her nightie because 'when the moonlight flits across your tits – Jesus Christ Almighty!!!'. One bloke had to go out because his beer had got some bones in it and he was choking on them, and a few other people smiled nervously; but a lot of the women had started to find that they'd got bits stuck in their teeth and were making lots of noise trying to get them out.

He didn't wait for the applause after that one but went straight into another one about a cock and an ass. It started off all right but it soon got well dodgy. It was about this old bloke who has this cock that's supposed to be a chicken, but you know there's a double meaning to it, and the old woman has a donkey, her ass, and there's an obvious double meaning to that too. Well it goes on all right for a bit but the cock gets out of order and jumps up on the donkey and it finishes with this bloke in court because, as the Judge says when he fines him ten pounds:

'I think things have come to a pretty poor pass
When you can't keep your cock from an old woman's ass!'

That was the last line of the song. Tommy finished, and there was total silence, not a murmur, though a couple more blokes had found that they'd got bones in their beer and one bloke was crying, though I don't think he'd found the song particularly sad.

Tommy just looked at the organiser with that terrible squint he has when he's drunk and said, 'Where's me pint?'

Well, a table went over, beer and all, and a bloke tried to grab Tommy but Tommy stuck one on him first. Women started screaming and somebody hit Tommy with the box they'd had the raffle in. I ran over and tried to get him away but someone tripped me up and I ended up under the piano with somebody giving me a good kicking. But the landlord came running in and it soon quietened down and when they grabbed the two of us, mob-handed, there was nothing we could do.

'You foul-mouthed swine, that was bloody disgusting!' says one bloke as they helped us out of the room.

'That was folk music, bonny lad,' says Tommy. But they wasn't convinced and we had to go, down the stairs and straight out.

'What about my pint?' says Tommy, but they ignored him and we had to go without our beer.

On the way home Tommy felt this big lump on his head from the raffle box.

'It bloody well was folk music,' he said. 'It wasn't written by no fuckin' chicken, anyway.'

The Virgin of the Discos

It was when Canon O'Connor went back to pick up the letters he had left on the pulpit steps while talking to Leach the sacristan, that he noticed the old lady kneeling before the votive candles in the Lady Chapel. Her cheap yellow scarf, now candle-lit and turned to shining gold, was curved about her face like the halo of the Blessed Mother in the darkening evening church. The old priest recognised her, and tried to turn away quickly and quietly without her seeing that he was there.

He liked the old woman. She was a simple soul with no harm in her at all, but she was lonely; once she got talking she never stopped and the Canon had a lot of paperwork to finish – and a card school tonight. But Mrs Donlan saw him, and crossing herself quickly, kissed her rosary beads, slipped them into her purse; then, with purse in one hand and her shopping-bag hanging from the other, she scuttled across the marble floor towards him as fast as her short rheumatic legs would carry her.

'God be good to her,' the Canon thought, 'she looks like an old crab. An old silver-haired crab in a worn black woollen coat with a Legion of Mary medal on the lapel.'

Outside the church, block-long snakes of city traffic were shunting through the grid of modern high-rise offices, disused cotton warehouses and old Victorian buildings, as the January evening smudged the streets with cold and damp, smearing the pavements with a thin, greasy film that mirrored the Christmas lights. For though it was now well past Twelfth Night, the city engineers had yet to dismantle the decorations; across the road from the old city church a Mickey Mouse with several long-dead bulbs waved at a short-circuiting and dim Pinocchio with a dull and sputtering nose. The Canon coughed. Somewhere, a block or two away, an ambulance siren keened, rushing its way through another story altogether. The old lady came close to the priest and peered up at him. He bent down towards her and they became two crow-black stick-shapes in the yellow light.

'Ah, Mary Ellen, how are you now?' He bent down towards her and raised his voice to pierce the blanket of her deafness.

'I'm fine, Canon, thanks be to God,' and she crossed herself. 'I still have the rheumatics in my shoulder, but at my age there's not a lot you can expect. And thanks be to God that's all I have wrong with me, so I mustn't complain you know. There's many my age that are far worse off.'

'And how was your Christmas? You'll have had a great time with the grandchildren, I don't doubt.'

'I did indeed. Fiona came over on Christmas Eve with Siobhan, and took me back to her house and I stayed there until the day after Boxing Day and it was grand. We had some great fun, and the house is beautiful. They're doing really well now, thanks be to God. John has a new job. He's gone higher up the ladder in the same firm. They think very highly of him. They couldn't do without him, Fiona says.'

'That's grand,' the Canon nodded. 'And how many grandchildren have you now?'

'Fiona has just the two still. Daniel is nearly three, and Siobhan is just seven. She's at the Convent of Our Lady of Perpetual Succour prep school. Oh you wouldn't know her now, she's a proper little lady with her red hair and her freckles. She's mad for the Irish dancing and her mother made her a lovely embroidered dress for Christmas – and didn't she look grand in it.'

'And what about Sean, did he come up to see you at all?' the Canon asked.

The old lady looked over the Canon's shoulder at the statue of Our Lady and there was a brief but heavy silence, for they both knew the answer to the question.

'Sure it's a long way for him to come from Northampton just for the three or four days, and with him being busy with his work and all. He hardly has the time to turn around these days. He's always driving all over the place in his job, and you know when it comes to Christmas he's that exhausted. He phoned me at Fiona's on Christmas Day, though, and we had a great old chat.'

'And there's no sign of him getting married yet?'

'What? I don't think that wan'll ever get married! Nearly forty he is, and the women still running round after him, washing his clothes for him and doing all his fetching and carrying. He's been courting that midwife now for nearly seven years, and has her running after him like a nursemaid. He'll end up leaving it too late, like his Uncle Manus did, stuck on an ould farm miles from anywhere, him and his dog and a couple of cows. He'll end up like an ould mountainy farmer!'

'In Northampton?' The Canon laughed and then looked at his watch. 'Well I must be off, Mrs Donlan, I've a million things to do. I'll give you my blessing, don't kneel down now.'

And the old lady, who was about to kneel on the cold stone floor, straightened up and stood with head bowed and her hands together clasping her purse as the Canon murmured above her, his right hand moving over her head in the sign of the cross. And if you had seen them from a distance that dark January evening, caught in the flickering light from the burning wax forest of votive candles, you might have said the priest's hand was a bird hovering over the old lady's head.

Three weeks later, close to midnight, the Canon was sitting watching the golf from Florida on the television with his collar off and his slippers on, sipping a glass of Black Bushmills with a knob or two of ice 'for medicinal purposes', when the doorbell rang. The Canon groaned. One curate was out on a sick call and the other was away for the night. He heard the housekeeper shuffle to the door and unchain and open it. There then followed the sudden explosion into the hall of a storm of noise and passion that made him turn the television sound down with the remote control and jerk upright in his wing-back chair.

'The Canon's just about to go to bed,' his housekeeper insisted.

'I have to see him. And you'll not stop me, Kitty McGlinn!'

'What's it about?'

'It's for his ears, and his alone. If I told it you, it'd be all over the parish in twenty minutes!'

The Canon opened his door. Mrs Donlan, all five foot of her, was squaring up to his housekeeper – a big milk-fed Kerrywoman with hair that had once been red but was now salt and pepper, and a mouth that one of his previous curates had described, accurately but uncharitably, as being the spitting image of a hen's ovipositor. The housekeeper stood to one side.

'It's all right, Kitty,' the Canon nodded. 'Come in, Mrs Donlan, and sit down and tell me all about it.' He closed the door behind him, knowing full well that his housekeeper's ear would be warming the varnish on the other side.

The old lady sat with her bag in her hands and when the Canon was in his chair again, spoke in a strained and urgent voice that was not far from tears. 'Forgive me for trespassing in on yourself at this time of night, Canon, but I had to tell you that tonight I've seen a miracle. I've seen the face of Our Blessed Lady in the sky.'

The Canon flinched and reached for the bottle, but the old lady didn't notice. Through his mind there processed a chain of images of weeping statues, statues that moved mysteriously overnight, statues of Christ that bled, statues of the Virgin that wept real tears and the crowds of pilgrims in perpetual vigil by a roadside in County Cork waiting for the Mother of God to appear on the face of a rock cliff. He saw headlines in the papers, his golfing holiday at Lahinch cancelled and his quiet city parish plagued by predatory television crews and gutter press reporters and above it all an old lady held up before the world, frozen in the flashlights, and all around her the braying of fools. He made a noise that started somewhere between a sigh and a groan but which ended disguised as a cough and, switching off the television, took out his cigarettes and lit one. His doctor allowed him five a day. This was the sixth, but his doctor had never bargained with Virgins in the sky.

He wafted the smoke towards the fire as he shook the match out and leaned forward. 'Now, Mary Ellen, I know you don't drink and I know that you're a sensible woman, so tell me slowly and as clearly as you can exactly what happened. You know how dangerous these things can be if people get to know about them.' He thought about the other side of the door and wondered would he be wise to switch the television back on and turn the sound up to drown their voices?

'Well, Canon, every word of this is as true as I'm sitting here, I swear on the Sacred Heart.' She crossed herself. 'I've just been to see Mrs Sloyan across the town. She's in Saint Dunstan's parish, but you might know her from all the work she did for the diocese Lourdes trip last year?'

The Canon nodded.

'Well she's been terrible with her chest since Christmas, you know, and I went over to sit with her for a while to have an ould chat. Anyway, I was coming home afterwards and I got off the bus at my usual stop and I was walking near the back of that railway place they're knocking down now and I just happened be chance to look up in the sky. The Blessed Lord himself knows what made me do it, but I looked up – and spread across the heavens, as plain as your own face I'm looking at now, was the face of Our Lady herself, the Mother of God smiling down at me from the clouds.

'I got down on my knees, there and then on the pavement and thanks be to God ten minutes or more I watched her smiling down at me and then the holy face just faded away, just faded slowly away into the clouds. Oh, but it was beautiful, Canon, absolutely beautiful.'

The Canon took another draw of his cigarette, looked into the fire and saw his golfing holiday vanishing in the flames. He heard a shuffling from beyond the door. 'Do you know, Mary Ellen, I think it would be better if you told no one else about this thing you've seen now. It could do more harm than good to spread a thing like this about. People don't always understand, you see. They can be jealous that they themselves haven't been blessed with such a vision as yourself, and they can be very uncharitable. You know, they might even accuse you of making it all up.'

'But for the love of God, why would I make such a thing up? That would be a terrible sin! That would be a kind of blasphemy, Canon, and, God forgive me, I'd never commit such a sin in my life.'

'I know you wouldn't, Mary Ellen. It's only what people would think that I'm worried about. You see, you might have been blessed with this vision tonight but perhaps nobody else saw it. Perhaps Our Blessed Lady only chose to show herself to you and nobody else. She has her reasons and they're not for us to question or seek to understand. After all, she chose to show herself to the little children of Fatima and to poor Bernadette of Lourdes and to little Mary McGloughlin at Knock' – and he thought of the airport there and the luminous statues of the Virgin, the musical holy-water bottles and the mountains of tat in the souvenir shops and sighed. 'Have you told anybody else what you saw?'

'Sure and didn't I come straight here after, instead of going home, Canon? I've told no living soul, only yourself.'

'Well, I want you to promise me now, before God, that you'll say nothing about this to anybody until I tell you to. You see, I believe that what you say is true. I don't doubt a word of it, and I'm sure that His Holy Mother chose to show herself to you tonight as a special sign; and maybe you need to look deep inside yourself for what that sign means. Perhaps she's just saying to you that, like you, she is a mother and understands what you have been through. I don't know. But you must keep this within your heart and soul and tell no one! Not your closest friend! Do you understand me?'

'Perhaps you're right, Canon. Maybe they will think I'm nothing but an ould fool, but I saw her with my own two eyes and oh God it was wonderful too! Her bright shining face looked gently down upon me with the most beautiful smile you've ever seen in your life. I'll hold that vision in my heart until my dying day.'

'And that's the way it should be, Mary Ellen,' said the Canon as he reached for the bottle and another glass. 'And now I'm going to give you a drop of good Black Bush to warm up the cockles of your heart before I put you in my car and drive you home.'

Before he went to bed that night, the Canon summoned the bold Kitty McGlinn to him and told her that if one single whisper of what Mrs Donlan had said was put about the parish, then there would be a ticket sitting on the sideboard for someone for the next boat home to Ireland. Slipping between the sheets, he prayed that he had averted the kind of fiasco that would have the Bishop roaring down his neck and God alone knew what other trouble rolling up the shores of his quiet little island in waves.

He slept a troubled and disturbed sleep that night. In one of his worst moments he dreamt he was playing golf at Lahinch with Michael Vaughan and just by the ninth they saw a vision of St Patrick driving snakes over the cliffs of Moher. In the morning he felt as though he was starting with flu.

The Canon told the curates, a day or two after the old lady's visit, to pre-warn them that any rumours they might hear had a factual base. But though the housekeeper, unable to keep a secret any more than her own water, spread the story as far as she could, it never really amounted to much beyond a few queer looks at the morning Mass when, each day, Mary Ellen took the sacrament along with a handful of schoolgirls and a few old ladies and men like herself.

True to her word, Mrs Donlan herself said nothing of what she'd seen to a living soul, though she prayed for a good half-hour each night that the Virgin who had shone so brightly for her should intercede for the souls of her dead mother and father and her husband and the soul of her baby Thomas who had died in an accident while still so young: and also that she would intercede with her own Son on behalf of Mrs Donlan's son and ask Him to give Sean the grace to do the right thing by that girl he was seeing, and get married and settle down, and perhaps come and see his mother more often. And she felt each night as she prayed that perhaps, now that she had shown herself to her, the Mother of God, as a mother herself, listened and smiled upon her with a new understanding and compassion.

At the end of the month, as though in a direct answer to her long and lonely prayers, Mrs Donlan's son Sean came home with his girlfriend to tell her that they had decided to get married that spring. He'd had a new promotion within the company, which meant he would be travelling less, and they both thought it was time they settled down and they were buying a house near the hospital where his fiancée worked.

Mrs Donlan was filled with a holy joy. As soon as she could she ran upstairs and knelt before the picture of the Virgin to offer up several Hail Marys and a cluster of Glory Bes in thanks. When she came down and made them a cup of tea they had another surprise for her. They were going to take her back to Northampton for a week's holiday to make up for the fact that he'd not been able to get up at Christmas, and also to give his mother a chance to meet his future wife's family.

And so it was that Mrs Donlan was away when the next Friday's edition of the town's evening paper was published. A copy of which flopped on to the doormat of the presbytery and was brought to the table by Father Hynes, the younger of the two curates. He well knew the story of Mary Ellen's Virgin of the Night Skies, and he was laughing as he came into the room.

He seated himself opposite the Canon. 'If it wasn't for the city council planning department, the Blessed Virgin would have been appearing over the rooftops every night.'

'What do you mean?' asked the Canon, looking up from his fish, and the curate read aloud:

'"Council Planners Pull Plug on New Light Show."' He went on, '"Marilyn's Speakeasy, Global Leisure Group's new disco in Saltersgate, was refused permission to shine a hologram into the sky over the city by the planning officer of the city council and by the civil aviation authority on Tuesday of this week after a demonstration of the hologram earlier this month failed to convince council leaders as to its safety and appropriateness. The beam, which can project a hundred-foot-wide hologram of the head of Marilyn Monroe on to the sky, was considered a danger to aircraft approaching the airport from the west. It was also considered unsightly and a potential nuisance by the planning officer. Martin Anderson, a director of Second City Developments PLC, the parent company of Global, commented, "This is ridiculous. We will definitely appeal. We had a special metal mask made of the Andy Warhol Marilyn picture, and it cost us more than a thousand pounds just to have it cut by a special laser process. The whole thing is totally safe and is controlled by computer. The council are just over-reacting. We consider that it would be a fun thing to see over the city. We're bringing employment to the area, and if the council was doing its job properly it would be encouraging firms like Global instead of making their job harder. We've every intention of appealing against the decision. Global Leisure have a disco in Glasgow called Play it Again Sam that projects a hundred-foot hologram of Humphrey Bogart above the Clyde from a disused shipping warehouse, and in three years of operation there have been no problems or complaints…" and it goes on a bit longer. There's a picture of the hologram, it's a bit dark but you can see it's her all right.'

He put the paper on the table. 'God bless her. Poor Mrs Donlan. Do you think I should go round and tell her that her miracle in the sky was a poor dim casualty of the Hollywood star machine who was certainly no virgin?'

'I think you should do no such thing. Does it matter,' asked Canon O'Connor, partly of himself and partly of Father Hynes, 'if the Blessed Mother of God chooses to reveal herself to a lonely old lady through a picture of a film star in the sky, and she sees it and we don't? We're not here as Holy Writ, you know, sole keepers of the Keys of Truth. Sometimes I only wish we were and then at other times I think even that certitude would be too terrible a burden. God knows, sometimes I feel as lost and helpless as Mrs Donlan. And if it's a poor old Hollywood trollop she sees as the Mother of

God, then didn't Our Lord himself wash the feet of Mary Magdalen, who was no better than she should have been? Kevin, it's enough that that poor lonely old woman believes that what she saw was the Virgin Mary, and if her belief gives her the strength to put up with her loneliness and the fact that she has a selfish ignorant rascal of a son, then that's something as God-given as a real miracle, and that's the most any of us can hope for.

'Now pass me the potatoes, if you don't mind, and see if there's a good second-hand BMW in there. That thing of mine is falling to bits.'

An Sasenach Fiarshúili

I could have killed Fergus for it after – and to tell the truth I haven't seen much of him since. Even if there's a session on somewhere that I might want to be in on, I'll stay away if I know he's playing. I know there are others who feel like me about it too – Aemon Clinch and Liam McDonagh for starters. I mean the guy was a real ballocks but when all's said and done what Walsh did was uncalled for. He'd have been better off telling him to feck off in the first place and stick his tin whistle and his bodhrán up his jacksie but he didn't, and I suppose we were all to blame too, in a way, for not doing anything to stop Fergus.

I don't know if you know Paidi O'Séa's? It's down near the harbour, by the ice store. It's the place that's painted red and cream, with the big wide window with the old pictures of musicians and the Guinness bottles and the dead flies stuck in it, in case you might be in any doubt as to what goes on in there. O'Séa's is famous all over the world for its music. An English record company made an album of Paidi and his brothers, Tomas, Dineen and Muirtin, playing in the mid-seventies and it sold all over the world. You'll probably have heard of it anyway. *The Blarney Pilgrim*, it was called; *Traditional Songs and Dance Tunes From the County Clare*. It wasn't a big hit like a pop record, you know – with a title like that you could hardly expect it to nudge Wet Wet Wet or Michael Jackson out of the charts – but it sold tens of thousands around the world to folkies and roots-music fans, and it put Ballysaggart on the tourist map.

Before that we'd just been a sleepy, old, small Irish fishing port with a harbour and a lot of bars and a market and a creamery where the red-eared, flat-capped farmers from the mountains would queue every morning with the ass and the cart and the two or three churns on the back. That changed a bit over the years, and the old ass was put out to grass and the farmers got cars and stainless-steel tanker trailers with their EEC grants. But still they'd block the road to the creamery every morning, talking in Irish about cows and pigs and sheep and dogs and the weather and the grants and whatever else it is farmers talk about.

Anyway, I was explaining.

The first tourists here came out at the turn of the century. They were Irish scholars mainly, people from universities in England and Germany wanting to study the Irish language. We're in the Gaeltacht, and people still use Irish as a first language, even though the television is taking us all over and a lot of the children are beginning to look down on it a bit. I don't have much Irish myself because I'm not from round here, but I learned enough of it in school to get by when I have to.

The scholars wrote a number of books on the language and folklore of the area and one of them, an Englishman to boot, got some of the native Irish-speakers to write their life stories, which they did. It's strange to think that if it hadn't been for that Englishman those old people would have died without having been known outside their parishes at all, and now their books are in every library and bookshop going.

It gave the place a bit of a famous name for a while and some Yanks even came to make a film, *Man of the West*. It was a sort of drama-documentary I suppose you would call it, and it was an awful lot of old cod with men smoking duídíns on the harbour steps and lepping into naomhógs to race off and harpoon whales. When they showed it here at the local cinema half the audience were sick laughing, and the other half said if they hadn't recognised the harbour front and the headland they'd have thought they were watching something from Mars.

The film crew built a 'traditional cottage' for the hero to live in because the real ones weren't folksy enough. They modelled it on Foxy Lennon's old thatched cabin, and after they'd gone Foxy charged people to walk up his boreen and look at it. For thirty years he made a small fortune in tanners and shillings and half-crowns; his son still does, though now it's nearer a quid a go. 'Come and see the House of *The Man of the West*' says the poster at the end of his yard and the cars stop and the idiots roll up and pay good money to see an artificial cottage that nobody ever lived in, while the original it was modelled on has fallen down and Foxy's son lives in a neat new bungalow.

Anyway, after the Irish scholars and the film crews, nothing much happened for years until the musicians came, and that was nearly all because of that record. A lot of younger people came from Dublin and Galway and the like, kids that were fed up of the show-bands and the Irish Country and Western: Big Paddy and the Panhandlers and such, great big beef-fed culchies from the Midlands singing in fake Yank accents about the Old Thatched Cottage on the Hill and the Green, Green Grass of Home and A Boy Called Sue and other crap like it.

It'd give you a pain in the ballocks listening to them singing on about the old stone-floored cabin and the turf smoke of home and the like, and they with their breeze-block castles, the central-heated bungalows with the concrete lions on the gateposts and the wife with a perm like a head of snakes and two weeks in Torremolinos every year. You see them coming home, falling off the plane pissed with their noses peeling and a stuffed donkey under their arms. They'd make you spit.

But it was hard to tell what was worse after a while, the Country and Shamrock mob or the invaders, because Paidi O'Séa's bar got mobbed out with people mad for the music. At first it was just a few Irish kids wanting to get back to their roots. Some of Sweeney's Men came out here, and after them Planxty and Da Danaan and what have you. Then Paddy Moloney from the Chieftains came down here for a weekend, and RTE did a big film on the pub and the brothers that was sold all over the world, and the foreigners started coming. English and Americans came here who would normally have been in carts going through the Gap of Dunloe being ripped off by the jarveys with their bullshit about Leprechauns and Banshees and all that Paddywhackery.

Then Germans and French and Japanese and God knows what else came, and they didn't all come to listen. Some of them came to play and, fair play to them, some of them weren't half-bad. Though it did come as a bit of a shock to find a couple of Germans speaking Irish better than myself playing flute and fiddle as good as the next man.

I've never understood why the Germans are so keen on Irish music, but someone said once that it was because Hitler destroyed their own folk music by using it for the Nazi Party and that they were hungry for any folk stuff they could get their hands on. But I don't know, I sometimes get sick of all this theorising. Maybe they just like it.

Anyway, over the years the pub got tarted up, old Paidi died and Dineen and Tomas took it over. They built a lounge on the back and ruined the place – formica-topped tables and bloody shillelaghs and sleans and plastic naomhógs hanging everywhere. But still people came from all over the world to bash their bodhráns and think they were hearing traditional Irish music when half the time the brothers were off drinking somewhere else and the room was full of students from Queen's or Trinity playing stuff they'd learned off records, and foreigners with tape recorders taking everything down as though it was holy writ.

And that's where I came in, I suppose. I was one of those students who came down here at weekends and stayed. I married a local girl and got a job in the town. I don't play much now, just the occasional session, and I play fiddle with a flute-player called Tony Trundle up at McCarty's on Fridays. That's the only regular gig I do. I'm not that good, but I like to play more for the crack than anything else. My eldest daughter, now, is learning – she'll be better than I'll ever be. She has a natural gift. She can hear a tune once through, and by the second time through she's joining in, by the third time through she's note-perfect. The middle boy is coming along on the tin whistle, too. I mean to buy him a flute this year, he's ready to step up to it.

We have good sessions in the bars in the winter, and I play for some of the dances. But in the summer the music in the town can sometimes be a bit Mickey Mouse, unless there's somebody here for a bit of a holiday. The bars have started paying musicians from away to come in for the season, some of the local lads too, and to some extent I think it's altered the way people play. You know there was a style of playing here that was local, that had never travelled out of the area at all until that record was made. Now there's all sorts of stuff coming in and it's changing the music. Everything seems to be played at the one speed, 'heads down, arse up and bang away'.

The worse thing was when the bodhrán players appeared. I don't know why it is, but everyone seems to think that a bodhrán is easy to play. Half a drum and a single stick – that's all it is, anybody can bang away on one. And there's a truth in that, anybody *can* play it – badly. 'The only way to play a bodhrán is with a pen-knife,' someone once said, and I think for most bodhrán players that's ninety-nine per cent true. There are exceptions, like Johnnie MacDonagh who's simply brilliant on the thing. A bodhrán played well can be a good solid base to a tune, it can work really well and move a set along. A bad one can be an insult to the goat that died to make it.

And we've changed somehow in the last ten years. It's almost as though the tourism has got too big, the balance has shifted. A lot of the old shops are closing and being replaced with tourists' stuff, craft shops and Aran sweater shops and the like. I know everybody has to make a living, don't get me wrong, but sometimes you feel as though it's gone too much the other way, that we'll all end up getting grants from the Bord Failté to go round dressed up like Darby O'Gill and the Little People, running round with bloody shillelaghs shouting 'top of the morning to you' at the visitors.

We've got a great reputation for hospitality in Ireland, but I tell you sometimes it wears a bit bloody thin.

Some of the pubs have started doing 'Laser Karaoke', for God's sake! And one of them even books traditional music 'stars' for the season. That's how Walsh got here. 'Fergus Walsh is up at O'Séa's,' someone said one night in Monaghan's, and we all poured up there to hear him. He'd been one of the best pipers around, back in the seventies. He was a bit of a legend in Ireland, and it turned out that Dineen had booked him for the summer season at O'Séa's. You could hardly get in the room, it was packed that solid with people and of course Tommy Moynihan was there with his tongue hanging out like a greyhound after the hare's arse. Moynihan is the worst guitar player and the biggest arse-licker in town and if anyone who's had a walk on part in Glenroe or whose face has appeared for two seconds on the Gaybo show comes into the place he's round like shit off a shovel hoping to be discovered. There were a few others like Moynihan too. Hangers on and glory grabbers.

Well, Walsh played like a dream that night, and for a few nights after, and musicians came in from all over the place to be in on the session. But it wasn't long before it was obvious to all but the aurally-challenged that Walsh's playing was only good until three pints of Black Mischief. After that it got fast and erratic and you'd find yourself racing after him, trying to keep up. Of course a lot of the punters thought it was great. They thought Irish music had to be wild and furious, even if it did end up sounding like someone kicking a crowd of chickens on speed to death.

It was early one night that the Englishman came in. You could tell he was a folkie because he had on a tee-shirt with 'Morris dancers do it with bells on', or some other such crap. He'd a pewter tankard hanging from his belt, a beer-belly like an overhang, his hair in a pony-tail, and he was carrying a leather case like drummers carry cymbals in. We all looked up from the corner we were playing in and thought, 'Oh, my God!'

There was Fergus Walsh, myself and Arty Hamilton half-way through a set of reels when he waddled towards us with a pint of Black Mischief in his mitt. He didn't even wait until we finished the set, he just plonked himself down beside us and unpacked the thing, rubbed a bit of Guinness into it to tune it, and began beating the shit out of it.

'How're you doing, boys?' he said when we finished, and then he introduced himself as Barry something or other and said his grandmother had come from Limerick or Athlone. I can't remember which. But none of us could look him in the face because, I tell you the truth, the poor bastard's eyes were jealous of each other. If he'd cried, the tears would have rolled down his back. He had the worst squint I've ever seen in my life.

Well, he played a few more sets of reels with us and though he wasn't the worst I've heard, he certainly wasn't the best, and thanks be to God there was only one of him. Then he pulls out a tin whistle and plays a couple of Kerry slides, and to tell the truth he was better than average. In the end he stays with us all night and tells us he's on holiday here with his girlfriend, camping down near the strand. And then we notice her at the end of the bar, talking to another girl; and wouldn't you believe it she's a beautiful blonde, Swedish-looking, and a figure like a dream.

Well, Walsh shouts to me in Irish that if love is blind then where's her white stick, and I tell him not to be so ill-mannered. The next night your man's back, and the next after that. I could tell that Walsh was pissed off by the guy, I think he was more jealous than anything else. He couldn't take his eyes off the girl, and kept making comments to us in Irish about her. I remember one time he said her arse was 'like two puppies fighting in a bag'.

On this particular night Walsh ripped into a hornpipe that none of us had heard before, so we all let him get on with it. 'What was that called?' asked the Englishman.

I forgot to mention that he was recording all the tunes we played on a little Walkman so that he could learn any he that didn't know. At the end of each set he would ask us the titles and he'd make a note of them in a little notebook he had with him, checking the tape index number and everything. He was like a trainspotter, very thorough. 'What was that one called?' he'd ask about any tune he didn't have and we'd tell him, if we knew. You wouldn't mind, it's the only way any of us get to learn tunes, but he was a bit of a pain in the arse all the same.

Anyway, at the end of the tune he asked what the hornpipe was called that Walsh had just played. 'An Sasenach Fiarshúili,' said Walsh. Arty Hamilton nearly choked on his stout, and I had to look away.

'You bastard,' I said to Walsh after he'd left, 'even if he doesn't know any Irish someone's going to tell him.' But nobody did tell him, and we heard that he was in An Béal Bocht a couple of nights later and he'd obviously learned the hornpipe because he played it, and when somebody asked him what it was called he said, 'An Sasenach Fiarshúili.' Half the pub, knowing Irish, fell about laughing.

Then we heard a few weeks later from Noel Linnane, the Dublin concertina-player, that your man had gone into O'Donoghue's and played the bloody tune and told them what it was called and the whole pub fell about. So your man asks somebody what it means. 'You don't know?' says some arsehole.

'No,' says your man.

'Well, it's hard to translate. It's very old Irish and there isn't really an English phrase that suits it perfectly, Irish being such a graceful language. But I suppose it would mean "The Squinting Englishman".' And the whole pub fell about again. Apparently your man just got up without saying a word, and left.

I felt bad when I heard that. The fellow was a bit of a ballocks, right enough, but he wasn't to know, and he had a respect for the music at least. I think it was terrible of Walsh to do what he did. And I'm not the only one who thinks so. I'm sure we'll all be glad when the summer's over and he pisses off back to Dublin.

Sahib Stories

By now Tsering could see that the big European slumped on the low bar like a bulky Sherpa's pack on a porters' wall was very, very drunk. The Sahib's body was waving from side to side on his stool, and his eyes were shutting and opening as though he was going to sleep. He was making noises through his nose, too, the kind of noises a baby makes when it is waking up and wants the breast, breathing hard and snuffling as though it doesn't know whether to smile or weep. Tsering looked at the big man's hands. They were twice the size of his own and looked very strong; but they were smooth-skinned, puffy and pink, and hadn't seen much in the way of hard work. That was the way it was, Tsering thought, with the Sahibs.

Outside, in the soft yellow light of the Kathmandu dusk, a bristle-headed American was turning slowly at the end of the open-air pool, half-way through the hundred lengths he had done every evening for the last five days. His arm, burnished like the arm of a golden Buddha by the last rays of the sun, pointed slowly at the night-coming sky, before it knifed lazily down into the water, arcing through the dim blue light; and he floated on, a half-mirage in the turquoise glow. Four fat memsahibs, silhouetted against the pool and the evening light, were comparing the souvenirs they had bought that hot afternoon in the noise and swelter of the Thamel area of the city. Prayer wheels in wood and copper, wooden masks with tin and brass plates riveted on to them, finger-bells and steel *kukri*s in leather and brass scabbards were spread out on the table. From other bags they brought woven belts, tee-shirts with pictures of Tin-Tin being chased by a Yeti across the snowy wastes of imagined mountains, and intricate and brightly coloured scrolled Thankas, imitations of the Buddhist religious paintings they had seen on their tour of the monasteries at Swayambunath and Bodhnath. The women's voices rattled on, tinny and sharp, cutting through the low muttering conversation.

The Sahib swung his head round, scanned the room and grunted. His eyes struggled to bring the four women into focus, managed to do so for a second, and then swept over the rest of the bar. He grunted again and stared over Tsering's head at the wooden masks hanging on the wall behind the spirit bottles. Tsering was very worried. It was his first night in charge of the bar and his English was not good enough to be able to handle this man if he got to be trouble, as the Sahibs sometimes did. This Sahib was a big Sahib with a very red face. His father had told him they ate too much meat and that too much meat made them red in the face and quick to get angry.

Now the big Sahib was breathing heavily through his nose again like a village pig, scattering salted peanuts across the polished mahogany as his hands scrabbled clumsily in the bowl, trying to lift the greasy nuts out like a badly driven grab crane. The Sahib sank into stillness again and stared ahead at nothing for a few minutes, his thoughts foundering in the booze-deep swamps of his mind.

Tsering began to feel more easy, looking out at the hibiscus slowly dancing in the warm evening breezes and the American Sahib shaking himself under the pool shower, long spokes of water spinning off his shoulders. As Tsering refilled the canapé bowls, the big Sahib before him slid slowly sideways along the bar as though he was going to fall, then jerked suddenly awake and steadied himself, looking about him at the people in the room. Drunken aggression and embarrassment flickered across his features and reality flowed around him, gravity-free.

'Another depth charge, Tsering,' he mumbled between wet, plump lips as he rubbed a soft hand across his thick sandy hair. He had taught Tsering how to make depth charges that evening when the bar opened and now he'd had nine, plus the three-quarters of a bottle of Scotch he'd drunk in his room. The conversation burred and dribbled on around him as he lifted the glass to his mouth, spilling a slobber of drink down the front of his safari suit.

Three neat and smiling Nepalese wearing dinner jackets entered through the bar door and walked softly and quietly to a cramped bandstand at the far end flanked by windows that looked out on to the pool and the night. They tuned up quickly and began playing some plangent half-recognisable melody, some standard from a long-forgotten show, the pianist leading the musicians haltingly on a piano that years of monsoon humidity had rendered slack-keyed and jangly. The drummer and bass player picked up the beat and the music spooled about the room in a smoke of minims and crochets.

Suddenly the Sahib snorted a question out loud that Tsering could hardly follow. 'You know who fucks these places up, Tsering?'

'Pardon, Sahib – I not understand.'

The Sahib almost shouted. 'I said, d'you know who fucks these places up?'

Tsering could not understand what he was being asked or why the Sahib was so angry, but he knew that fuck was a bad word because the Sahibs used it a lot when they were angry. Or if they wanted a woman, then they would ask him where they could find one to make fuck.

'Please, Sahib, no make trouble.'

'People like me do it. People like me fuck these places up.'

Now his voice was carrying across the room and some of the other customers in the bar had picked up the waves and were beginning to listen.

'I called it "An Earthly Paradise", see. "The last Shangri La".' The Sahib waved his arm in a wide arc, a drowning swimmer in the cool dry air of the bar. 'Two thousand words and half a dozen pictures. The article was syndicated in the travel sections of damn near every major newspaper in the Western world. I was a travel journalist, Tsering, that was my trade, butchering the truth with a biro on a bellyful of free meals and booze, courtesy of your local friendly tourist board. You scratch my back, I'll scratch yours, and we'll both sit back and watch the touro-dollars roll in. "I'm bent – fly me!" Fly me anywhere, get me pissed, give me the press handout from the PR people and I'm as happy as a sandboy. All I did was spew out what the PR people wanted to hear. They got a good press, I got paid for fuck-all and everybody was happy.'

Tsering smiled a nervous smile. 'Is good you happy, Sahib. Everybody should be happy.'

'Do you know that song, Tsering, it's a very old English folk song, called "My God, How the Money Rolls In"?'

Tsering shook his head and the Sahib began singing in a crackling voice to the tune of 'My Bonny Lies over the Ocean' a rugby song he'd learned in some club-house an eternity before:

'My father he works in the clap house,
My mother makes counterfeit gin,
My sister gives blow-jobs to vicars,
My God, how the money rolls in.
Rolls in, rolls in; my God, how the money rolls...'

He turned to the rest of the bar and started conducting with a cocktail stick, but nobody joined in. Instead people either stared at him with curiosity or gazed deep into the bottoms of their glasses. The four Englishwomen carried on looking at their souvenirs. They hadn't heard him, yet. He stopped half-way through the last line in a ratchet of coughing, cleared his throat loudly, took another mouthful of drink and turned to address the room, his eyes glassy and wet.

'I didn't do it on my own, you know. I wasn't the only Judas. There were shit-loads of us. Yanks, Krauts, Ozzies, Swedes.' He thumped his fist on the counter and the peanut bowl overturned.

'No trouble, Sahib, please!'

Even the souvenir ladies were listening now, and the trio, aware as all musicians are that there has been a subtle change in the atmosphere, played with one eye on the bar.

The Sahib's face had a thin sheen of sweat and a fish-belly pallor had taken the place of the high red colouring of a few moments before. He groped in the breast pocket of his shirt and pulled out a small notebook and a pen, dropping them on the bar top. He turned away from the room, opened the notebook and began studying it, seeming to read whatever was there with difficulty. It was his journal, and the entry for that day read:

'Today is the sixth day of the festival of Dasira Dashain, one of the most important festivals in the Hindu calendar. In Kathmandu it is the festival at which sacrifices are made to the Hindu deities. Every family, no matter how poor, brings an animal to the temples to be slaughtered. I remember being here half a lifetime ago on the days of this very festival and I remember being happier than anywhere else I had ever been in all of my young life. Now all of that has changed.'

But what the Sahib could not see was that the most grievous change was inside himself and not out there in the streets. He had spent the day wandering round the city, a place he had known some thirty years earlier, when he had first come to Nepal as a young journalist. He had fallen in love both with the city and its people. Their warm unquestioning hospitality, and the depth and passion of their religion, had made a deep and lasting impact on him. And although the idealism and optimism of his youth had sloughed off him like a skin as he climbed the Fleet Street ladder through the tumbling years, still Kathmandu had rooted itself in his mind as a symbol, as somewhere immutable.

Now he was Travel Editor of a major Sunday Newspaper and when the chance came to return there to cover the first All English Women's attempt at the summit of Everest, he had taken the job out of the hands of a younger female journalist and had opted to cover the expedition himself. Most of his colleagues were foxed by his decision. 'What does an old soak like you want to be covering that for, James? You're twenty years too old and four stone too heavy. You'll never make it to base camp,' one of his fellow editors had said.

But he knew that what he lacked in ability his paper could more than make up in cash. In less than a week he had flown direct from London to Kathmandu, met the fixer, and paid a great deal of money to be choppered up to base camp the next day, with an oxygen bottle and a doctor just in case of altitude sickness. He had done the interview using the expedition's own photographer, bought an exclusive on the life, and got himself back to Kathmandu. The rest of his time he could now spend making occasional radio contact with base camp, faxing copy back to London, and wandering round the city enjoying himself.

But what had happened to him on his first free day had driven him, earlier than usual, into the arms of his very good friend the bottle. If there is a sliver of truth in the belief that Hell is personal, something that we each carry around with us wherever we go, then the Sahib that day was lugging a Hell with him worse than any hump on his back.

As he stood in the heart of the city and saw the changes around him, he saw more than the – perhaps inevitable – ending of an untouched innocence. He saw his own ideals, the principles and passions he had squandered down the years, running through the dust like the blood and waters of Dashain. He saw his own life as shabby and shallow, a slow but steady slide from ideals through compromise to cynicism. From youth to middle age, with the city at either end, he saw a tableau of truths distorted, friends and ideals betrayed, two dead marriages, children who were strangers now, and of years spent drowning in an ocean of ambition and booze.

The festival was approaching its end and thousands of small animals and birds, kids and chickens, geese and ducks, had been ritually slaughtered in the forecourts of the temples; the stones and the brass pillars and the great bronze gods on their pedestals were thick with the scarlet of the blood and the saffron of marigold petals, while the air was sweet and warm and heavy with smoke and incense and slaughter. He had walked through areas of the city which had once housed small shops and workrooms but which were now crammed with stalls selling 'genuine' antique masks, temple bells, bamboo flutes, tat and gee-gaws. There were whole streets that seemed to consist only of souvenir shops, cafés, trekking equipment shops and agencies advertising white-water rafting, treks and tiger-watching.

Buzzing knots of young Westerners with clear excited faces wandered about the streets and squares in shorts and tee-shirts with swarms of sellers and hustlers swirling about them, like piranhas round lumps of meat. It didn't bother them that thirty years ago there had been no stalls and bells and Tin-Tin and the Yeti tee-shirts. What they saw was a city of noise and bustle and wonder. But what had gladdened the young people had depressed him greatly, and the Sahib had taken a rickshaw back to his hotel at lunchtime and had started into his bottle of duty-free. By mid-afternoon the anaesthetic had begun to take effect and he had wandered out again.

He took a cab across the city and, telling the driver to wait for him by a batti stall, took the steps down to the river by the monkey temple at Pashupatinath, a stranger to himself and to the world. At the burning ghats a group of Nepalese were cremating a body.

The son and brother of the dead man, dressed only in white loincloths, their heads shaved, walked three times round the pyre. A burning torch was held to the mouth of the corpse to signify that the soul had passed on into the afterworld, then the fire was lit and the brand cast into the sacred river. The Sahib watched it sail slowly down the muddy brown, slack, slow water. Then the pyre caught and the smoke rose, oily and dark, towards the blue cloudless sky. Through the heat haze above the flames the Sahib could see the shaking colours that were women washing on the far bank, their children splashing in the shallows on the river steps. The fire cracked and howled and the dead man's hand, the sinews tightening in the flames, raised as though in a farewell salute.

The Sahib heard a cackle of laughter and looked behind him. Above the ghats, a gaggle of Japanese tourists were climbing on the temple walls, laughing and calling, pointing down at the cremation, cameras clicking. Two of them, a young man and a woman, sat on the wall, their arms round each other, laughing. Another straddled an idol while his wife took his picture. Another raised her hand in the air, waved a white flag and the rest of the Japanese trailed after her in a crocodile of leather jackets, chatter and cameras.

Thirty years ago there had been no tourists. The hippies of Freak Street and the mountaineering expeditions on their way to climb the high peaks of the Solo Khumbu or the Annapurna range had been the only Western faces here. Beyond that the West had hardly impinged on the consciousness of the Nepalese at all. Then there was nobody hustling you to buy hash or change money.

Now the Sahib saw that more than money was changed. For the new consumer travellers of the first world, culture was not something to experience or share or try to understand; it was something to photograph and buy, to possess and take away home with you. Mass marketing, big business and the years had gnawed at and eroded a culture without price, until within thirty years it had turned the city almost completely over to tourism, and the open and friendly eyes were becoming cloudy, narrowing and dimming, weighing up the Westerners like so much meat. But, worst of all, he saw too that he had played a part in it all.

'Are you happy, Tsering?'

'What you mean, Sahib?'

'Are you really happy, working in here, serving these wankers?'

An Englishwoman sitting nearby froze rigid and looked hard-eyed and tight-mouthed at her husband across the table. He stared into the air over her shoulder as though he'd noticed something really interesting about one of the high fans.

Hearing her noise her disapproval with a tutting sound, the Sahib turned half-round on his stool: 'I'm sorry madam, I should have said us wankers.'

A table of Americans in a far corner stopped talking and stirred slightly in their seats.

'Sahib, please, no trouble.' Tsering thought of his boss, Mr Hauptman, and how angry he would be if there were complaints. Tsering needed this job. His promotion to barman was very important. If he made a mess of this first night alone at the bar, he would have to go back to being a waiter and he would lose money and face.

'No, Tsering, there'll be no trouble. I'm just interested, that's all. What brings all these fat old people half-way across the world out here? People like me, that's who. Travel-writers, sitting on their fat arses in air-conditioned bars the third world over, saying, "Come and peek at the natives. Thrill to their quaint customs. Buy their temple ornaments and their pots and pans and take them back home to Hamburg and stick them on the fucking wall!" D'you know where I went tonight?'

'No, Sahib.'

'I went to your hotel's so-called Nepalese cultural evening. Twelve bored boys and girls and three bored musicians performing for the tourists. One of those dances I knew. It was a sacred Sherpa Mani Rimdu dance, and it was being sent up. The tourists were laughing at it. That's what it's come to now. We go round the world, laughing at little brown people. And if we'd kept quiet, if we'd written "Asia is closed", what would we have condemned you to? To being yourselves a little longer, that's all. Your own songs done for you, not for a lot of fat car-workers from Detroit or fast-food executives from bloody Milton Keynes to snap and video. Kodak culture vultures. Travel doesn't broaden the mind, it broadens the arse.'

191

One of the Americans, who had caught part of the last sentence, shouted, 'What's eating that guy?'

'Throw the bum out!' said another, loudly.

The Englishwoman and her husband signed their bar bill and left, heads down and in a hurry. The Germans were looking around at the Sahib, wondering what was going on.

'Hey, buddy, you'd better go sleep it off,' another American voice shouted.

The Sahib lurched to his feet like a ship hitting a rock, and waddled towards the Americans' table. He was well over six foot and, though fat hung around his waist like a money belt, he was very broad and muscular too. The Americans went quiet.

'I'd like your opinion on this country.'

'Opinions are like ass-holes,' said one of the men. 'Nothing much good comes out of them, and everybody's only interested in his own.'

The people at the table laughed, but it was a nerve-edged laughter made apprehensive by the presence of the large drunken Englishman.

'That was quite witty for an American,' said the Sahib. 'I want to know what you think about this country? Why you're here?'

'We're here because we're on holiday,' said one.

'Cos we paid a lot of goddam' good money to come out here and to look around,' said another. 'What the hell is it to you, anyway?'

'You aren't good enough to drink these people's piss.'

There was a momentary silence. Murderous static crackled in the air. The band stopped, and the two biggest American men stood up and moved towards the Sahib. One of them pushed him in the chest and he stumbled slightly.

'We all think you'd better go before we bust your dirty mouth for you, Mac. Where we come from we don't use language like that in front of ladies.'

As the Sahib struggled to focus, swaying gently and trying to form words that would not come out, Tsering suddenly came between the two cores of violence as though he had appeared from out of the air like a pantomime devil.

'Sahibs sometime liquor too much,' Tsering smiled and shrugged. He took the Sahib gently by the arm and, to everyone's surprise, the big man followed him back to the bar like an old dancing bear with sore feet. The pianist caught the eyes of his fellow musicians and nodded as a sign for them to start playing again. He led them into 'Feelings' with much arpeggio work, his podgy right hand fluttering up and down the keyboard, unconscious of any irony in his choice.

The Sahib sat on his stool and stared wildly ahead of him. He was muttering now, a thick string of curses in a monologue of despair.

'Depth charge!' he suddenly shouted at Tsering.

'Sahib maybe too much liquor. Maybe better if Sahib go to bed.'

'Just gimme a fucking drink, Tsering. Just another fucking drink!'

Tsering looked at the white man with his rich clothes. The money for his watch alone would have fed his village for a month.

'Maybe better Sahib go to bed.'

'I think, sir, you ought to go and sleep it off.' A new European voice echoed in his mind.

He turned to curse whoever it was and found a man in a dinner jacket and tie at his side, smiling stonily while gripping his arm with a hand like a claw. 'I think we would all be happier if you left the bar, sir.'

'Who the fuck are you?'

'My name is Mr Hauptman. I am the manager, and if you do not leave the bar immediately I will call the police. And though the Nepalese are normally respectful towards Westerners, the police can be quite heavy. They are small; but many of them are ex-Gurkhas and they are very, very tough. The gaols are not nice places and tonight you have a choice between a nice hotel bed and a filthy stinking cage. It's up to you.'

The Sahib tried hard to focus on the big Austrian. In the troubled murky pool of his mind he formed words that never surfaced, and for an instant he half-thought of taking a punch at him. But some basic survival instinct warned him against it and, without speaking, he slid off the stool and turned his body in the general direction of the door. The manager let go of his arm and the Sahib lurched between the tables, trying to hold himself with some dignity but falling instead into raw, cold comedy.

At the door he spun suddenly towards the room and bawled in a slobber: 'Fuck you, fuck the lot of you!' Then he swivelled heavily about and was gone.

The manager turned towards his customers and shrugged an apology. The band carried on playing where they had left off, and the tables erupted in a hubbub of chatter as the incident was sifted through over and again.

Instead of going to bed the Sahib rushed through the reception area and out of the glass doors of the hotel, past the saluting Gurkha doorman, and down the marble steps to where the noise and bustle of the city wrapped round him like a fog. Young men swam from the shadows of this undersea world like moray eels. 'You want taxi? Change? Hash? You want make fuck?' But he waved them away and lurched towards the lights of the main street.

And as the grains of light that were the first stars of evening spiked the purple bruised sky above Kathmandu, his shaking legs took him past the brightly lit windows of Yeti Travel and the Sherpa Trekking Company, past the offices of the Elephant Lodge Safari Park, past the small man threading his way through the bicycle rickshaws with his rosary of seven goats, and down through a web of city streets to the river.

He came after a long time and many falls to the bridge, where he leaned exhausted on the parapet, swallowing great mouthfuls of the cool dark air. A few lights showed on the far bank across the great brown waters, while below him on the burning ghats the blurred image of a man dressed all in white was coming and going, smudged into the mists that were rising off the river. Singing a low soft prayer, the man moved as though in a saraband, seeming to float on the thin fine mist as he swept the last glowing ashes of the dead into the sacred waters.

Turkey Legs

When I was about seven years old or so, in those innocent days of giants, miracles, Flash Gordon and First Communion strawberry breakfasts, I believed that Father Christmas was Irish. It was not a belief that I had discussed with anybody or thought about very deeply; it was just something I knew in the depths of my inner soul. It had entered my credo in what the priests called, much later in my life, a 'Holy Ghost Leap of Faith in the Dark'.

This leap in the seven-year-old dark night of my psyche was based on the fact that my grandad came from Dublin and was the most Santa Claus-like person I knew. He was well over six feet tall, a big-boned, long-nosed, pink-faced, bald-domed man who looked, particularly after drink had made him more than usually mellow, the image of every Father Christmas you've ever seen, only without the beard.

He lived in Liverpool, where he worked as a master tailor, sitting cross-legged, so my mother told me, on a wooden bench, like the tailor in the fairy story about the tailor and the elves, making suits for what Nanna called 'the big nobs and the Coleman's Mustard'. He made all his own suits and overcoats, of course, so that this big Irishman from the slums of Dublin looked every bit as smart as the shipping magnates and cotton importers he tailored for.

He always looked, Nanna used to say, 'every inch and every half-inch a gentleman'.

That was until he opened his mouth, and then a voice that was pure Dublin rang out of his long nose like the trumpetings of a Celtic elephant. He was a terrible spendthrift both with his words and with his money, throwing them about him in showers of notes and coins and sayings and stories like some magical prince and storyteller from the Arabian Nights. Every year he left Liverpool and came by train to stay with us for Christmas and New Year, and every time he came he would press a ten-shilling note into my hand as he walked through the door.

Ten bob was no small beer in those days. Usually my mother, the amateur banker in our household, would take it into her safe keeping and give it back to me a little at a time in case I overdosed on aniseed balls or liquorice root. You could get four Uncle Joe's Mint Balls for a penny and a seat at the local cinema, the Globe Picture House (we knew it as the 'Bug Hut', because of the friendliness of the denizens of its seats) and watch Flash Gordon, the Three Stooges and Tweety Pie for a tanner; while a whole shilling would take you all the way to the countryside and back.

So, in my seven-year-old world, Christmas with its largesse, its spendthrift nature, its roasting fires and coloured streamers, its joke-telling uncles and giggling girl cousins, its crackling hot turkey and creamy trifles, was associated in every shining and all its warmth with a tiny baby swaddled and warmed by the breath of beasts and with a big tipsy tailor from Dublin lurching off the Liverpool train. His shadow cast itself hugely about that feast, eclipsing all the Christmas-card Santas, all the red-nosed brouhaha and reindeers, even St Nicholas himself. The Father Christmases I saw in their grottoes in the department stores in Manchester I knew for fakes. They weren't real, they had false beards, painted noses and, even worse they had flat Manchester accents. They could never have said:

'Mother of God, will ye give the child a taste of porter.'

'Jaze, he's as fit as a barrel of fleas.'

'Yer man has a mouth so big he takes Holy Communion off a shovel.'

'He has the eyes of a travelling rat.'

'He'd mind mice at cross-roads.'

The only similarity between the stores' Santas and Henry Joseph Patrick O'Neill was, that like him, they smelt of drink and had stomachs that left you with very little lap-room to sit on.

My great-grandmother lived with us at the time. She was my grandad's mother and I called her Nanna. She was the only person in the whole world that my grandad was afraid of. She was a beautiful lady more than eighty years old, with long white hair held up in a thick bun by some mysterious arrangement of combs and pins. At times she would let it down, and then it would fall in a shimmering cascade into her lap. I thought that Rapunzel in the story would have hair like Nanna's, long and thick – and white.

I could never really picture Nanna as my grandad's mother, somehow; they seemed to be both so much of an age. In childhood people pass before you down the tunnel to infinity, hitting a stage called 'grown-up' somewhere round nineteen or so, when they stop jumping walls and shouting after cyclists and grow bosoms and shave instead. Somewhere round thirty they become 'old' and are married and tell you to get off chairs and give you looks that say, 'If you were my child, I'd saw your legs off,' then they pat you on the head and smile at your mother. Round about fifty, greying and balding, they become 'very old', and always ask you what you're going to do when you leave school and tell you these are the best days of your life. But when they get to the age of my grandad and great-grandma they are as old as time itself, old as the rocks and the stars. They knew Julius Caesar and Robin Hood and St Patrick, they saw dinosaurs roaming the swamps before the coal was made and they also have one foot in that forward-looking door marked 'infinity'.

Nanna was a bright and burning world of stories and songs and from the time when I was a baby on her knee to this Christmas when I was seven she had filled my head with music, stories, banshees, ghosts and her own brand of republicanism and socialism. But she suffered fools not at all and had a temper and a fiery impatience that made her more than able to deal with her errant son.

If she had one weakness, it was her love of good food. We didn't get much beyond plain stuff for most of the year. My mother was on a war widow's pension and Nanna had only her 'Lloyd George' money so there wasn't much room for more than the basics: lots of fish and potatoes but meat only once a week, on Sunday. Christmas was the time of the blow-out: chocolates, ham, tongue, pickles, meat pies, mince pies, gravy, sherry trifle... And the big one – the turkey.

As we waited each Christmas for my grandad to come, Nanna would sit by the living-room fire while my mother, in the scullery, cooked the bacon ribs and cabbage that we always had when he came home because they were his favourite. Nanna would sit in the fireside chair spelling her way through *The Universe*, the Catholic newspaper, her soft mouth forming the words soundlessly as her eyes foraged through the print. Every ten minutes or so she would look up at the clock on the mantelshelf and call out to my mother, 'I wonder how big it will be this year?'

'It' was the turkey, the chief of the feast, the sacrificial god around whom this whole festival revolved. Without the turkey, Father Christmas and all the elves, fairies, donkeys and mangers would fade away into the darkness of the Manchester streets and the days would become just like any other days. My grandad brought the turkey with him from Liverpool each Christmas. It was not an ordinary bird.

The turkeys my grandad brought were the biggest, the meatiest, the tastiest and the juiciest birds that had ever strutted on the face of the earth. He had some sort of secret (and whispered and winked and nodded about) arrangement with a butcher in Liverpool whereby he made the butcher a suit from the butcher's own material and the butcher gave him a special turkey – 'The pick,' my grandad used to say as he thumped it on the table, 'of the whole bloody bunch,' and for once Nanna wouldn't tell him off for swearing. For some reason the turkeys had increased in size each year; whether this was because the butcher had got fatter over the years meaning bigger suits meaning bigger turkeys I don't know, but some of them had been monsters.

'Be God,' said Nanna, looking up from an article on the African missions, 'the thing he brought last year wasn't a turkey at all. 'Twas an oystritch. There wasn't the room for half a spud in the oven after it went in. You'd be ruined with the gas you'd use cooking the thing. If he brings one like that monster this year we'll have to saw it in two, or build a fire and roast it outside in the yard.'

The thought of us all roasting a giant turkey in the back yard on a fire made her laugh, and that set her off to coughing and that set her off to sneezing and that set her off to blowing her nose. She used to blow her nose on newspaper and fling it on the fire. She saw no use in handkerchiefs – 'filthy things' – and so her nose always had a black patina from the newsprint. My mother would remind her of this two or three times a day and she would go into the scullery and wash it off.

I sat, this Christmas Eve, on the stool beside Nanna, looking into the fire. We had a large black iron range in the living-room with ovens either side and cranes and things to put the pots and smoothing irons on. I would sit for hours watching faces and making worlds in the fire, dreaming it was the surface of one of the planets on my favourite radio programme, 'Journey into Space'. Volcanic and turbulent, strange raging fires burned round blocks of obsidian, clouds of smoke hissed from cracks in the earth, then a lump of coal would eject a jet of gas which would ignite, burning like a miniature of the sun-spots in the nature book in school. Here, writ small, was all the power of the universe.

'You'll burn the eyes out of your head staring into that,' said Nanna.

'Is Hell like this, Nanna?' I asked.

'Hell,' she said, thinking for a second, 'Hell is a million times worse than that. That fire there, son, is a pinprick compared to the raging, never-ending fires of Hell. The torments the sinners in Hell endure are not just the fires but the endless pain, the screams of other sinners, the tortures of the devils with their forks and the fact that because they damned their eternal souls they will never ever set eyes on the face of God or his son Jesus,' and she nodded her head at the word 'Jesus'.

'Will I go to Hell?'

'Not at all, come on out of that! You'll not go to Hell, not if you say your prayers and grow up decent and become a priest maybe.' She looked at me slyly and I knew what question was coming next. 'Have you never thought of becoming a priest?'

I said that I had, though I hadn't. I wanted to be a spaceman and zoom off through the asteroid belt and destroy man-eating plants with a death-ray gun. My answer seemed to satisfy her.

'Good.' She smiled. 'To have a priest in the family is a great thing.'

I wondered if perhaps I could be both a priest and a spaceman, flying back for confession and mass. Priests only worked two days in the week; maybe I could be a spaceman the other five?

Then another thought came into my head. 'Who will go to Hell, Nanna?'

'Hitler and Stalin and Winston Churchill.'

I knew the answer to that question already. Nanna had a hatred of Hitler bred from the number of nights she had spent sitting in a cold shelter while Piccadilly and Ancoats went up in flames. She had no love of the English establishment, but allied with them over the war with the Nazis. Stalin she hated because of what he had done to the Roman Catholic church in Eastern Europe, and Churchill she hated because of what he did at Tonypandy, his attitude to Ireland, his father's complicity in the secession of the Six Counties, but mostly because he represented to her everything she hated about the upper classes and British imperialism.

'Will grandad go to Hell?'

'He will, son. As sure as water runs downhill, he'll burn in Hell if he doesn't stop that drinking and being a Communist.'

My grandfather's brand of Communism was really a bedrock socialism, but because he was slightly more left-wing than Nanna, and because he was an atheist, my great-grandmother thought he was in the pay of the Kremlin. He could always get her going on politics and religion and the rows they used to have were monumental things, the great-grandmother and grandfather of all rows.

One had started when my grandad picked up a Catholic magazine sold in aid of the African missionaries – *The Word*, I think it was called. 'Missionaries!' he snorted down his trunk. 'The storm troopers of imperialism. They go out to these countries with the Bible in one hand and a bottle of fire-water in the other, subduing the natives and turning the poor blacks into slaves. St Joseph's Penny is Judas's thirty pieces of silver, betraying happy darkies into serfdom. *The Word*, huh! Is that what they call it? Spreading the White Man's poison and diseases and putting brassieres on the black chests of Africa!'

'I'll wash your mouth out with soap, using language like that in front of the child!' said Nanna. And the two old people glared at each other until my grandad, sensing he'd gone too far, backed down and went into the scullery to put the kettle on.

On the eve of this Christmas, my grandad was later than usual. He arrived most Christmases at about eleven o'clock, having gone through what had become a fixed ritual. He would finish work in Liverpool at lunchtime, have a few drinks with the butcher when he went to collect his turkey, another one or two with his fellow tailors in the Royal Vaults and, when that closed at three o'clock, a few more with the man he talked politics with in the bar of the Adelphi Hotel. At opening time he would have a few more in the Philharmonic with a flute-player who was very good on the horses because he had a brother in the stables, and before he got on the train he would always have a last drink in the station bar with a lady that he knew in Liverpool.

A fog of whispering mystery surrounded this lady. When Nanna spoke to my mother about her their voices disappeared and only their lips moved as they talked. This 'me-mawing', as it was called, was a Lancashire custom, developed by mill-girls for talking over the noise of machines. My mother and Nanna and almost all the women in our street were expert at it. Why they talked about the woman that my grandad knew in Liverpool in such a voice I don't know. My grandad's wife was not with him any more, although I was told she was not dead.

If I asked any more than that I was told that little pigs had big ears, which I knew was like empty vessels making the most noise and long roads having no turnips, and that I would hear no more on the matter; and in any case it was probably past my bedtime and had I cleaned my teeth and where were my pyjamas? The matter of the woman that my grandad knew in Liverpool was a mystery like the Holy Ghost and how Flash Gordon managed to escape every week from the clutches of the Emperor Ming.

So, after having a last drink with the woman that he knew in Liverpool, my grandad would get on the train to Manchester. When he got to Manchester my Uncle Bobby met him off the train and they would have a drink in the station buffet and then meet a man called Laherty in a pub called the Douglas.

My grandad called him 'Laherty', but Nanna called him 'Laherty, hunh!', the last bit of his name being a noise made by blowing down her nose while she looked into the fire as though Laherty, hunh! was somewhere in there. Laherty, hunh! was the man who talked to my grandad and Uncle Bobby about politics. He seemed to know an awful lot about everything to do with what was going on in the world.

According to my grandad, he had studied to be a doctor but had ended up as a printer because his family had no money; but he had read every book and newspaper there was and knew more than many a college professor. Laherty, hunh! was quoted in argument by my grandad a lot and whenever he started a sentence with the words: 'I was talking to Laherty the other night in the pub...' or 'Yer man Laherty, he was talking about Roosevelt the other day...' or 'Laherty was telling me about this book he's read...', Nanna would go 'Laherty, hunh!' into the fire or even sometimes sing out 'Laherty, Laherty, Laherty,' in the way we children used to sing 'Tell-tale-tit, your tongue will split, and all the little birds will have a little bit' in the street.

Laherty used to keep my grandad out late, which was another thing she didn't like about him. I never met Laherty, though I knew if I did I would like him. Being with Laherty made my grandad very happy and when my grandad was happy it was Christmas all the time.

'He'll be rolling round the pubs with Laherty,' said Nanna, breaking off from her silent rosary, the beads pooled in the lap of her pinny, and looking up at the clock with the holly and the balloons fastened to it.

'Will he be long, Nanna?' I asked, looking out at the pavement of our street, now dusted with a fine coating of frost under the gas-lamp.

'Long, child? If him and Laherty and your Uncle Bobby have got their teeth into the troubles of the world and their tongues stuck down the bottom of a pint glass, they could be there till the cows come home.'

I had a mental picture of my grandad with his false teeth stuck in the model of the globe like the one we had at school and his tongue reaching all the way to the bottom of the big glass, waiting at the door of the Douglas for a big black and white cow to get off a bus outside.

I went back to the window and stared out. The carol singers had been and gone. Reg, the drunk, who threw bottles through bus windows, had staggered past singing a song about buying a paper doll to call his own and had vanished rubbery and shaking into his own little house at the top of our street. I saw our cat coming back from a night prowling the dustbins, fighting other cats and killing the rats outside the chip-shop back gate. He paused underneath the gas-lamp, looked around to see if there was anything else to fight, then tripped neat and aloof up to our house door as though he owned it.

'Nanna, the cat's here,' I said, opening the door.

'Eileen, cover the meat, the cat's back,' called Nanna as the cat rubbed against her legs and fell on the hearthrug before the fire to wash himself.

People were setting off for Midnight Mass and I was turning from the window, thinking that my grandad would never come, when the noise of a taxi pulling up outside the door dragged me back to the window with my nose stuck to the pane, like one of the snails on the glass of the fish tank at school.

'He's here!' I shouted back to the room.

'He'd be late for his own wake,' said Nanna to herself.

I watched him peel himself from the taxi, a massive-looking man seeming almost too big for the puny little door of the black cab. He paid the driver and lurched up the pavement. I ran to the door and opened it.

'Hello! How are you? You are looking grand,' he said to me, answering his own question before I could so much as open my mouth. Then, thundering down the dark lobby like a dinosaur, a brown paper parcel with his pyjamas and shirt and socks in it swinging from his hand, he bawled the same question as he burst into the room ahead of me like a surfacing whale.

'Aragh, the back's still as bad as it was, and the rheumatics in the hand have me crippled,' said Nanna, 'but apart from that I'm fine, thanks be to God, and how's yourself? You've put a lot of weight on,' she added. as my granddad sank into the chair at the side of the table, snorting through his long nose like a walrus as he dragged the cigarettes out of his pocket. He still had his overcoat on, the parcel by now was on the floor. He lit a cigarette and blew smoke out as a plate of ribs and cabbage arrived steaming on the table.

There was something wrong with my grandad's eyes. They looked as though they had somehow slid closer together and developed a life all of their own. Wet and shiny and bright, they seemed to be flicking from side to side like little fishes. It was obvious to me that he had met Laherty, hunh! and Uncle Bobby and had had lots of pints and was very, very happy. He picked up a big bacon rib torn from the sheet, opened his mouth and missed. He had another go, got it right and winked at me as I sat, elbows on the table, chin on my hands, opposite him.

'Take your coat off, Dad,' said my mother.

'I will in good time,' said my grandad. 'Be God, it's bitter outside. I was expecting to see Eskimos coming down the street in a sledge any minute.'

'Did you get a good bird, Henry?' Nanna asked almost peevishly, eager to see tomorrow's god in all its uncooked pimply glory.

'Be Jesus, I got a Jack Dempsey of a bird. If it was any bigger it would be an eagle.'

'Have you left it in the lobby?'

'Not at all. I tied it by the legs round me neck to leave me bloody hands free,' he said, and he stood up and opened his coat.

But there around his neck, like a strange version of the stole that the priest wore in church, was nothing but a piece of hairy white string with a scaley red turkey leg on each end. The rest of the bird was missing.

'Be God! It's escaped!' said my grandad, looking down at an abundance of nothingness.

'God save me, I brought up an eejit,' Nanna said scornfully. 'Mother of God, the thing'll have a job running off wit' no legs. Where in hell's name did you go before you came here at all?'

'I was in the Douglas with Bobby and Laherty,' said my grandad.

'Laherty, hunh!' said Nanna. 'You'd better go and get Laherty to chase your turkey!'

My grandad sat down with a silly grin on his face. 'Be God, that's a clever bird he gave me this year. It must be one of them homing turkeys,' and he started to laugh to himself.

Nanna on the other hand just stared into the fire gloomily and angrily. I could tell she was furious about him losing the bird but, seeing how drunk he was and what sort of a state he was in, thought twice about starting an argument at this time of the night on Christmas Eve. For half an hour or so my grandad ate his ribs and cabbage and drank his tea and ate his bread and butter, a thick crust cut from the end of the loaf spread heavy with butter the way he liked it.

He asked me how I was going on at school and what I hoped to be getting for Christmas, winking at me all the time. He asked me how I was doing at school again, although I'd already told him once that I'd got gold stars for everything except sums, and asked me could I swim yet and did I know that a man had once swum over the Niagara Falls in a barrel according to Laherty – but not one word came from either my mother or my great-grandmother.

Then there came a heavy banging at the door and Nanna looked up at the clock and wondered out loud who could that be at this time of night in the name of God? I ran down the lobby and opened the door. There, in the cold dark gas-lamp night, with the beginnings of a snowfall swirling around him and melting in white specks on his black jacket, stood a man with a walrus moustache, sad eyes and in his hands a hat and something wrapped in newspaper.

'Is that old man here I dropped off before?' he asked.

'It's my grandad.'

'Who is it?' said Nanna.

'It's a man,' I called back.

'It's the taxi driver that brought that old drunk home,' shouted the man.

'He's got grandad's hat,' I shouted down the lobby.

'Me hat,' said my grandad, feeling for it on his glossy pink dome and looking wildly around him.

'Bring him in,' said my Nanna. I returned to the door.

The man followed me down the lobby into the living-room. 'You left these in me cab,' he said, unwrapping the newspaper and holding out a massive legless turkey and an expensive man's hat.

'Thanks be to God,' said Nanna.

'You nearly got me locked up, pal,' the taxi driver told my grandad, in a serious voice.

My grandad snorted down his nose. 'What the hell are you talking about?'

'I'll tell you what I'm talking about, pal. You left this bloody bird on the seat of my taxi, right? And your hat's fallen on top of it, right? So I gets back to town, right? I don't know it's there, do I? So I pick up a fare at Victoria, a woman, fur coat, plenty of money, wants to go to the Midland, right? Gets through Albert Square, doesn't she? She screams blue murder, doesn't she? Opens the window giving it "Murder! Police! Murder!"

'So there's two bobbies on the corner, isn't there? They're over in no time and they've pulled me out of the cab, haven't they? She's in hysterics, screaming, and points in me cab. So the police have a look in, and there's this thing looking like a dead man's head on the seat...' He stuck the hat on the turkey. With its big breast-bone for a nose and its wings for ears, it looked every bit like my grandad.

'Be God,' he said, 'that bears a powerful resemblance to a man I met in a pub tonight.'

'I tell you what, pal, it's caused me some bother, this bird has.' The driver planked it down on the table. 'I could have been done.'

'Not at all,' said my grandad, through his nose. 'Would you come on out of that!'

'It's good of yourself to bring it back to us at all, mister,' said Nanna.

'The police said I had to, love.'

'Well, I still think it's good of you.'

I could see that my grandad was dying to burst out laughing, but he pulled a pound note from his wallet. 'There you go, get yourself a drink. Have a happy Christmas. All the best, and compliments of the season.'

The taxi driver looked at the money, looked at my grandad and then looked at the money again for a second, looked as though he was about to say something, seemed to think better of it, took the glass of sherry that my mother had brought from the scullery and offered to him and drank it in one.

'Well,' he said, 'I suppose there was no harm done in the end. Anyway, it is Christmas, isn't it? Suppose it couldn't be helped really, you didn't do it on purpose. Anyway, Merry Christmas to you all, all the best, missus.' He went off down the lobby, still muttering. I closed the door behind him.

'Well thanks be to God for that,' said Nanna, looking at the legless bird. 'At least there's some honest men still walking this world.'

'He said the police made him bring it back,' snorted my grandad, 'that's not the sign of an honest man, is it?'

'It's a wonder they didn't come and lock you up for disturbing the peace,' said Nanna.

'Not at all. I was nowhere near the place, why should they lock me up? I wasn't in the bloody cab.'

My mother took the bird into the scullery. 'It won't fit into the oven,' she called out. 'I'll have to take it to the chip shop to see if Doris will cook it in her big oven in the morning.'

My grandad wasn't listening. 'If the police hadn't made him bring it back it would have been on his table tomorrow,' and he winked at me.

'Mother of God, have you no charity in your heart?' said Nanna.

'Charity,' snorted my grandad. 'Charity? What are taxi drivers anyway but the lackeys of the capitalist oppressors of the working classes. Taxi drivers are a symbol of the serfdom of the proletariat.'

'What the hell are you talking about, you eejit? You came home in a taxi yourself,' said Nanna.

My grandad looked puzzled for a moment, then he lit another cigarette and decided to change tack. 'Laherty says some of them taxi drivers earn twenty pounds a week.'

'Laherty, hunh!' said Nanna. 'The day Laherty drives a taxi or does anything else in the way of earning an honest bob will be the day that turkey clucks!' And she threw another lump of coal on the fire.